Final Round

By N.L. Hudson

SOUL Publications

 This book is a work of fiction. Names, characters, places, and incidents either are the product of the author's imagination or are used fictitiously and are not to be construed as real. Any resemblance to actual persons, living or dead, business establishments, events, or locales or, is entirely coincidental.

Saadiq

A few hours after the incident…

"What you're telling us is that a ghost was driving the vehicle?" the detective asked. I was in an interrogation room with two officers. One was black and the other one was white. They were trying to play this good cop bad cop shit with me.

"Y'all muthafuckas tryna be funny. Hell nah, it wasn't no ghost!" I barked.

"Who was it then? When we got there it was only you and Jon-Jon at the scene. We know it wasn't him driving because he was dead underneath the truck. Unless you can tell me someone else was there, all the evidence points to you," the baldheaded, fat sloppy white officer said. I released a deep breath. Even though Brisham left me to deal with this shit, I still couldn't bring myself to snitch on my little cousin. I was stalling these muthafuckas out while waiting to see if he would turn himself in. I didn't know how long I had been here, but it was longer than I wanted to be. My throat was dry as a desert, my body was weak, and I was exhausted as hell.

“Saadiq, this isn’t looking too good for you, man. Right now you’re not giving us nothing. You’ve refused to take a sobriety test and I feel you’re lying about what happened tonight. At this point, we should just lock your ass up since you don't wanna cooperate,” the black officer shouted.

“Man, do what the fuck y’all wanna do because I’m done talking to y’all. Matter fact I want my phone call, and I want a lawyer.” They both ice grilled my ass before turning to each other.

“Alright, fuck it. He’s gonna go down for this anyway,” the black one uttered.

"Yeah, you're right. That's actually better for us. Now we won't have to deal with his black ass. I can go home to my family." That was the white one talking. I shook my head as I sat back in my seat.

"Racist muthafucka, and yo’ Uncle Tom ass dumb as fuck for working with this bitch," I snarled at the black officer.

He slammed his hand on the table. "Shut the fuck up!"

"Whoa, calm down there." The white officer patted the black officer's chest.

"Yeah house nigga, calm yo' ass down." I smirked. That time he just looked at me and frowned.

I could see they were pissed as hell. They stood up and walked out of the room without uttering another word.

"Fuck," I gritted as I put my head in my hands. *This shit cannot be happening*. Just a few hours ago I was enjoying my family and making plans to start a new life. Now I was stuck in this bitch wondering what the future held for me. I should have listened to Gee when he told me something was up with Brisham. Maybe my boy would still be here if I noticed the signs. I felt guilty like somehow this shit was my fault. Suddenly the door opened, and I glanced up. "Unc, I told these muthafuckas this shit wasn't on me, but they won't believe me," I said, thankful to see him.

"What are you talking about, what wasn't on you?" He looked at me strangely.

"I didn't wreck that truck, man."

"Listen Saadiq, I understand this is all scary for you. Jon-Jon was one of your close friends, so you feel bad about killing him. However, lying isn't gonna help you out of this," he stated. I frowned as I stared at him. This nigga wasn't even trying to ask me what happened. Right off he was telling me I'd done it without getting the full story.

“You ain’t hearing me. I didn’t do this and I ain’t confessing to shit,” I barked.

My uncle pulled out one of the chairs and brought it around to my side of the table. He faced it towards him before sitting down.

“I want you to hear me out. If you do not tell them the truth, they will give you life without parole. This is a serious situation, and I need you to start treating it as such. The judge ain't gon' give you another slap on the wrist like they did when you were younger. Someone’s life was taken tonight. Do you hear me?”

“What the fuck are you talking about?” I yelled.

“Just come clean and tell them that you made a mistake. The judge will show leniency if he sees that you’re remorseful.”

“But I didn’t do this shit. It was your fuckin’…”

“Shut the fuck up! Do you hear me?” My uncle leaned towards me and gritted. I lifted my eyebrow as I glared at him and shook my head.

“I guess that nigga told ya?” I finally asked.

“I don’t know what you’re talking about. Who?” He smirked.

“You know exactly who he is,” I whispered angrily.

"I don't know what you're talking about. I just got a call that someone had been killed during a DUI. When I came in, I saw the driver was you and the victim was Jon-Jon. I spoke with my officers and they informed me you weren't cooperating. I came in here to offer you some advice."

As I bit the inside of my jaw, I shot daggers at my uncle's bitch ass.

"Get me a fuckin' lawyer nigga. And I want my phone call!" I bellowed.

"Alright you'll get your phone call, but first I want to make sure that you understand me. Take your time. There will still be an opportunity for you to box and do whatever else you wanna do. If you try to fight it, then you're only gonna make it harder for yourself and those around you. I'm sure you don't want Talya and Jenny suffering from your mistakes, do you?" My uncle looked me dead in the eyes as he spoke. I didn't need him to spell this shit out any clearer for me because I got exactly what he was saying.

"I want my phone call," I repeated. My uncle nodded while standing. He stepped over to me and grabbed my shoulder.

"I'll make sure your books are taken care of, and I'll keep my eye on your family too."

That was it. I lost all the restraint I had left. I jumped out of my seat and hit my uncle with an uppercut to his chin. His neck snapped as his head flew back. The two detectives ran into the room and immediately grabbed me. They threw me against the wall while forcefully gripping my hands behind my back. "That's another charge. You just keep digging yourself further into a hole," the black detective chuckled as he roughly threw the handcuffs on me.

"Fuck all y'all muthafuckas!" I boomed with spittle flying from my mouth. I didn't give a damn about shit. My life was ruined, and it was all Brisham's fault. I didn't have shit else to lose. As the detective started to walk me out of the holding room, my uncle called out to him.

"Hansen."

"Yes Chief?"

"Let's forget about this incident. He's lost his best friend, his career, and now his freedom all in one night. I should have been more understanding when he asked me for his phone call. Trust me when I say this is not his usual behavior. I'm sure my nephew is gonna do the right thing by telling you guys everything. Right Saadiq?" my uncle questioned. I glowered at him. As much as I wanted to expose my uncle for this crooked shit, I knew I couldn't do that. It was my word against him and his punk ass son.

"Yeah I'll tell you the truth," I finally spat. My uncle winked at me while holding his jaw.

"Well sit your ass down and start talking," the detective ordered while pushing me back towards the table.

Kiana

"What do you want from us?" I cried as I stared up into Jacobi's cold eyes.

"First I want this nigga to show me where that money and work at. Then I want you to suck my dick. Since you can't seem to keep your mouth closed, I'mma help ya out," he spewed.

"So you doing all this just because I told your girl about you and Landi?" I frowned in disbelief.

"That's part of it. Because of that lil stunt you pulled my girl left me. She stole all my money and took my daughter. I told you before you talked too fuckin' much. This time I'mma make yo hoe ass back that shit up."

"Nigga, you brought all this shit on yourself. You was the one fucking me and that damn girl at the same time. It was yo' bullshit that caused me to lose our baby. I didn't even know you were gonna be at her spot. If anybody needs to be blamed, it's you. Your dick is the one that got you caught up," I snarled.

Whap!

Suddenly, Jacobi hauled off and slapped the taste out of my mouth. I grabbed my face and glared at him, as Brisham jumped up and tried to charge him. "Sit the fuck back down before I shoot you and this bitch!" Jacobi pointed his gun at Brisham's head.

"My nigga, if you gonna do something then gon' ahead and do what the fuck you gotta do. I ain't sitting hur' while you bitch about this soap opera shit y'all had going on." *Pow!* Jacobi fired a single shot, hitting Brisham in the leg.

"Keep talking that hot shit nigga!" Jacobi barked. I glanced up at the other guy that was with Jacobi, and he smirked at me.

"Fuck you nigga. You might as well kill me now. If you don't, I'm coming for you bitch." Brisham held his leg as he grunted.

"I'mma handle that as soon as you show me to that money and work. I been watching you for a while, so I know you working with Marcellus. You sitting on something nice and I gotta have a piece. Now show me where it's at," Jacobi said, revealing something I didn't even know. I shot my eyes at Brisham. This shit with him just got deeper and deeper.

"Muthafucka, I ain't giving you shit," Brisham seethed.

"Oh you ain't?" Jacobi once again pointed his gun at Brisham. I jumped up and stood in front of him.

"Please stop!" I screamed.

"You better tell yo nigga I ain't playing!" he yelled in my face.

"Brisham, please just give him whatever it is that he wants," I turned to him and pleaded. Brisham clenched his teeth. "Please!"

"Aight nigga, what you want?" he asked Jacobi.

"I already told you I want that work and money."

"I got about twenty-thousand in the back room along with a quarter ounce of work. Take that shit and do what you want with it," Brisham stated nonchalantly. I sat with my eyes damn near bulging out of my head. Brisham hadn't let me know shit about having that stuff in this apartment. What if the police would have come here searching for something? They would have hauled my ass straight to jail, and it wouldn't have been shit I could've done. If I wasn't done before I was definitely done now. He obviously didn't give a fuck about me or my freedom.

"Where that shit at in the back room?" Jacobi asked.

"In the closet; it's a garment bag hanging up," Brisham explained.

"Go to the back and get that bag out the closet," Jacobi ordered the other guy. He was a young thug looking dude. I figured he had to be one of Jacobi workers.

"Jacobi please just let us go. We both did our part in this shit so ain't no need for you to kill us. Please don't hurt me, I'm pregnant," I confessed.

"So you pregnant with this nigga's baby? This shit gets better and better." He let out a sarcastic chuckle.

The other guy came back with the garment bag. "It's in here man," he told Jacobi.

"Cool! Count that money right quick. Once you confirm it's all there, we gonna handle them and get the fuck outta hur'." My eyes widened in fear. I couldn't believe Jacobi was actually gonna kill us. *Think, Kiana. You gotta do something to get out of this situation.*

"So you really gonna kill us?" I questioned. Jacobi cut his eyes at me, but he didn't say anything.

"Kiana don't ask that nigga shit else because it's pissing me off. What the fuck you think he gonna do?" Brisham snarled.

"Shut the fuck up! This shit is all your fault 'cause I told you not to bring that damn gun out!" I snapped. Jacobi started laughing.

"Looks like trouble in paradise," he jested.

"Fuck you Kiana. I was trying to look out for yo ass," Brisham spat.

"Well look where that shit got us." I frowned at him and rolled my eyes. Somebody knocked on the door.

"Who the fuck is that?" Jacobi asked.

"How the hell am I supposed to know and I'm in here with you?"

"Bitch shut yo' smart mouth ass up and see who the fuck that is," he whispered harshly.

Boom, Boom, Boom!

Whoever was on the other side of the door beat again.

"Hurry yo' ass up and check that shit out. And you better not say shit," Jacobi threatened. When I looked out of the peephole, my eyes widened.

"It's the police," I whispered.

"Hell nah," Jacobi said while speed walking towards me. He pushed me out of the way so he could look out the peephole. Turning back around, he stared at me with wide eyes. "It's the police."

No shit. "I told you."

"What the fuck is the police doing hur'?" I shrugged my shoulders just as the knock came again. Little did Jacobi know, it was Brisham's daddy at the door. Of course I wasn't going to tell him that.

"Nigga, we gotta get the fuck outta here," the other guy told Jacobi.

"Aight. Grab that shit and we'll go out the back door." Jacobi was now looking around frantically like he didn't know what to do. All that toughness he had was gone.

"What about them?" the guy questioned as he gathered up the drugs and money.

"We'll deal with this shit another time. I ain't about to get caught with this shit," Jacobi whispered.

"I know y'all in there, I can hear someone moving around. Open up now!" Mr. Kamen demanded. I glanced at Brisham and we locked eyes. He knew what I was doing, so he didn't say anything. Jacobi and the other guy hurriedly gathered everything. A few seconds later they were headed for our backdoor.

"We'll see each other again nigga," Jacobi threw at Brisham on his way out.

"Be ready bitch," I heard Brisham grumble as I rushed to get the door open. I snatched it open without waiting to see if they were gone.

"What took you…" Mr. Kamen cut himself off when he saw Brisham laying on the floor. "What the fuck is going on?"

"We just got held at gun point and robbed," I told him.

"By whom?" He questioned with a nonchalant tone. He didn't even try to pretend he cared.

"We don't know Pops. Can you please just get me some fuckin' help. This shit hurts like hell." Brisham breathed heavily.

"I came here to tell you all that Saadiq was on board, but I had no idea all this was going on. Are you sure you don't know who the person was?" Mr. Kamen pressed.

"Nah Pops, they were wearing masks. Can you please just call for an ambulance?"

"What did they take?" he asked as he removed his cell from his pocket.

"Just some money I had. They shot me because I didn't wanna give it up at first," Brisham continued with his story.

"I tell ya, it's always something with your ass."

While Mr. Kamen called for help, I sat on the couch and rubbed my head. Not only did we have Saadiq's situation hovering over our heads, we now had to deal with Jacobi. *What the fuck am I gonna do*? It didn't seem this shit would ever end.

Saadiq

One week later…

"Kamen let's go. You got a visitor," the female guard informed me. I stood and grabbed the bullshit orange pullover shirt. When I got to the bars of my cell, the guard had me slide my hands through so she could put the handcuffs on.

"I can't believe that you in here. Wait until I tell my friends I met Knockout!" the guard squealed, and I frowned. Here I was facing jail time and this bitch was talking about some boxing shit. I shook my head. When we got to the visiting area, the CO took my handcuffs off and pointed me towards the tables. The sad look on Talya's face when I approached the table was the first thing I noticed. That shit broke my heart.

"Saadiq baby." She jumped up when she saw me. She tried to hug me, but the guard shouted that there was no touching. Talya went back to her seat. "I didn't know," she whispered.

"It's all good," I told her as we stared at each other.

"How are you holding up?" She went to grab my hand but quickly snatched it back.

"I'm aight."

"We spoke to the lawyer and he told us that you refused his help. Why would you do that?"

I briefly glanced away. I hated to tell her I was taking the plea deal, but I guess I really had no choice.

"Because it's best if I cop to the plea deal they're offering me. I'll get five years, and with good behavior I could be out in two or three years," I explained.

"You made the decision without discussing it with me first?" Talya frowned.

"Nah, I haven't told them shit yet. If I try to take the case to court, I'm looking at 25 years…minimum."

"For what…a mistake? They gotta know this wasn't intentional," she snapped.

"They don't look at the shit that way. I killed my best friend. This shit ain't just about me driving drunk and crashing the car. My day one nigga is gone because of me," I told her.

"Is that why you refused the lawyer's services, because you feel guilty?" she questioned.

"I didn't see no reason for y'all to waste money on a lawyer when I'mma do time anyway. I figured this would work out for all of us," I told half the truth.

"What about the plans we made, the move to Vegas, and your promise that you'll never leave me? Did you think about any of that before you made that dumb ass decision?" Talya snarled. Tears were falling down her cheeks as she went off. She was mad at me, and I really couldn't blame her. If only she knew I was doing this for her.

"I know I fucked up," I mumbled.

"You damn right you fucked up, but I'mma still stick this out with you." She wiped her tears and gazed into my eyes. Hearing those words would have been like music to my ears if I was a selfish nigga. However, I couldn't just let Talya put her life on hold for me. I'd always told her I would do whatever to protect her, and that's exactly what I was gonna do.

"I appreciate that shawty, but I feel like you need to go on with your life. My life might be fucked up, but it doesn't mean yours have to be."

"What the fuck are you talking about go on with my life? You making it seem as if you're turning your back on me," she spat vehemently.

"I'm not turning my back on you. A nigga would love for you to ride this sentence out with me, but five years is a long ass time for you to wait. C'mon Talya, don't make this any harder for me."

"No it's not. How the hell you gonna tell me? Only I can decide what's too long, and right now I'm saying I'mma be here!" she yelled.

"I'm not saying when I get out I don't want us to be together. But for now, I want you to go on with your life. It's not fair for me to hold you back." I thought that would make her understand but Talya was stubborn.

She glared at me with tears steadily falling down her face. "I guess you never loved me like you claimed, huh?" she hissed, and I frowned at her.

"I'mma let that slide 'cause I know you upset, but don't ever question my love for you again."

"I wouldn't have to if you weren't trying to push me away," she spat. I sighed.

"It's not like that." I tried once again to explain but she held her hand up to stop me.

"I'mma give you some time to think about what you're saying. Obviously, all this got your head fucked up so I'mma leave for now." She stood up and stared down at me. "I promise Saadiq, if you don't allow me to be here, I will never forgive you for this. You might as well consider yourself dead to me at that point." Her words came out slow and deliberate, and I could see the seriousness in her eyes. This wasn't just Talya being angry, she meant every word.

When she walked off, I kept my eyes on her until I was no longer able to see her. When the CO came back and escorted me to my cell, I laid on my bunk and thought about everything. I wanted Talya to be here, but I was afraid if she continued to visit, I would slip and tell her the truth. I couldn't have her or my momma getting hurt. It was best to just let her walk away to prevent that. Tomorrow I would take her name off the visitor's list. From this day forward, I didn't want any contact with the outside world. It would be the only way for me to get through this shit.

Brisham

A week later…

After being released from the hospital, I went to my boy Bird's crib. I couldn't go back to the old spot, so he let me crash here. Before I was released the police came by questioning me about that supposed 'home invasion.' I told them the same story I told my Pops. I didn't need them handling nothing. Me and that nigga Jacobi was gonna handle this shit street style once I healed. He violated when he came into my home, so he had to see me. Aside from dealing with him, I had Marcellus on my back. I was supposed to take him a payment a week ago. Telling him about the robbery wasn't going to help me. Marcellus was the type of nigga that didn't give a fuck if you were on your death bed.

Kiana still wasn't fucking with me. She stayed with a nigga the whole time I was in the hospital. As soon as they let me go, she got ghost. I guess I couldn't blame her. She wasn't supposed to get caught up in this bullshit, but that's just how it went down. She could be mad, but she needed to keep her mouth closed.

My phone rang and I snatched it up. When I looked at the caller ID, I saw it was the lil broad Kylisha calling. We'd chopped it up a few times since the day I hit, but we hadn't hooked up again. "What's good?" I answered.

"Hey, is now a good time?" she asked.

"Yeah wassup?" It was a good thing she was calling because I was out of Mollys. Maybe I could get her to cop some for me. The pain pills the doctor had prescribed wasn't doing shit for a nigga.

"Um, we need to talk asap," she said.

"We talking now," I told her with a slight chuckle.

"No, this is not something we need to discuss over the phone." Her tone sounded serious. *I hope this bitch ain't trying to set me up with Marcellus.*

"You gon' have to tell me over the phone. I just got out of the hospital and can't leave the house."

"What happened to you?" she questioned.

"I was shot but fuck all that. What you wanna discuss?" She released a deep breath.

"Aight, I'mma just say it…" she paused.

"C'mon shawty, spare me with the theatrics. What's going on?" I pressed her to continue.

"I'm pregnant Brisham," she blurted out, and my heart damn near leaped out my chest.

"Fuck you just say?" I frowned as I pressed the phone closer to my ear. Clearly I hadn't heard her correctly.

"I'm pregnant," she repeated.

"Aight, so what you saying?"

"Are you slow? I just told you I'm pregnant, and yes this is your baby," she spat. I shook my head.

"I thought you were cool people. Why you playing games?"

"Nigga, this is just as much of a shock to me as it is to you. I ain't plan this but shit happens." I got quiet as I listened to her talk. What really messed me up was I knew it could be my baby. I'd skeeted all in her the time we fucked. I was pissed at myself for being reckless.

"Damn," I mumbled.

"That's all you gotta say?" she asked.

"I mean what else is there to say?"

"Are you gonna step up and be a father?"

"To be honest, I got another seed on the way. I ain't ready to have two."

"What that got to do with me?" she snapped.

"You ain't hearing me. I ain't trying to have another kid right now. I'mma just hit you with some ends to take care of it." Kylisha got quiet. "Aight?"

"Fine, I'll get the damn abortion." Her voice cracked.

"This for the best shawty. We ain't ready for all this."

"Whatever Brisham," she cried as she hung up in my face. I sighed as I laid back. *When it rains, it fuckin' pours*, I thought.

***

A few days later…

"Wassup Pops?" I answered my phone.

"He just signed the deal," he told me.

"So everything is good?"

"So far it seems that way. They sentence him in three weeks. Do *not* try to come. We don't wanna rock the boat. I'll just come up with a lie to tell Talya and Jennifer why you're not there," my Pops explained.

"Aight 'preciate it—"

"Muthafucka, you been hiding out from me," I heard a familiar voice say as I tried to ease into the apartment.

"Hello…Brisham?" my Pops yelled.

"Let me hit you back." I ended the call as I turned to Marcellus. I was just coming back from copping some Mollys from this dealer around the corner. I wonder if his bitch ass set me up. Nobody else knew I was here.

"I was gonna hit you up today," I lied. Marcellus glared at me.

"Oh yeah?" He slowly nodded.

"I been in the hospital. I was shot," I tried to explain.

"Nigga, do it look like I give a fuck about what you were laid up for? I wanna know where the fuck my money at?" he barked.

"I gotcha money, man."

"Where it's at muthafucka?" I glanced at the baby gansta s in training he had with him. I was wondering if I should run or just tough this shit out.

"It's in the house," I uttered, deciding it wasn't worth the risk.

"Go get it. If you ain't out in two minutes I'm sending them in after you," he threatened.

I went into the house where I been sleeping and headed for the closet. When Jacobi took that money back at the crib, he didn't know I had another forty thousand in a shoe box underneath the bed. The nigga called himself robbing somebody, but his dumb ass didn't even make sure he got everything. I owed Marcellus like thirty-one thousand for the two bricks he gave me on consignment. He let me cop them for some killer prices; fourteen thousand for the bricks, and he only charged me ten percent interest.

Initially, I had enough to pay him plus walk away with a hefty profit. Once I handed this over, I was back at ground zero. *Fuck it, that shit is all a part of the game.* I would just have to get it how I lived. After peeling off the money I owed Marcellus, I went back outside and gave it to him.

He handed it to one of the dudes while never removing his eyes from me. "Count that shit," he instructed the lil dude. "Now what's this shit I hear about you getting robbed? Is that why yo' ass been hiding out?"

"How you hear about that?" I wondered.

"Nigga don't worry about it. Just answer the fuckin' question."

"Yeah, somebody ran up in my spot a few weeks ago and hit me for some cash and work," I admitted.

"Why are you just telling me this?" Marcellus folded his arms across his chest as he leaned on the railing.

"Because I was tryna handle it on my own. I know who the nigga is."

"Did you take care of it?" He asked.

"Not yet, but I plan to get on it real soon."

"Maybe your ass could be on your business if you weren't out here getting high," he smirked.

I shook my head in bewilderment. How the fuck did this nigga know everything? As if he was reading my mind Marcellus said, "Yeah muthafucka… Don't shit get by me in these streets. I own this city."

"Look man—" I started but he cut me off.

"After this transaction, consider our business done," he told me straight up.

I threw up my hands. "I gave you the money."

"Nigga, I don't give a fuck about that. I had to come looking for you. Then you out hur' getting high and shit. I don't fuck with pill heads," he bellowed before turning to walk away.

For a second I stood there thinking 'fuck this nigga, but then it hit me. Marcellus was the only connect who could put some real dough in my pockets. To get what he was offering I would have to go out of town. I didn't have time to establish a relationship with a new connect. I needed to get back to this money.

"Wait Marcellus," I called. He turned around shooting daggers at my ass.

"Lil nigga I got shit to do," he gritted.

"What if I hit you with the cash first? Can we do business then?"

"Yo' broke ass ain't got no money to hit me up front," he spat. The lil dudes with him starting giggling and shit.

"Not now but I will soon if you know what I mean. C'mon man, I ain't trying to be out here like this begging. I need to get to this money." Marcellus was silent for a minute like he was seriously considering it. "C'mon, fuck with me," I asked.

"Aight chill out." He laughed. It was nice to see he found humor in me begging. "You know what? Usually when I make a decision, I stick to it. However, I'm in a good mood today. Let's go to my car to chop it up, and I'll tell you what you can do to get me to reconsider working with you again," he stated. Excitedly, I rubbed my hands together while nodding.

Ain't no telling what this nigga had up his sleeve, but at this point I would rob my own Pops if he wanted me to. Speaking of my Pops, it was probably best if I told Marcellus he was the Chief of Police before that shit came back to bite me in the ass too. I didn't want nothing else fuckin' with my money. I was about to get on for real.

Natalya

A year and a half later…

"Say cheese Kacen," I said to my baby boy as the camera man took what felt like the hundredth picture of us. His cute lil chubby cheeks dented in as he grinned hard as hell. Once we were done snapping it up, I thanked the camera man and walked back over to the table. I'd rented out Monkey Joe's amusement center and invited all my close family and friends to celebrate my baby's very first birthday. When Kiana heard about it, she asked if we could do a joint party. My goddaughter Raegan, which was her daughter, had just turned a year old about a month before Kacen. The party was filled with some of everybody from both of our families. We'd just cut the cakes Kiana and I ordered, and now we were getting ready to open the gifts.

"You want me to get him for a minute?"

"Nah baby, that's okay." I smiled.

"You sure? 'Cause lil man been glued to you since we got here. You'on need no break?" Marcellus offered.

"It's okay. I don't mind him being stuck to me, we a team. Ain't that right lil man?" I tickled Kacen's neck, and he smiled the infectious smile that always melted my heart.

"You got his butt spoiled." Marcellus shook his head before bending to put a kiss on my lips.

"I spoil you too," I told him, and he grinned mischievously.

"Shit, can I get spoiled later? Can you make that happen?" He smiled at me while stroking his goatee.

Aight, so I know you're wondering how I ended up with Marcellus. Well that's a funny story. After I found out Saadiq blocked me on his visitor's list, I was completely devastated. I did everything I could to reach out to him, but nothing worked. All my letters came back returned and I never received any calls. Hell, he didn't even reach out to Ms. Jennifer once they sentenced him. It was like he'd just shut himself off from the world.

Most of my pregnancy was spent crying over his ass, but then one day I had an epiphany. I figured if Saadiq really loved me, he wouldn't have turned his back on me. When I was seven months pregnant, I ran into Marcellus again. We started talking on the phone and then we began to hang out. By the time I hit my nine month mark, we were already in a committed relationship. He was there at the hospital with me when I gave birth to Kacen. He'd even cut the umbilical cord. We moved in together around the time Kacen turned three months, and we'd been rocking ever since. For the most part I liked being with Marcellus. We had a lot of fun together and our sex was amazing. My only dilemma is that I don't love him.

"Yeah, I can make that happen. Now c'mon and help me open these—" I was suddenly interrupted by the sounds of someone shouting. I glanced around and spotted Marcellus' baby momma speed walking in our direction.

"Marcellus, we need to talk!" Ariel shouted. I sighed. See this was the shit I wasn't about to deal with today. This was part of the reason I couldn't completely give my heart to Marcellus. He didn't know how to keep his baby momma in check. Me and Ariel had several run ins since Marcellus and I have been together. She was always doing shit like this, and it was starting to get on my last nerve.

"You need to handle that right now," I told Marcellus through clenched teeth. I looked around to see if anybody was looking and all eyes were on me. I was so embarrassed.

"I'mma handle it baby. I promise," he swore as he took off for Ariel.

"Talya I don't know who that bitch is, but I tried to stop her. She was talking about how I needed to get Marcellus right now. I had to let her ass know she wasn't running shit up in hur'," my cousin Nene ranted as she approached me. She was my older cousin on my dad's side of the family. Over the past few months we'd grown closer.

"Girl, that's just Marcellus' baby momma. Her daughter is Emani," I explained. She sucked her teeth and rolled her eyes. Nene was a little over average height and was my complexion. A lot of our family said we resembled each other, but I didn't really see it.

"You want me to beat her ass? 'Cause you know I will," Nene spat. I giggled. My cousin was ghetto as hell.

"Nah, that's okay. If she wasn't Emani's momma I might consider it." I laughed.

"Aight cuz, let me know." Nene walked away while holding her fist to her palm. I shook my head. Kiana came up just as she walked away.

"What was that about?" She asked me.

"You talking about the shit with Ariel?" I questioned as I bounced Kacen on my knee.

"Yeah, wassup with her? What was that shit she was talking about?"

"I don't know what that is about. I just know she getting on my nerves. It's like she pops up wherever we are. Then her ass be calling all the time. I thought we handled this shit in the beginning, but it just seems to be getting worse." Kiana looked at me and frowned.

"Am I'm still talking to the same Talya?"

"What are you talking about?"

"Bitch, you need to make Marcellus handle that. You're his woman, not that hoe," she spat.

"It's not him, it's her," I admitted.

"Nah Talya fuck that! That's his baby momma, so he needs to handle it. You shouldn't have to deal with her popping up at your son's birthday party."

"I try not to nag him about the situation. I know he hates to be stuck in the middle, but tonight when we get home I'mma have to gon' and say something."

"Hell yeah. Matter fact give me lil man. You need to gone out thur', get your man, and bring him back in here to his family where he belongs." Kiana gave me a stern look like she was my momma.

"Bitch you crazy." I laughed.

"Nah, you crazy if you sit by and let her take your man away. Now go handle yo' business. Don't be no punk." After handing Kacen to his godmother, I made my way through the building. When I stepped outside, I immediately spotted them near the side of the building. What caught me off guard is that they were kissing.

“Marcellus!” I shouted, and he looked at me. I charged straight for them.

“Look, it ain’t what you think,” he said while pushing Ariel out the way.

Kiana

A few days later…

I was out at the St. Louis Galleria doing a little shopping for Raegan. Since today was my off day, I'd decided to spend it with my baby. After we finished here we were going to go have lunch somewhere. I loved being a momma. It was the only good thing I had going on in my life. Raegan and I stayed together unless I had to work. Brisham was in the streets so much he barely had time to spend with her. I guess he'd finally gotten what he wanted because he was now pushing major weight.

Me and him wasn't on good terms at all. He still tried to act like we were together, but I let him know wasn't nothing popping off. The most he could do was make sure he hit me with some ends to take care of our daughter. The situation with Saadiq made me not want to have shit to do with him. I'd kept my word not to tell Talya, but I swear every time I was around her it ate me alive.

If that wasn't enough, the shit with Jacobi messed with me for the longest. I moved out of the place me and Brisham used to live in and got me a spot in a better neighborhood. I kept thinking Jacobi was going to come looking for me. Everywhere I went I was looking over my shoulder. That is until one day when I saw a news report that he had been shot multiple times. Whoever killed him dropped his body at the city's dump. One of the men working on site found him underneath a pile of trash.

I knew for a fact Brisham was behind his death. Even though he never mentioned anything to me, it just had his name written all over it. That's why he didn't tell the police what happened because he wanted to handle it. Sometimes I questioned if what went down was my fault, but I just figured Jacobi had brought that on himself. I didn't owe him any sympathy after everything he did to me. Stepping over to a rack that had dresses on it, I picked up one that was in Raegan's size. Just as I was getting ready to check the price, a little person ran into my leg.

"Are you okay baby?" I asked the little girl. She looked to be about six or seven. Her skin was a pretty brown, she had long jet black hair, and pink lips. Her little cute ass looked like a real-life baby doll.

"I'm sorry," she whispered.

"It's okay." I reached out my hand to help her up.

"Macy where you at?" I heard a deep voice say just as I grabbed the little girl's hand.

"I'm over here, daddy!" she yelled.

"Girl, what did I tell you about running off?" This extremely tall, light brown guy with a curly mohawk and a toned body suddenly stepped over to us. I stood back for a minute, stuck in a trance as I looked him over. Ol' boy was fine as hell. He was dressed simple in a pair of shorts, a white tee, and tennis shoes. He had two sleeved tattoos on his arms that gave him this ruggish look. *Mmm, mmm, mmm!*

"I'm sorry daddy," the little girl said, and the gorgeous guy sighed. I let go of her hand as I stared her father down.

"Don't be hitting me with that sorry daddy stuff. I don' told you not to run off," he continued and then he looked at me. "My bad about that."

"It's no problem. I was just helping her up because she fell. By the way, she's so cute," I complimented.

"'Preciate that. Is that your daughter?" he asked, pointing to Raegan.

"Mhm," I mumbled.

"I can see. She's pretty just like her momma," the dude said. I blushed as I bit my bottom lip.

"You're the first I heard that from. Most people say she look like her daddy," I told him.

"Well I don't know what he looks like, but from what I see that's all you right thur'."

"Thanks!" I continued to smile.

"So what's your name?" he questioned while stroking his goatee.

"Kiana. What's yours?" I asked.

"Lex," he stated.

"That's wassup. It was nice meeting you Lex." I started to walk off, but he stopped me. "Yeah wassup?" I asked nonchalantly.

"How about you let me get that number? Maybe I can take you out sometime, that is if you ain't got a man." He grinned.

I looked him up and down before replying. "Let me ask you a question."

"Aight shoot."

"Are you still with your daughter's momma?"

With a straight face he told me, "Nah we ain't together." I glanced down at Macy to see if she would give me any indication that her father was lying. Surprisingly she didn't. I thought about it for a second. Really, I wasn't trying to get with nobody. My focus had been strictly on my daughter, but I guess it wouldn't hurt to at least see what he was talking about.

"Give me your phone," I finally told Lex. He went into his pocket and retrieved his phone. He took the lock code off before handing it to me. Once I stored my number, I gave the phone back. "See you later," I said, sashaying off.

"Hol' up. What's the rush?" he asked.

"Today is mommy daughter day. I would like to finish having my time with my daughter." I glanced back just as Lex was checking me out.

"I can dig it. I'mma hit you later if that's okay." He smiled.

"That's fine." I told him. Before I could go back to what I was doing, I heard Lex's daughter say something that made me stop dead in my tracks.

"Daddy, why did you tell me to run over where that lady was?" Macy questioned.

"Aye girl," he chuckled. I glanced back and noticed the look on his face. It was priceless. He was embarrassed that his daughter had busted him out. I actually thought it was cute that he used her to help him talk to me. Finally turning to walk away, I made sure to put a little extra twist in my walk since I knew he was looking.

Marcellus

Later that night…

I took my hands and gently opened her legs as she slept peacefully on her back. Her body shifted a little, but she didn't wake up. After pulling off the black lace panties she was wearing, I wasted no time attacking her sweet tasting center. Almost immediately her soft hand grabbed my head as her legs spread wider.

"Mmm," she moaned. Her lower body lifted from the bed. Gripping hold of her legs, I pinned them down with my arms and latched onto her pearl. I then stiffened my tongue and pushed her legs back towards her ears. Just like that, shawty's juices spilled onto my tongue.

"Oh my god, Marcellus!" Talya screamed.

"You like that shit?" I asked between kisses. When she locked down on my head with her legs, I got my answer. I was eating that pussy up when it finally hit her.

"Mhm…No, wait! What the hell you think you doing?" She suddenly pushed my head away.

"I'm trying to make up. Now lay back and let me take care of you." I grinned up at her.

"No, I'm still mad. Now move," she hissed. I got up while wiping my mouth with the back of my hand.

"You still pissed about that shit? I already told you she kissed me."

"Hell yeah I'm still mad. You got me out hur' fighting and shit like I'm some teenager. This is not what the fuck I signed up for."

"Aight, let's talk about this shit." I let out a sigh.

"What do you want to talk about? Maybe we can start with how you let your baby momma control whatever time we spend with Emani, or maybe we can talk about how she still wants you. Oh, and let's not forget how she ruined my son's party. Which one you wanna start with?" She went on and on.

"Aight, I get it."

"If you get it, then why are we having this conversation? Your baby momma been wrong, but what have you done to put that bitch in her place?" Shawty was so pissed she was rolling her neck and shit as she talked. It was kind of funny to see her professional ass act like this. I knew better than to laugh while she was on her rant though.

"You make it seem like I'm letting her do this shit," I said with a half grin.

"See, you think this shit is funny," she spat.

"Nah, I'on think it's funny. I'm just trying to figure out why this is my fault."

"Because somehow you made her feel comfortable to do everything she does. How can you not see that?"

"But I'on be doing nothing," I told her.

"That's a lie. The only time a woman won't let go is if the nigga is leading her on. Ooh, I swear I wouldn't have to go through all this—" She suddenly cut herself off.

"You wouldn't have to go through all this if what?" I questioned.

"Nothing," she mumbled.

"Nah, gon' and say it." I slid off the bed and stared down at her. A nigga was cool at first, but she'd just pissed me off.

"I told you it's nothing." She shifted her eyes, trying to look everywhere but at me.

"Don't sweat it shawty. I'll handle the situation," I sputtered. I turned and headed for the door.

"What's wrong with you?" She had the nerve to ask me. I turned and snarled at her ass before continuing my way. "Marcellus!" Talya called my name just as I got to the door.

"What the fuck you want Talya?"

"Where are you going?" she asked.

"Out."

"In the middle of our conversation?"

"Ain't shit else to discuss. You said you wanted me to handle it, and I told you I would."

"Don't you think it's kind of late for you to be going out?" I had to bite my tongue because I almost called her out her name.

"Nope! I'm a grown ass man and don't have no curfew. I'll be back in a minute." I opened the door.

"Really Marcellus?"

I ignored her ass as I kept going. One thing about me is that I didn't argue. Besides, if I would have stuck around any longer, I was bound to do something I would later regret.

Saadiq

A few days later…

"Did you check on that for me?" I asked as soon as I approached the table. I was just in the rec room about to work out when one of the COs told me I had a visitor. I made my way out here as fast as I could.

"Hello to you too," she said.

"My bad, how you doing?" I gave her a half smile.

"I'm fine Saadiq. Thanks for asking," she smirked.

"C'mon girl, don't start tripping. You know it ain't like that," I told her with a sly grin.

"You would think I could get a simple hello since I'm the one that comes to visit every week." Adore' playfully rolled her eyes at me. I shook my head as I sat back and looked at her.

When everything went down, Adore' and her father stuck by my side. They were the only ones I allowed to visit. We became fast friends, and I was cool with that because she was easy to talk to.

"I hate to be the bearer of bad news, but it seems she has moved on," Adore' stated.

"What you mean she moved on?"

"I went to the address you gave me, but the new owner told me she doesn't live there anymore. They said she moved in with…" Adore' said and paused midsentence while glancing off.

"She moved in with who?"

Adore' looked back at me with this blank expression on her face. "Are you sure you want to know Saadiq?" she questioned.

"Yeah go ahead," I muttered. She cleared her throat before speaking again.

"She moved in with her new boyfriend. I believe they said his name was Marcus, Marcel, or something like that. I can't remember."

I ran my hand down my face. "You serious right now?"

"I couldn't make this up even if I wanted to. You just don't understand how hard this was for me to tell you. That's why I didn't make it to the last visit because I was trying to bide my time. This is not something you should have on your mind right now," she said. I leaned back in my seat and looked straight ahead. "Are you okay?"

"You know what, it's all good. I told her to move on with her life while I was in here, so it ain't like I didn't know it was possible. That shit probably ain't even serious.

Once I get out, she'll know what's up," I uttered. Adore's big brown eyes lowered towards the table again. Her ass had something else she wasn't telling me. "What else?" I questioned.

Sighing, she looked up at me. "I mean, you pretty much have what you need. There is no reason to torture yourself. Just move on Saadiq," she told me.

"Just tell me what you know," I gritted through clenched teeth.

"Alright, I'll tell you." Adore' threw up her hands. "The couple told me she now has a newborn baby."

That time I sat all the way up in my seat as I looked into Adore's eyes. "Boy or girl?" I snarled.

"They didn't say. I'm sorry."

I bit down on my tongue so hard I started to taste blood. "So she did it like that?" I said more to myself.

"I'm so sorry Saadiq. I know this is a hard pill for you to swallow. Whatever I can do to help you get through this, you know I will." I continued to look at Adore' and then I stood up. "Wait, where are you going?"

"I'm leaving," I grumbled.

"But visitation isn't over." She had a confused look on her face.

"I ain't in the mood to talk no more. Just come back next week." I quickly walked away without saying shit else.

"Saadiq!" I heard her say. I kept walking until I made it back to the door where this female guard, Eva, stood waiting. Eva was about 5'8 with a caramel complexion, brown eyes, and was sort of on the thicker side.

"You okay Knockout?" she asked as she opened the door. I'd fucked Eva several times since I been in here. Matter fact, I'd knocked down a few of the female guards. It wasn't shit serious, and they all knew about each other. Crazy thing is they didn't give a damn that they were sharing the dick. As long as they got their piece, everything was all good.

"Nah, I need to let some steam off."

"Okay baby. Go get ready and I'mma come get you in about thirty minutes," she whispered.

"Don't forget the rubbers, and don't have me waiting too long. I need to handle this asap," I threw over my shoulder as I trudged to my cell.

Brisham

As soon as I stepped foot into the house, the foul stench of something hit my nostrils. "Yo, what the fuck is that smell?" I frowned my face in disgust.

"Your son just shitted," Kylisha snickered.

"Goddamn! What that lil nigga eat?" I covered my nose as I went and sat on the couch. Kylisha walked over and immediately dumped him in my lap. "Damn, he ain't a package," I grumbled.

"Boy, I'm tired as hell. I been with him all day, and I need this break." She snaked her neck as she bent down to pick up a blunt that was in the ashtray. When she got ready to spark it up, I frowned.

"Fuck is you doing?"

"I'm about to smoke…duh," she stated with that smart ass mouth.

"Aye, what the fuck did I tell you about that? Don't smoke that shit in front of him. If you want to smoke, take yo ass outside."

Kylisha looked at me and rolled her eyes before stomping towards the door. "What's wrong with your momma, huh?" I asked my son as soon as her ass was gone.

About six months ago I'd gone out and copped me a house in Maryland Heights. It was a five bedroom home located in a cul-de-sac of a quiet neighborhood. I let Kylisha move in with me after I found out she hadn't got the abortion I gave her the money for. She took my bread and disappeared for a few months. When she popped back up, her ass was eight months pregnant. By then it was too late for me to even be mad. We did a DNA test when my son was born, and the results came back he was 99.99999% mine.

We named him Skylar Lyndell Kamen. He was now nine months old and looking more like me by the day. I still hadn't told Kiana about my son because I knew her ass would bug out. Every time we saw each other all we did was argue. If she knew I had a baby with somebody else, she might be lowdown and try to keep my daughter away.

As far as me and Kylisha, we were just co-parenting. Actually, I wouldn't even say co-parenting. Her ass was more like a babysitter. She only kept our son while I was out hustling. The minute I came in she dumped him on me. The bitch didn't cook, clean, wash clothes or do shit. All her trifling ass did was get high and beg. She didn't know shit about being a momma.

After being gone for over thirty minutes, Kylisha finally came back into the house. I glared at her trifling ass in disgust. Before she had Skylar, she at least took better care of herself. Now all she wore were the same dingy Joggers and my big t-shirts. The only reason I let her stay here so she wouldn't be ripping and running the streets with my son.

"You wanna fuck," she asked me, and I frowned.

"Hell nah. You look like you ain't washed yo' pussy in days. That shit probably reek. I'm good on that." I frowned.

Kylisha flipped me the middle finger. "Fuck you then. Ugh, I'm so tired." She let out a long yawn before stretching out on the couch.

"Maaaa," Skylar attempted to say her name in his baby voice. Kylisha acted like she didn't hear him.

"Say man, don't you hear him calling you?"

"Mmm mmm. It's your time to be with his lil whiney ass. I be with him all day," she mumbled. I shook my head while shooting daggers at her back.

"Why you don't get up and cook or something? All you do is get high and sleep."

Kylisha snapped her neck back. "You better go over to that bitch you still in love with house and get her to do all that wifely shit. 'Cause nigga that ain't me. We had an arrangement, and it didn't have nothing to do with me cooking, cleaning, and all that extra shit you be trying to get me to do," her smart mouth ass spat.

"You's a pathetic broad, you know that?"

"Whatever Brisham. I'm about to take a nap. Let me know when you leave so I can get up with him." Kylisha rolled over on the couch and went to sleep. *What the hell was I thinking when I fucked around with this hoe*? You know you couldn't stand a broad if you didn't even want to fuck. What nigga turned down in house pussy?

"C'mon lil man. You can ride out with yo' daddy," I told my son. He started to smile like he understood what I was saying. As I held him in my arms, I went to his room to gather his stuff for his diaper bag. Once I had everything I needed, me and him left Kylisha right where she was. I hated this was the shit I had to deal with. I never had these issues with Kiana.

Natalya

One week later…

It had been almost two weeks since Marcellus stormed out on me. I knew why he was angry. I'd almost made a mistake and said I wouldn't be going through this bullshit if I was with Saadiq. I hadn't meant to go there, but all this baby momma drama was stressing me out. Why couldn't he just keep her in check? The day I'd caught her kissing him, I snatched that bitch by her hair and started to beat her ass. When it got too bad, Marcellus jumped in and broke it up.

Even with her face messed up, Ariel just kept talking shit. The bitch had the nerve to tell me I was just a temporary filler until he got his mind right. I tried my best to get to that bitch again, but Marcellus wouldn't let me. What really pissed me off is all Marcellus told her was to chill out. In my eyes, it was as if he enjoyed seeing us fight. She might have been fighting for his ass, but I was making a point.

The first few days after the situation I'd seriously considered leaving him. I didn't give a fuck if he did say she kissed him. Once I calmed down, I thought about everything. Honestly, I didn't want to leave because I wasn't ready to be alone. Still, I wanted Marcellus to learn a lesson. I was walking around ignoring the shit out of him until he turned the tables on me.

Looking in the mirror, I put the finishing touches on my makeup and fingered through my curls. Once I saw they were popping, I went into the bedroom where I'd set up rose petals, candles, chocolate, and massage oils. I had Ms. Jennifer keep Kacen so Marcellus and I could have the whole evening to ourselves. He was decent enough to call home and let me know he would be here soon. That was almost two hours ago, so hopefully he would be coming in at any minute.

Once Marcellus saw what I put together, he wouldn't be able to keep his hands off me. It had been two weeks since we last had sex, and a bitch was horny. After waiting for another forty minutes, I finally heard the front door open. I quickly hopped on my knees and waited for Marcellus to come into our bedroom. Ten minutes later he entered the room eating an apple. His eyes briefly scanned the room before landing on me.

"Surprise!" I shouted, and Marcellus smirked. I ignored the unpleasant look he had on his face and stuck to the task at hand. "You like?" I asked as I stood up on the bed. I wanted him to get a good look at the crotchless, see through lingerie bodysuit I was wearing. I ordered it from one of those sexy lingerie shops online.

"What's this?" he questioned nonchalantly.

I twisted my lips at him. "What does it look like?"

Marcellus tossed the apple into the trashcan by the door. "This shit ain't gon' fix our problems Talya."

"I know it ain't but c'mon baby, you gotta appreciate the gesture. If nothing else, I thought you would get a kick out of seeing me in this. Look at my body." I turned around, poked my butt out, and glanced over my shoulder.

Again, Marcellus didn't display any form of happiness. I sighed as I plopped down onto the bed. "Okay, what's the problem? It's been like two weeks and we haven't fucked. That's really got me feeling some type of way. Are you cheating on me?" I folded my arms over my breasts.

"You know exactly what the issue is because if you didn't yo' ass wouldn't be going through all of this. Stop trying to insult my intelligence," he barked. I pressed my lips together.

"You're upset about something I almost said."

"Nah shawty, it's deeper than that. I wanna know why you even thinking about him. You claim you been over the nigga, but I don't believe that. You stay going to his momma's house like you just waiting for him to come home."

"She's my son's grandmother. I'm her only connection for them to have a relationship." I frowned, not understanding why he was even bringing this up. I now realized we did have a bigger issue than I thought.

"You act like that lady ain't raised two sons on her own. Lil man will be good without you being there."

"It's not even like that Marcellus. Ms. Jennifer has always been like a second mother to me, even before Saadiq and I got into a relationship. I'm not gonna end my relationship with her just because we ain't together anymore."

"Aight, what about me asking you to spend some time with my momma? You go over there but it's only with me. She wanna hang out with you too, but you be acting like you ain't got no time."

"Oh my God! I was trying to do something that would break the ice, but I see you're just trying to find some way to flip all our issues on me. I don't know why the hell I even bothered," I huffed.

"I don't either because it's not like you really did this shit for me anyway. You did it to make yourself feel better."

"What are you talking about now?" I asked, and Marcellus chuckled. This wasn't going anything like I planned.

"We been together for a year and a half but you ain't ever said you love me. You so worried about the next bitch moving into your territory, but you ain't even secured your own spot," he spat before marching back out the room.

I blinked my eyes rapidly as I sat there dumbfounded.

***

Later that night…

I was laying on my back staring at the ceiling. No matter how hard I tried, I couldn't stop thinking about what Marcellus said. Even though he claimed he wasn't feeling Ariel in that way, I knew for a fact he liked the attention she gave him. If she snatched up my man, I wouldn't have nobody but myself to blame.

I was so stuck on Saadiq I hadn't paid attention to the man in front of me. But why was that when Saadiq basically gave me his ass to kiss? He allowed another man to come in and raise the son he should be raising. So again, I asked myself, *Why the hell am I even thinking about his ass*?

Just then Marcellus entered our bedroom. Quietly, I laid and watched him as he removed his clothes and tossed them into the hamper. Knowing he was going to ignore me like he'd been doing, I closed my eyes and prepared to go to sleep. To my surprise, Marcellus walked around to my side of the bed and sat down beside me.

"Wake up shawty," he said.

"I'm not sleep," I mumbled as I opened my eyes.

"I apologize about how shit went down earlier. I know you went through a lot to get all that together, and I ruined everything."

"It's okay," I sighed. None of that mattered. I just wanted things to return to how they were.

"Nah, it's not okay. To keep it real, I been tripping lately. I guess a nigga just get a lil jealous sometimes."

"But you shouldn't. I'm with you, and this is where I plan to be," I told him.

"You already know. You mine, and forever gon' be mine," he said, and my heart fluttered.

"Aww baby," I said, rubbing my fingers through his beard. "I'm sorry for everything. I just wanna make sure we're good."

Marcellus gazed into my eyes before nodding. "Yeah, we're good." He finally grinned.

I lifted my eyebrows. "You're sure? I don't want you to feel some way. If you want me to stop spending time over there so much, I will."

"That ain't my place to tell you that shawty. Y'all had a relationship before I came in the picture. I was out of line to even tell you that," he said. I nodded. "I got a little surprise for ya."

"What is it?" I asked with a big grin.

Marcellus smirked as he got up and grabbed his phone. When he returned to the bed, he handed it to me.

"What's this?" I asked as my eyes scanned the content on the screen. When I saw that they were plane tickets, I started screaming. "You taking me to Dominican Republic?"

"You said you ain't ever left St. Louis, so I figured a spot like the DR would be a good place to pop your travel cherry."

"You really do love me, huh?" I smiled.

"Not really. A nigga just love that pussy," he joked.

I busted out laughing. "You are so silly."

I hopped out of the bed and pushed Marcellus back. Since he'd given me this surprise, it was only right I properly thanked him. While seductively removing his boxers, I gazed into his eyes. I was still wearing the crotchless lingerie that gave me easy access. I wasted no time climbing on top and sliding down his already erect penis. Marcellus tried to grab my hips, but I slapped his hands away.

"Un-un, no touching. You been a bad lil boy," I said as I started to work my hips in a circular motion.

"Goddamn shawty, she good and wet." He closed his eyes and bit his bottom lip.

"Ain't that how you like her?"

"Hell yeah," he mumbled as I started to rock back and forth. Marcellus' penis was a nice size. It was about nine inches; not too big and not too small. As I started to ride him nice and hard, I could already feel my essence leaking out. It was making a loud squishy sound that echoed throughout the room.

"Ooh yesss!" I moaned while bouncing harder. Marcellus raised me up and down his length. My ass cheeks slapped against his thighs each time he brought me back down. I leaned forward so he could suck my breasts. Knowing exactly what I wanted, Marcellus lowered the top of my bodysuit and popped a tittie into his mouth. He sucked slowly before gently biting on my nipple. At that moment, I creamed all over his dick. He knew just what to do to send me over the edge.

"I'm coming," I moaned with my eyes rolling to the top of my head.

Marcellus went harder, repeatedly hitting my g-spot. As soon as I recovered from one orgasm another one hit me. I wrapped my arms around his neck and allowed him to fully take control. The sounds of our sex filling the room had me so turned on. It was then I realized this was where I wanted to be. Even if I didn't love Marcellus, at least I could say he was here for me. That was a lot more than I could say about Saadiq.

Kiana

One month later…

"Thank you! This is the most fun I had in a long time." I laughed hysterically.

Lex wrapped his arm around my neck and looked into my eyes. "Glad I could put a smile on your face," he said.

"You definitely did that," I told him as we walked out the building. We'd just come back from seeing Michael Blackson in stand up at the Helium Comedy Club. It had been so much fun, and dude was funny as hell.

For the past month or so, Lex and I had been getting to know each other. We talked on the phone all the time, but this was our first time hanging out. When he picked me up this evening we went to dinner at a Steakhouse. After we ate until we were almost about to burst, we left and hit up the comedy show. This date had been nothing short of amazing.

"So what you wanna do now? The evening is still young and the sky's the limit," Lex stated as we got into his G-Wagon. I glanced at him with a devious grin.

"I know something we can do," I said, reaching my hand over to his lap. Lex glanced down at my hand.

"What?" he asked.

"Let's go to a room, or we can go back to my place. My auntie has my daughter, so I don't have to get her until tomorrow." I smiled at him seductively.

Lex looked as if he was pondering my suggestion, but then he said something I never thought I'd hear a man say. "Nah, how about we go somewhere and talk?" he responded.

"Talk?" I asked incredulously.

"Yeah talk." He laughed. "How you think we supposed to get to know each other if we don't talk?" I looked at his ass like he was crazy. "What?" He laughed.

"What's up with that? I'm trying to skip all the formal bullshit and move us to the next level. But you saying that you wanna talk." I shook my head because I didn't get it.

Lex let out a deep sigh. "Having sex is cool, but I'm trying to find out what's up here rather than what's down there." He pointed towards my head and then my pussy. "We got plenty of time to do all that other shit."

"Wow! Nigga, what planet did you fall from?" I laughed.

"So because I want to get to know you something gotta be wrong with me?"

"I'm just saying, most guys—" He cut me off.

"Let me stop you right there. I'm not most niggas, and you'll soon find out I carry myself completely different from how every other man does. I like fucking just like the next man, but I'm not trying to be on that right now. I wanna get to know the real you so when we do cross that line it will be more than just a fuck. I don' had my fair share of women, and most of them thought they could hook me with sex. It didn't work because I didn't connect with them beyond that. I'm feeling you so I want to do things differently," he explained.

Well damn. You couldn't do nothing but have respect for a dude who was coming to you on his grown man shit. Not only was Lex a gentleman, but he had his own place, car, took care of his daughter, and owned a tattoo shop. If all he was spitting was true, then I might just make him mine.

***

Thirty minutes later…

"I know we talked about you not being with your baby momma, but you never told me why y'all broke up. What, you cheated on her or something?" I inquired. Lex and I were out having drinks at this lil spot called One Night Stand where they did karaoke. The music was nice, the atmosphere was laid back, and the crowd was chill. This was my first time doing something like this, and I was enjoying it.

Lex glanced at me with a smirk. “We didn’t break up,” he said. *Oh shit. Here we go*. She died about two years ago,” he revealed. My mouth dropped.

I felt so stupid for thinking the worst of him. “I’m so sorry Lex. I didn’t know.” *Why did I always have to talk so damn much?*

“It’s all good. The first year it was hard to talk about it but now it’s don’ got a little easier.”

“If you don’t mind me asking, how did she die?”

“She was killed. Some dumb ass thought stealing her car wasn’t enough, so they shot and left her to bleed out on the school campus.”

“Wait, I think I heard about that. Was she on her way home from a night class or something?”

“Yeah, she had just finished her last class and was going to graduate a few weeks later,” he explained.

“Damn, that’s messed up. Did they ever catch the person who did it?”

“Nah, you know how muthafuckas are around hur’. They ain’t finna say shit even if they know. The case been cold for a year.”

"That's a damn shame. Again, I'm so sorry," I said glancing up at him.

"'Preciate it."

"Do you have custody of your daughter?" I questioned.

"Yeah, and I went through hell just to get it. Her grandmother tried to fight me for custody. Me and her ain't ever seen eye to eye. She swears I'm this dog ass nigga. After my baby momma passed, her momma was hollering I wasn't capable of raising Macy. I mean, I know I did some fucked up shit, but that didn't have nothing to do with my parenting skills. We went back and forth to court for over six months before the judge finally awarded me custody. She hated that shit too, but she really ain't have no choice but to accept it. She should just be thankful she got visitations."

"I'm glad everything worked out for the best. You seem like a really good father."

"I try to be. That's why I'm trying to settle down with one female. She don' been through enough, and the last thing she need is to see her daddy bringing around a bunch of different women. I gotta be the example for the type of man I want her to end up with." I nodded.

"Trust me, you're doing the right thing. I wish I would have had a father figure to look out for me when my mother was killed."

"Damn, yo' moms was killed too?" His face was full of shock.

"Yup, so I can definitely relate to your daughter."

"I'm sorry to hear that."

"Thank you. It happened when I was younger, so it doesn't hurt as much as it used to."

"But that pain will never completely go away," Lex ran his head down his face.

"You're right about that." We both became silent for a minute as we seemed to be caught up in our own thoughts. Lex finally broke the silence after a while.

"Anyway, what happened to you and your daughter's father?"

I paused being caught off guard by the question. There was no way I could tell him the real reason why Brisham and I had broken up. "Um…we just grew apart," I uttered. It wasn't completely a lie, but it wasn't the whole truth either.

Lex looked at me skeptically. "So y'all don't have no dealings? Ain't no backtracking, late night booty calls or no shit like that? I'm feeling you but if your situation ain't over then I don't wanna step on no toes."

"No, it's none of that." I looked him dead in the eyes and told the truth.

"You sure?" Lex questioned.

"Positive." I gave him a big smile.

"Aight, that's wassup." Lex suddenly leaned across the small table and we engaged in a kiss.

Damn his lips are soft, and his breath smells good. Mmm...I just wanna fuck him right now. Why does he have to be such a gentleman?

"What you smiling for?" Lex asked when we pulled away from the kiss.

"Oh nothing." I blushed as I gazed into his eyes. *You about to be my man, that's what.*

Marcellus

One week later…

For the past week I was busy as hell trying to get all my affairs in order before me and Talya made this trip. Just a few minutes ago I'd finished a meeting with my crew to make sure everything was lined up. I didn't have no right-hand man because I didn't trust no damn body. Niggas weren't loyal these days, so I handled most of my shit on my own. I had my street runners I fucked with, but I took care of all my big transactions. Them niggas didn't know shit about no drop offs or pickups.

I'd been in this game since I was a teenager. So far, I hadn't got knocked majorly. I served a few months here and there but that was it. The reason I felt my shit was solid was the fact I didn't tell nobody anything that could get me hemmed up. Sometimes this shit could get stressful, but I would rather do it this way than to live with regrets. In a few years I planned to retire a free man, so it was very necessary I kept all my ducks in a row.

Walking out of my office, I headed to the front of the building. I had a little spot in East St. Louis. It wasn't flashy; it was real low key. Matter fact, the only way to access it was through this soul food spot in the front of the building. The older black couple who owned the business had allowed me to rent the space. To show my appreciation, I always had my workers buy food as part of my support. When I finally made it to the front, I told one of the waitresses standing by to bag up my plates. I always brought dinner home on Thursdays so Talya wouldn't have to cook.

Quandra the waitress, smiled at me before running off to the back to get the order. Once she returned she handed me the bag. "When you gonna quit playing and let me get some more of that? It's been a few months," she stated.

I eyed her as I took the bag from her hand. "You remember I got a girl, right?" I was sure that shit didn't mean nothing to her, but I figured I would throw it out there.

"Didn't you have a girl the last time we fucked?" she asked. For the most part, a nigga tried to do right but at times it was hard as hell. Being in the position I was in, I always had pussy being thrown at me. I wasn't thirsty, I had restraint not to take all the bait. Every now and then I did like to get my dick wet though. Any street nigga who said he didn't at least get some head or pussy on the side was a straight up liar. That's just how shit went. It was in our DNA to step out at times. That didn't mean you didn't love your gal.

I grinned while looking at Quandra. She was a voluptuous chick who prided herself on her looks. She kept her hair, makeup, nails, and toes done. When she was outside of this restaurant, shawty looked like a completely different person. Not to mention she had that wet wet and some bomb ass head.

"You wild shawty." I slightly chortled.

"Shit, I'm serious. We can go to my place, blow back, and then I will suck your dick until your toes curl," she whispered, and my dick thumped.

"You don't make it easy to resist yo' ass, do you?"

"Nah, I'm trying to get some of that asap."

"I'mma hit you up," I told her.

"No you ain't. You said that last time. I'm starting to think you don't like fuckin' with me anymore." Quandra smacked her lips.

"I'mma hit you up," I told her again as I left out. See the shit I'm talking about? It was damn near next to impossible for me to be faithful with all this temptation.

Twenty minutes later I was headed back to my house with the food in tow. I'd also stopped and got Talya some of the Moscato she loved to drink. I had plans to feed her then serve her up some of this dope dick. When it came to the bedroom, shawty wasn't no slacker by a long shot. I had my own little super freak, but at times I felt that was all it was on her part. She had no problem sucking and fucking a nigga to oblivion. It was her heart I still didn't have. I was a patient nigga, so I was trying to give her time. Sometimes she made that shit hard though. I just kept reminding myself to look at the big picture.

Just as I was about to step out of my whip my phone rang. I snatched it out of my pocket and looked at caller ID. I sighed when I saw it was Ariel. "Yeah?" I answered.

"I need you to come over here and fix our toilet. It's running everywhere," she said.

Goddamn! It was something always going on with her ass. "Nah, I can't come right now. I just got back to the crib."

"What am I supposed to do? It's leaking water everywhere. My shit gon' be flooded in a minute," she huffed.

"Call a plumber mane."

"But it's late in the evening. They ain't gon' come out until tomorrow. What about your daughter?" She tried to hit me with that same shit she always used.

"Don't yo' momma got a place? Y'all can just go over there for the night."

"I already called her, and she said she got company."

Her ass lying. "Aight mane. I'mma come through but we gon' have a talk."

"About what?" Ariel questioned nastily.

"I'll talk to you when I get there," I said before ending the call.

I was starting to see exactly what Talya had been talking about. Ariel was always calling on a nigga, and it was starting to get on my fuckin' nerves. It was time for me to dead this shit asap.

Natalya

A few days later…

"Alright, so here is his teddy, teething ring, snacks—"

"Talya, will you quit acting like I've never kept my grandson before?" Ms. Jennifer pursed her lips together.

"I'm sorry but you know this is my first time leaving him for a week."

"I understand, but this boy is going to be just fine. Ain't that right granny's baby?" She tickled Kacen's chin and he cracked up with laughter.

I smiled as I watched their interaction. My baby loved his grandma, and she loved him. "I know he's going to be fine," I mumbled.

"Exactly, now quit tripping."

"Alright, well I guess that's it. Bye baby, I love you. Be good for your grandma." I kissed Kacen on his chubby cheek and headed for the door.

"Talya wait. There was something I wanted to show you," she stopped me.

"What is it?" I questioned with a raised brow.

She placed Kacen in his playpen and held up a finger. "Be right back with it."

I stood there wondering what it could be. When Ms. Jennifer finally returned a few minutes later, she had what looked to be an envelope in her hand.

"What's this?" I questioned.

"After all this time, my baby finally wrote!" She squealed with excitement. My heart fell to the pit of my stomach as she handed me the letter. Blankly, I looked at the writing on the envelope before quickly passing it back to Ms. Jennifer. A part of me was jealous she'd received a letter and not me.

"Um, that's nice," I mumbled.

"Nice… Girl, this is great news! Ain't you happy?" she asked.

"For you, yes," I stated blandly.

"What's with the sudden attitude?"

"What do you want me to say?" I shrugged.

"He asked about you. That's why I gave you the letter because I wanted you to read it," she said.

"If Saadiq wanted me to read a letter, he would have personally sent me one." I folded my arms over my chest as I looked off. Tears had started to sting the brim of my eyes, and I was trying to stop them from falling.

Ms. Jennifer slowly nodded, finally understanding why I was so upset. “It’s okay Talya. At first I was angry that he’d shut us out too, but after reading the letter I finally understand. Why don’t you read it? Maybe you’ll have a change of heart too.”

“I don’t mean no disrespect, but I don’t care what he had to say,” I barked. Ms. Jennifer looked taken aback.

“Excuse me?” she asked.

“I don’t wanna know what he gotta say. Do you know how long it took me to get over him? I ain’t trying to go back there again. I’m glad he finally reached out to you, but I don’t want to hear about him. I would appreciate it if you don’t mention Kacen,” I said.

“Wait a minute Talya. You know I love you like a daughter, but this is my son you’re talking about.” Her white face turned beet red as she glared at me.

“Yeah, your son that abandoned me and his son.” I lashed out.

“He didn’t know about the baby because you didn’t tell him.”

“That’s because he never gave me a chance!” I shouted.

“You know what, let’s just calm down. I thought you would be happy to hear that he’d finally wrote.”

"Well I'm not. You think I'm supposed to jump for the skies just because your son finally decided to stop being selfish? Hell no! It's obvious Saadiq only cares about himself. He was only thinking about himself when he got behind the wheel of that car and decided to drive, and he only thought about himself when he got his stupid ass locked up. Now after all this time he's still thinking about himself. He probably only reached out because he wants money on his books or something." I was so angry that my throat was burning, tears were pouring out of my eyes, and my chest was heaving up and down.

Ms. Jennifer glared at me angrily while sliding her tongue across her teeth. "I never thought that I'd have to say this to you, but I want you to leave my house right now. What Saadiq did was wrong, but I'd been damned if I stand here and let you talk shit about my son. That's still my child and I don't give a damn what he did. You will not disrespect him in front of me," she hissed. I shrugged my shoulder while wiping my eyes.

"That ain't no problem, I'll leave. All I ask is that you respect my wishes. Don't mention my son to him. He doesn't deserve to know about my baby." I turned and stomped off, leaving Ms. Jennifer standing there.

Brisham

A few days later…

Angrily, I glanced around the messy living room that looked as if a damn storm had come through this bitch. It was food containers, beer bottles, the guts from several cigars, trash, and all other types of filth scattered about. The longer I stood here the angrier I became. It had been a few days since I'd been home. Me and one of the chicks I messed with was at the hotel laid up. I left Skylar and Kylisha here thinking everything was cool.

I should've known I couldn't trust this bitch. Storming through the house, I quickly went in search of my stupid ass baby momma. A few minutes later I found her ass passed out on the bed between this white couple that lived down the street from us. The female was dirty looking, and her dude looked like he was on meth or something. I glared at all their naked bodies entangled, and my blood started to boil.

"Aye, what the fuck is going on in hur'?" I yelled. The first one to wake up was the white chick.

"Oh my God…Kevin, wake up!" she exclaimed as she quickly sat up. By the time her dude woke up, he was staring down the barrel of my pistol.

"Look man, I'm sorry. Please don't kill me," he pleaded.

I took my pistol and smashed him across the face with it. Blood squirted everywhere while his bitch started screaming to the top of her lungs. I'd asked them before not to hang around the front of my house when I saw them sitting out there. Now to come home and see them in my shit, had a nigga pissed off.

"Shut the fuck up!" I roared.

Kylisha's hoe ass woke up looking around frantically. "Brisham, what the fuck you doing?" She had the nerve to ask.

I took my pistol and slapped her across the face with it. She howled out in pain. With my gun now pointed at the other two muthafuckas, I dragged Kylisha's hoe ass out the bed.

"Aye, y'all get the fuck outta my house right now, and you better not let me see y'all out," I barked. They were lucky my son was in here or their asses wouldn't be leaving this bitch breathing.

The couple immediately hopped up, grabbed their shit, and hauled ass.

"Brisham, why are you doing this?" Kylisha cried.

"Bitch, didn't I tell you I ain't want nobody in my shit? You got them crackhead looking muthafuckas in here. What the fuck is up with my house, and why the hell you got my son in there screaming to the top of his lungs? You must don' really lost your mind?" I seethed as I dragged her through the house.

"Brisham, you're hurting my head!" she screamed.

"Bitch you think I give a fuck about yo' head? I wanna know why the fuck you neglect my son while yo' hoe ass laid up?"

"Let me go please. Stop!" she yelled as I dragged her to the door. "Please Brisham, don't kick me out. I don't have nowhere to go."

"You gotta get the fuck outta hur'."

"Noooo!" she screamed as I snatched the door open. I had to pry her hands off my shirt because she'd latched on tightly. Once I finally got her hands loose, I tossed Kylisha right on her ass. Snot and tears were mixed on her face as she stared up at me.

"I don't have nowhere to go," she sniveled.

"Not my fuckin' problem no more," I gritted. Her naked body trembled as she glared at me.

"I want my baby." She had the audacity to say.

"Bitch you ain't getting my son. Now you got two minutes to get the fuck off my doorstep."

I watched as Kylisha peeled herself off the ground and dusted her butt. She glared at me with an evil look. "Fuck you nigga! I'm coming back for my son."

"Fuck out of hur'!" I spat before slamming the door in her face. I heard her beating as I went to Skylar's room.

When I picked him up, I noticed he was soaking wet. His clothes were dirty and dried up snot and tears were all over his face. I carried him straight to the bathroom. While holding him in one arm, I ran some warm bath water with my free one. I then got him undressed and put him in the tub. It took about ten minutes for me to clean him thoroughly. I took him out the tub and dried him off. After getting him dressed, I fixed my lil man a bottle and fed him. In less than five minutes he gulped that shit down. Ain't no telling how long it had been since he'd last ate. While rocking him to sleep I thought about what my next move would be. I was too heavy in the streets to be a fulltime dad, and just putting him off on anybody wasn't an option either. I needed somebody I could trust to watch him while I was out handling business. One thing was for certain, ain't no way I would let Kylisha's ass step foot back in this house or get my son.

Marcellus

A few days later…

We had been in the Dominican Republic for a little over four days now. My boy Jue and one of the broads he messed with had accompanied us on the trip. We rented a villa at this resort in Las Galeras. I had to admit, a nigga couldn't even remember the last time I'd had this much peace. Working from sun up to sun down had become the norm for me. During the times I was able to travel it was usually just for business or small weekend getaways.

Being with Talya had given me a new perspective on life. In just these few days I'd learned it was a lot more to life than hustling. We'd been doing everything we could think of from clubbing to sightseeing, snorkeling, fuckin' in different places, and even jet skiing. Talya tried to get me to try zip lining, but that was where a nigga drew the line. On top of spending this QT with my shawty, I was happy to say I hadn't heard from Ariel. After that conversation back at her house she called herself mad at me. I didn't give a fuck, just as long as she calmed that shit down.

"Baby what do you want to get into today?" Talya asked as she walked onto the balcony. Pulling on my Kush filled blunt, I looked my shawty over. She was wearing a short spaghetti strap dress that showed off those toned legs and brought plenty attention to them big melons of hers. Her wide hips protruded on the side. I couldn't lie, Talya was bad.

"You know I'm down for whatever," I told her as I allowed the smoke to seep from my nostrils.

"I'm glad you said that because I was thinking…" she began.

"What?" I gave her this sideways look. She wanted a nigga to try everything. I guess since she had never been anywhere, she was determined to make the best of this trip.

"There is this place I been researching. It's called the Cave of Wonders and it's a tourist spot. I want to check it out."

I took one more toke of the blunt before putting it out. "Aight, we can go."

Talya arched her brows. "Wow that was easy!"

"I told you before we got here that it's your world. The way you been throwing that pussy on a nigga, I will go to the moon if you wanted me to," I told her straight up.

She busted out laughing. "You are so nasty."

"Shit I'm serious."

Talya walked over and put a kiss on my lips. The kiss started off slow and before long it quickly picked up. She rubbed her hands up and down my chest while sliding onto my lap. Without putting much thought into it, I raised her dress up and yanked my shorts down all in one swift motion. "Un-un baby, it's daytime. Somebody may see us," she panted.

"So what? You scared of a lil peep show?" I questioned as I slid my dick inside, not giving her the chance to object. Just like a snug glove, her walls immediately gripped my shit, making it the perfect fit. I took my hands and moved her hips around.

"Mmm," Talya let out. With her feet planted firmly on the ground, she began to make that ass pop all over me. "Ooooh," she cooed as I sucked her neck while she rode me. At the same time I smacked her ass, encouraging her to keep the rhythm going.

She placed her hands on my chest and went all in. I leaned my head back with a smile on my face as she twerked all over a nigga's shit. Suddenly, she stood up and climbed onto me backwards. When I saw her plump ass cheeks facing me, I gripped hold of them and slammed Talya down onto my rod. Her body twitched which indicated she was about to release. I did it again, and again, and again until we both came at the same time. I leaned forward wrapping my arms around her waist, then put soft kisses on her shoulder.

"When you gon' give me a lil one?" I decided to ask.

Talya glanced back over her shoulder. "Boy quit playing." She laughed.

"Why you think I'm playing? I'm serious as hell right now."

"First off, we don't need any more kids at this moment. Between your three and my one, I be about to go crazy when we got all of them. Secondly, before I pop out any more kids, you gon' have to put a ring on this finger."

"So that's the only way that I can get a baby?" I hoped that her ass wasn't trying to hit me with an ultimatum.

"Yes, that's exactly what I'm saying. Don't get me wrong, I ain't in no rush to get married. But before we bring another life into this world that's how it's gonna go down. You had kids with those other women, so I would want something different to know what we have is special. You feel me?" She laughed. I shook my head because she'd just hit a nigga with his own words.

"Yeah I feel ya." I leaned forward and put another kiss on her shoulder. This was why I dug shawty. Most broads would have jumped at the opportunity to have a nigga's seed, but she didn't operate like that. She wanted me to prove myself to her and not try to use a baby to solidify her spot in my life. You couldn't do shit but respect her mind.

***

"Pussy whipped ass nigga," my boy Jue faked sneezed as I kissed Talya on her lips.

"Leave my baby alone," Talya told him.

"Yeah Jue, leave that man alone. Not everybody is like you. Some men don't have a problem showing their affection," Jue's date, Hope, said.

He shot his eyes at her. "Fuck that. Ain't that much love in the world. His ass been attached to that girl like he her shadow."

All I could do was shake my head at this fool. I met Jue when we were just jits. We'd been cool all the way from grade school until now. Jue was one of them niggas who would never settle down. He changed females like he changed his clothes. Because we'd always done dirt together, it was hard for him to accept I was back in a relationship. He'd been saying slick shit since we been out here.

"Your boy is a mess." Talya giggled.

"Yeah, that nigga som' else."

We had just left the cave Talya told me about earlier. After being there for about four hours, we were now headed into this damn museum. I was all for giving shawty what she wanted, but a nigga didn't really want to do no more exploring. At this point I was just tagging along because I knew it would make her happy. I wrapped my arms around Talya from the back and pressed my dick in her ass.

"Let's just go back to the room," I whispered as I walked behind her.

"We can once we check out this museum."

"C'mon shawty, ain't you had enough of sightseeing?" I licked the side of her neck, and she giggled.

"No Marcellus. You promised I could do whatever I want," she whined. "And quit trying to distract me with yo' freaky ass kisses." Talya walked out of my arms. Looking at her ass in them shorts made a nigga hard. I swear shawty had me infatuated with her.

On the way into the museum this Indian looking lady wearing a long white dress with one of those fortune teller hats stopped us. "You wanna get your palm read?" she asked. Talya looked at me with a big grin.

"Hell nah shawty. This where I draw the line," I told her. A nigga didn't fuck around with this witchcraft shit.

“C’mon baby, it’s just for fun,” she whined.

“Nope, that shit is a gimmick.” I shook my head.

“I know but I’ve never had anything done like this. I just want to see what she’s going to say.” She poked out her bottom lip to make a nigga give in like she always did.

“Nigga if you do that shit, I’m done with yo’ ass. You ain’t supposed to be fuckin’ around with this voodoo shit,” Jue spat.

“Shut up Jue,” Hope told him.

“Don’t tell me to shut up. I’m serious as hell.”

“Y’all ain’t gotta get it done. I just want to do mine,” Talya said.

“Go ‘head shawty, but I ain’t fuckin’ with it,” I told her, and was dead ass serious.

“Whatever. Hope, you getting it done?” Talya asked.

“Yeah I’ll do it.”

“Thank you! At least somebody wanna have fun.” Talya rolled her eyes.

“Y’all gon’ fuck around and be like that lil girl on *The Exorcist*. If you start throwing up green shit, I’m leaving y’all right hur’,” Jue jested.

“Jue would you shut the hell up? You’re so negative,” Talya told him, and he laughed.

"Nah y'all broads just crazy. Hurry up so we can go back to the room. I'm trying to get blunted," he told them.

"Girl, how you put up with his ass?" I heard Talya say as they walked to the table where the lady was sitting.

"Dawg, you turning soft on me. That broad got yo' ass wrapped around her finger. We been running up behind they ass this whole time we been here. What happened to doing the shit we wanna do?"

"This trip wasn't about me. I'm doing this for her. What you think we supposed to be doing?" I asked.

"Not this shit," he spat.

"Quit nagging like a bitch, nigga. You didn't have to come with us."

"Nah, I had to," he stated.

"Mufucka, you ain't have to come."

"Yes I did. Cause that was the only way I could get Hope ol' Eddie Munster head ass to give me some pussy."

"Nigga, you a damn fool!" I roared with laughter. "Shawty head is big as hell."

"Hell yeah. Bitch got the nerve to be 'round hur' acting like she got options and shit. I almost told her booty head ass to bounce. Her pussy ain't even that good for me to be doing all this caking," Jue ranted.

I continued to laugh as I walked towards the table. Just as I made it over, the woman was doing something with Talya's hand. I couldn't believe shawty wanted to do this. She took being adventurous to the next level.

"There is someone close to you holding a secret," the lady began.

"Yeah yo' ass," Jue mumbled, and I chuckled.

"What kind of secret?" Talya asked.

"A big one, very devastating. They don't want to hold it, but by telling you they fear it could end your relationship," she claimed.

"Nigga, she might be talking 'bout yo' ass. You better put an end to this shit quick," Jue leaned over and whispered.

"Nah I'm good," I said, and he smirked.

"Do you know what the secret is?" Talya questioned.

"No, I don't know what the secret is," the lady mumbled, and I shook my head. How the hell was she gonna say somebody had a secret but couldn't tell what it was? I knew her ass was fraud. Jue had already walked off, and I was getting ready to do the same when I heard her next words.

"Something recently happened that keeps you from being happy. There is much pain in you because—" Suddenly her ass paused and glanced at me.

I looked at the bitch wondering why she stopped. "What is it?" Talya urged her to continue.

"Maybe it's best if we end here," the lady said. Now she had piqued my interest. Why did she want to stop?

"Nah, I want to know what else you see. Am I going to die soon or something?" Talya ass was getting all worked up.

I figured I would put an end to this. "C'mon shawty, let's just bounce."

"No, I want her to tell me. What is it ma'am?"

The bitch darted her eyes towards me again before looking back at Talya.

"Look, can you please tell me what it is?" Talya spat. I could see she was getting mad.

"Shawty fuck this, let's just go. This bitch wants you to offer her ass some money."

"It's not about the money but if she wants me to do it, fine." She reached out and roughly grabbed Talya's hand. I knew her ass was full of shit. At the mention of money, she was suddenly willing to talk. "Someone from your past will soon come back into your life. This person has been around since childhood. That's who will make you smile again because you truly love them. You two share something special that no one else can come in between. That is all," she concluded with a smirk.

"Whatever lady. You don't know what the hell you talking about." Talya told her and jumped up. "C'mon baby, let's go."

"Move out my way Talya." I pushed her hand away when she tried to grab me and walked off towards the shuttle.

"Really Marcellus? You believe her?" she called to me.

"Yo, what the fuck happened?" Jue questioned when I approached him. He was sitting on a bench smoking a blunt.

"This trip is over. I'mma catch an earlier flight back."

He looked at me confused. "Aight dawg, it's yo' call. What about Talya?"

"Fuck her ass," I snarled as I hopped on the shuttle. With the way I was feeling she could stay here.

Kiana

Two weeks later…

"What's the matter boo? You look like you lost your best friend," I said as I slid into the booth. Talya called earlier and told me she needed a drink. I knew something was wrong from the sound of her voice.

"I did," she mumbled.

"Girl, tell me what happened."

She started to tell me about what went down with her and Marcellus while they were on vacation.

"Wait, did she specifically mention Saadiq's name?" I asked.

"Nah she didn't mention his name, but she brought up a lot of our history."

"Did she give detailed events or just general stuff?"

"She mentioned him being in my life since I was a kid, and she said he was going to make me happy again."

"I'on really believe in them people, but that is crazy."

"I know right," she mumbled.

"Is Marcellus still mad at you?" I asked.

"Yup, he barely talks to me and he won't touch me. I think he's cheating on me too," she revealed.

“Hol’ the hell on. What makes you think that?” I squawked.

“Because his phone is always ringing. I know what he do, so I know he get a lot of calls. At the same time, I feel like it’s more than just customers calling.”

“So what you gon’ do?” I asked.

“I’on know.”

“I’mma be real with you. I feel you are settling right now. You don’t even have that same spark in your eyes like you did when you were with Saadiq. To be honest, that lady may have just picked up on the same vibe everyone else been getting. You ain’t completely happy with Marcellus. You try to paint this picture that you are, but everybody can see through that shit. Even auntie said she didn’t think you and Marcellus would last. No offense boo, but he ain’t your soulmate.”

“Maybe I’m not in love with Marcellus, but that don’t mean I’m going to leave him. He’s been there for me, and I wouldn’t feel right turning my back on him,” Talya suddenly snapped.

“Whoa! Calm down boo.” I laughed.

“I’m serious Kiana. I feel bad I don’t love him like he loves me. I just hate that everything happened. Why am I still thinking about Saadiq after all this time?” she asked with her voice cracking. I looked at her and swallowed hard. This was one of those times when I felt like shit. How could you truly console someone when you were a part of their pain?

"It's gonna be okay honey. Maybe you just need to take a step back from your relationship with Marcellus and get your head right." I reached across the table and grabbed her hand. It was the best advice I could offer. Talya glanced up at me.

"To be honest I don't think I can do it. I'm afraid of being alone. Too much time by myself would cause me to think of Saadiq," she explained.

"I get it boo. But staying somewhere you ain't happy won't make the situation better."

"I didn't say I wasn't happy. I like Marcellus and the way he treats me and my son. It's just…" her voice trailed off.

"Don't worry about it. Sometimes your feelings can be hard to put into words."

"How did you get over the break up with Brisham?" she asked.

"Shit, I guess I just forced myself to do it."

"You are so strong. I admire that about you," she said.

If only you knew…I'm not as strong as I put on. "I don't really have a choice but to be strong," I mumbled. Talya nodded.

"So anyway, what's up with you and this Lex dude?" She changed the subject. I was thankful because I was about to break down with her. It was getting harder and harder to hold on to this secret.

A big smile suddenly covered my face at the mention of Lex. "Talya, he is so different from all the guys I'd ever met. I really like that man."

"Whatttt? I can't believe I'm hearing you talk like this!" she squealed.

"Yes bitch, he is the full package."

"Damn girl, do I hear you got a new man?" she asked.

"Hell nah. It's too early for all that. We're still in the stage of getting to know each other. Besides, I need to see what that dick do before I commit to him."

Talya's eyes got wide as saucers. "Wait a minute! Y'all haven't had sex?" she questioned.

"Nope." I shook my head.

"How long have y'all been talking?"

"It's been about two months since the first time we went out, but if you include when we started talking on the phone, I would say close to three months now."

Talya jumped out of her seat and walked around the table. I looked at her strangely when she put her hand on my forehead.

“Bitch, what the hell are you doing?”

“I’m trying to see where my friend is at?” She giggled.

I pushed her hand away. “Girl sit yo’ ass back down. Don’t act so damn surprised.”

“I’m just saying.”

I shot her a mean, playful look. “You just saying what?”

“Nothing girl. Now finish telling me everything.”

“It really ain’t that big of a deal. He’s really cool, I’m just so sexually frustrated.” I slapped my hand on the table.

“Ah, you’ll be okay. Like you said, it ain’t the worst thing. I’m proud of you for holding out.”

“Bitch this ain’t my idea.”

“So it’s his idea?” She raised an eyebrow.

“Yeah it is. He said he wanted to get to know me better before we took it there.”

“You don’t think he’s gay, do you?” Talya questioned.

“Nah, he’s just a gentleman.” I found myself blushing at the thought of Lex. Actually, I wasn’t mad that we hadn’t slept together. It really did give us the opportunity to connect. Talya started clapping. "Bitch, what the hell are you clapping for?"

"Because somebody has finally tamed my friend," she said, and I busted out laughing.

"You special." I shook my head.

"I may be but at least I'm not horny," she shot back.

***

After hanging out with Talya, I went and got my daughter from Aunt Delano. On my way there, Lex called and said he wanted to see me. I suggested for him to come over and he agreed. This was going to be his first time visiting, and I was so happy. When it came to him, a bitch was like a school girl with her first crush. He said he would be at my place in the next hour or two. That gave me enough time to put Raegan to sleep and take a quick shower.

I went to the kitchen to fix my daughter a bottle and heard my phone ring again. Jogging back into my room, I snatched it off my bed. When I noticed the unfamiliar number on the screen, I frowned. Rarely did I answer unknown numbers but for some reason I decided to answer this time.

"Hello?" I answered.

"Is this Kiana?" The light feminine voice asked.

"Yeah this me… Who dis?" I asked as I tucked my phone between my ear and shoulder. I walked back towards the kitchen.

"Um, this is Kylisha."

"Okay. What can I do for you Kylisha?"

"I'm calling about our baby daddy…"

"Whoa! What the hell are you talking about…our baby daddy?"

She started to giggle. "Oh, he didn't tell you?" I put the bottle down I was fixing and focused on the call.

"Who didn't tell me what? And what the hell is so funny?" I didn't know who this trick was, but she was already pissing me off.

"Damn shame," she mumbled. "Aight, since he didn't tell you, I guess I'll introduce myself. I'm Brisham's other baby momma. We have a son together that's almost eleven months old. I can't believe he didn't tell you this." My heart beat rapidly as I listened to this bitch tell me about a baby Brisham had without my knowledge. "You still there?" She had the nerve to say.

"How long have y'all known each other?" I questioned.

"We met almost two years ago."

"Hol' up. So y'all been fucking around all this time?"

"Yup. Me and him got a place together. I just thought it was messed up how he was keeping our baby a secret, but I don' been around your child. Matter fact, I just had her last week when she came over."

My blood started to boil. "So what exactly is your point for calling me?" I was trying my best not to let her know that I was bothered.

"I just told you why I called. Since our kids are siblings, I thought we should finally get to know each other."

"Nah, that ain't why you called. You did this shit to prove some type of point. Bitch you ain't got to do all that. Me and Brisham ain't together so you can have his ass."

"Hol' up, I didn't call you out your name so don't call me out of mine. All I was trying to do was put yo' ass up on game."

"I don't need you to do a muthafuckin' thang for me. What you need to be worried about is why your nigga is still trying to get with me."

"Girl please. Don't nobody want your used up pussy."

"What bitch?" I snarled, but she hung up.

I snatched the phone away from my ear. My body was on fire as I hurriedly dialed Brisham's number. He didn't answer so I hung up and called right back. When his voicemail picked up, I left him a heated message.

"Nigga, you need to be calling me back right this muthafuckin' minute." I hung the phone up just as I heard a knock at the door. *Damn.* I had forgotten all about Lex coming over. I hadn't even had a chance to feed my baby or wash my ass. This shit had thrown me completely off. Stomping towards the door, I snatched it open with a scowl on my face.

"Wassup shaw… Damn, you aight?" he questioned.

"No, I'm not aight," I sputtered while walking towards the kitchen. I was so angry I could kill somebody.

I heard Lex close the door before he came into the kitchen.

"Aye, what's going on?" he questioned as I went through the kitchen slamming things. He walked over and gently grabbed me. "Talk to me." His voice was so soothing and caring that it made my heart melt. "You gon' tell me something or will I have to guess?"

"Before you came, I got a call from this girl. She's claiming to be my baby's daddy other baby momma."

"Let me guess, you didn't know he had another baby?"

"No, I didn't know," I mumbled. Lex nodded his head.

"Aight, let me ask you this. Are you upset because you had plans to get back with him, or just because he failed to tell you?"

"No, I don't have any intentions of getting back with him. I told the bitch she could have him. He just should have told me."

"I feel ya on that. He should have kept it real with you, especially since y'all have a daughter together. At the same time he is her father, so you gotta know he wouldn't let anything happen to her," Lex stated, and I pursed my lips together.

"When it comes to good judgment, that's something he ain't got."

"So why you have his seed if you couldn't trust him?"

"Honestly, we ended up together on some default shit. I've known him since I was younger. He went away for a few years and came back around the same time I was dealing with another situation," I explained.

"I know we ain't been talking for a long time, but I'on like to see you crying and stressing over this shit. I can't do nothing to change the situation with your BD, but I can be a good shoulder for you to lean on. It's all on you though. Do you want me to stay?" He looked into my eyes.

"Yeah, I want you to stay. I just need to go feed my baby and make sure she's good."

"Aight, go ahead. I'll be out hur' waiting until you get back." Lex pulled me into his arms before engaging me in a very passionate kiss. This wasn't our first time kissing. We'd done it a few other times, but this one was by far the best. As our tongues wrestled with each other, I fought hard to restrain myself. He was making me all mushy inside. Just that fast he'd taken my mind off all the bullshit.

"Aight, go take care of your baby. I'll order us something to eat and we can chill out the rest of the night. Macy is with her grandma, so I don't have to get her," Lex said.

"Okay." I smiled as I finally grabbed the bottle and left the kitchen. Although I was still pissed at Brisham, I now felt a little better with Lex here.

Natalya

A few days later…

"Girl his lil ass took off running like the police was after him," Ms. Jennifer said, and I laughed.

"I knew his butt was going to be a handful when he started walking, but everybody was rushing for him to do it," I stated.

"Mhm. Now he getting into everything. And he be knowing what he doing too 'cause he'll look at you and bust out laughing," she continued.

I'd finally decided to have a sit down with Ms. Jennifer to clear the air. We'd never gone this long without at least checking in on one another. After I apologized for the way I acted, we fell right back into our usual mother-daughter bond. For the past thirty minutes she'd been telling me about all the things her and Kacen did while we were away.

"That is too funny," I snickered as I wiped my eyes.

"You gon' have to make sure you childproof that house."

"I know. Can you believe he's growing up so fast?"

"Exactly, and he looking more and more like his daddy everyday too," Ms. Jennifer stated. I got quiet and glanced off. I didn't want to make it seem like she couldn't even mention her own son's name in my presence. Still it was a sore topic for me, and I didn't know how to deal with it. "I'm sorry Talya. I know this situation is a lot for you to deal with, but you can't deny the fact you still love my son. That's why you got so angry at me before you left," she asserted. I crinkled my face.

"How did you know?" I asked.

"Girl, I been knowing you most of your life. On top of all that pain, there is still a lot of love."

"Maybe so, but I know for a fact we're not getting back together."

"Never say never. Some things we just can't control."

I briefly thought about everything she said. Saadiq had broken my heart and I didn't think I could forgive him. Plus, there was my relationship with Marcellus I had to think about. Although he was being a complete asshole right now, I still couldn't turn my back on him.

Ms. Jennifer stood up. "I'mma get started on dinner. You staying?"

"Nah, I'mma head on home. I have a faculty meeting early at work in the morning."

"Aight. Let me get a kiss from my grandbaby before y'all leave." I stood up with Kacen on my hip and walked to Ms. Jennifer. Once she gave him a big kiss on his cheek, I let her know we would stop by later in the week to see her.

A few minutes later when I was leaving the neighborhood, I spotted Tarmika pulling onto the street. I'd seen her a few other times in passing, but this was the first time that I'd seen her up close. We locked eyes with one another. Something about her looked so different to me. It was like she'd aged a lot over the years. A huge part of me wanted to turn around because she'd never met her grandson. The stubborn part of me wouldn't allow me to go there, so I kept it moving.

Marcellus

Later that evening…

"Damn girl, you gonna swallow a nigga's shit whole, ain't you?" I grunted.

She pulled my dick out of her mouth and gazed into my eyes. "You already know how I get down. I'm a beast when it comes to this shit," she boasted.

I grinned as I pushed her head back down. Like the true pro she was, Quandra commenced to sucking the skin off my dick. With my hand wrapped in her curly weave, I laid my head back and closed my eyes. I swear getting head was always a sure way to cure a nigga's stress.

Ever since we'd been back in town, I'd been on another level. The last night in the DR had me like fuck everything. If I wasn't already feeling like Talya still wanted to be with that nigga Saadiq, then I would have just chucked that shit up. But even I couldn't deny that at times I knew she was with me because he wasn't around.

Wasn't no way I could even come close to competing with the history they had. Before I heard that shit, I was still willing to make our situation work. But after basically hearing what I already knew, it was like I just snapped. No longer did I care about protecting shawty's heart when she didn't give a fuck about mine. That's why I told myself from here on out I was going to do me regardless. I wasn't ready to walk away just yet, but I'd be damned if I sat back like a chump and let a bitch play me.

"Argh shit! I'm about to nut," I told Quandra as I tightly gripped her hair.

Her soft, wet lips slurped harder as she continually pulled me in and out of her mouth. Before long, she was bringing me to bust the biggest nut I'd ever released.

"Muthafucka!" I gritted as I bit down on my bottom lip.

"You good baby?" She asked.

"Yeah, you did yo thang." I gave shawty her props.

"I know this!" she stated while popping her lips. I shook my head.

"Do me a favor and go grab me a towel baby."

"I gotcha daddy." She walked away just as my phone started to ring. After snatching it off the coffee table, I looked at the screen and saw it was Talya calling. She'd been calling since earlier this evening. Sighing, I tucked that shit back in my pocket. I didn't have no words for her. Keeping it real, I was madder at myself because I'd fell hard for a broad that didn't feel the same way I felt.

You know how much pussy I'd passed up on for her ass? Bitches were constantly throwing that shit at me daily. I felt like a real sucker right now. No woman could say I'd ever shown them as much love as I'd shown Talya, not even my kids' mommas. In just this year alone I'd dropped over a quarter mill on that bitch. I went out and copped her a brand-new Audi just so she could ride in style. If I was going to be riding clean, then so was my bitch. We'd been on plenty shopping sprees. Now she was rocking labels that only you would see celebrities wearing. She had over a dozen Louis bags, some she hadn't even removed from the boxes. We won't even get started on how much I'd bought lil man. Just thinking about this shit was pissing me off.

A few minutes later Quandra finally returned with a warm towel. After she cleaned me off, I got up and redressed. "What's going on with you?" she asked.

"Whatcha mean?"

"You don't seem like yourself."

"It ain't nothing. Just got a few things I'm dealing with. Not too much I can't handle."

She pursed her lips together. "It's cool Marcellus. You can talk to me. Just because we fuckin' don't mean I can't give you advice towards your relationship."

“How you figure it’s something with my relationship?” I questioned.

“Cause you here. Before whatever happened, I couldn’t get you to even dial my number.”

“You wild shawty. So you’ll listen to me talk about my relationship with the next broad?” I questioned skeptically.

“Why wouldn’t I? I’m a woman so maybe I can give you advice,” she said staring into my eyes.

Usually this wasn’t me, but for some reason I just started spilling everything to shawty. I mean, I didn’t leave a single thing out. I was desperate to know why Talya wasn’t giving me her heart like other women had.

“To me it doesn’t sound like she’s ungrateful. You’re just going about this all wrong. See, most women love emotionally, whereas most men love physically. Y’all will go out of your way buying us shit and making sure home is good. You probably think giving her everything she wants is going to make her love you more. It’s not.

“You gotta connect with her on an emotional level. It’s like she’s struggling because she seeing you go hard for her. That’s probably why she hadn’t left. At the same time, it’s hard for her to reciprocate it because you’re not giving her the love she requires. Maybe that’s what her baby daddy did, and that's probably why he still has her heart," she explained.

"That's deep shawty… 'Preciate that advice," I told her. I had never thought about shit like that.

"Yeah ain't no problem. So anyway, what's up with a job?" she asked.

I chuckled. "Don't you already got work?"

"Man, that bullshit money I make there ain't even enough to pay my full rent. A bitch been out here trying to get it how I live. I'm barely surviving."

"I'on know mane. I don't really like to mix business with pleasure."

"Trust me, I know how to keep shit strictly business when it's that time. I'll never let anything we got going on affect work. You know how I get down."

I pondered on her offer for a minute. A nigga could use another runner to help with deliveries. I'd been short one ever since Kylisha got pregnant and couldn't put in no more work.

"Let me think about it, aight?" I glanced at her.

"Okay baby. I appreciate it." She smiled. I stood up and put my shoes back on before grabbing my keys.

"I'mma hit you later."

"Cool! See you later," Quandra said as she got up and let me out of her apartment.

Jogging out to my truck, I hopped inside and pulled off. I figured since I'd been out most of the day, I would finally take my ass home.

***

Twenty minutes later…

Walking into the house, I was immediately hit with a surprise that my daughter Emani was here. She was sitting down on the floor, watching one of those weird ass Disney shows. Peeping the Dora the Explorer pajama clothes she was rocking let me know she'd been here for a minute.

"You don't see me?" I said.

"Hey daddy," she waved like I was just some random.

"Oh, it's like that? No hug or kiss, just a wave?" Her lil ass sighed like I was getting on her nerves. She stood up and ambled to me, I bent down so I could give her a hug.

"That's what I'm talking about. You supposed to always show your daddy some love."

Emani nodded her head, but I could tell she wasn't paying attention to what I was saying. Her ass was too focused on that damn show. "Gon' on girl and finish your show."

She immediately ran back to her pallet on the floor. I shook my head as I went in search of Talya. I found her in our bedroom laying across the bed. Lil man was knocked out next to her.

"Aye, how did Emani end up over here? I wasn't supposed to get her until the weekend." Talya didn't say anything. She just continued to look at her phone like I hadn't said shit. "You don't hear me talking to you?" Again, her ass didn't say nothing. "Here we go with this childish shit," I mumbled.

Suddenly Talya's head shot up from her phone, and she shot daggers at me. "Excuse you?"

"I'm trying to figure out how my daughter got over here."

"Well if you would have answered your phone, then you would know. Your ignorant baby momma just dropped her off and said she needed some me time. I tried to tell her it wasn't our time to get her, but she just pulled off."

"I was out handling business," I lied.

"And you couldn't have taken a minute to answer and see what I wanted?"

"Nah, what I was doing was important," I stated nonchalantly.

"But you call me childish? Fuck you Marcellus," Talya seethed.

"Oh, fuck me?"

"Yeah, fuck you. Go back to wherever you just came from because I'm not about to deal with you. Matter fact, let me just leave before I lose my cool." She got up and stomped to the dresser. As she started to snatch out clothes, I walked up behind her.

"Where you going?"

"I'm leaving. Nigga I don't have to put up with this bullshit. You walking around hur' mad about some shit a random person said instead of listening to what I've been telling you. Then on top of that, when I call you ignore me. Basically, what you're saying is fuck me. So like I said, fuck you too!"

I snatched the little shorts she was trying to put on from her hands. "Nah, you ain't leaving this late with him."

Talya frowned. "You can't stop me from leaving. I'm a grown ass woman."

"I don't give a damn about that."

She glared at me. "You are so full of shit. Yo' ass probably been laid up with a bitch, but you want to come in hur' and tell me I can't leave? Nigga please! Give me my damn shorts!" she yelled.

"Aye, you need to calm down before you wake him up."

"I'mma have to get him up anyway. Now give me my damn shorts." She jumped up and down trying to get the shorts that I was holding over my head.

"I told you I ain't letting you leave." I smirked as I eyed her. I don't know why, but it was slick turning me on to see her showing her ass. She'd never acted this way before.

"You know what? I got plenty other clothes. You can keep the damn shorts," she barked. When I noticed her grabbing some more clothes, I snatched those out of her hands too. "Stop playing with me Marcellus. You can't make me stay here." She stomped her foot, and I laughed.

Turning her back to me, Talya tried once again to gather more clothes. That time I wrapped my arms around her waist from the back and pressed my dick into her ass.

"Get the fuck off me." She bucked her body, trying to get out of my grasp.

"Aye, calm yo' rowdy ass down. Now I don' already told you I ain't letting you leave, so you might as well get that out of your head." I put a soft kiss on her neck, and she brushed it off.

"Don't put your lips on me," she hissed.

"So I guess you mad now?"

"Damn right I'm mad. You've been disrespectful as hell lately and I don't deserve that."

I pulled away and turned her around to face me. Lifting her chin with my hand, I forced her to look me in the eyes. "You right, I have been tripping. I apologize about that. A nigga just don't want to lose you," I admitted honestly.

"Well say that instead of playing these childish ass games. You doing all this other bullshit ain't gonna make me stay with you. All it does is piss me off."

I nodded my head. "Aight, you right," was all that I could say. Talya walked around me and sat on the bed. "You still mad?"

"To be honest I am, but I do forgive you. Just don't do that to me again."

"You got that," I told her as I bent to put a kiss on her lips. Surprisingly she kissed me back.

When I pulled away, I looked at her and grinned. No matter how much I tried to tell myself this was not where I wanted to be, I just couldn't deny that I had mad love for shawty. She had my heart. I just wished I could have the same effect on her.

Brisham

"Aye Kiana, I'm not finna sit here and let you keep calling me out of my name. I told you I apologize for not telling you. What else can I say?"

"How about you keep it real. When were you going to tell me that you had another child? Then you had that bitch around my baby. That's real fucked up Brisham. What if I left Raegan with another nigga you didn't know?"

For the past thirty minutes I had been trying to do damage control on that fucked up shit Kylisha pulled. I guess she went through my phone and got Kiana's number. Now she had us beefing and shit.

"We would have a problem. She ain't about to be around no other nigga like that."

"What nigga…are you serious right now? You just had her around some random bitch but telling me I can't do the same."

"Hell nah you can't. I left her with Kylisha maybe one or two times while I ran out to handle some business. Besides, she ain't no random female." Kiana's face contorted.

"She is to me! I don't know nothing about that bitch. She could have poisoned my child or done something to hurt her. Then what? I wouldn't have no clue what went on because you can't just keep it real."

"Look, what's done is done. Ain't shit I can do to change that. You ain't fuckin' with me anyway so what you tripping on?"

Kiana stood there shooting fire at a nigga. "You right about that. I will never be with yo' ass again. Ever since you came into my life it has been nothing but pure hell. You claim you love me but you're always doing something to hurt me. Do you know how hard it is to face my best friend and not tell her the fucked up shit I know? I'm disgusted at myself for keeping it a secret, but I do it so you can continue to walk around a free man. All that shit ends today though. I'm no longer having your back if you can't have mine."

I bit the inside of my jaw. "So what you saying? You plan on telling somebody?" I gritted.

"Nah, I'm not going to say anything. At least…I won't say nothing right now." Her ass paused for a dramatic effect.

"What the fuck you tryna say?"

"You got something on me, but I got something even bigger on you." She folded her arms over her chest and smirked.

I snarled at her. "You wanna play dirty, huh?" I asked while rubbing my hands together.

"Nigga, you started this shit. I'm so sick of you trying to ruin my life. I don't want you around anymore. Matter fact, I don't even want you in Raegan's—"

"Bitch, you got me fucked up. I'mma be in my daughter's life!" I bellowed as I walked into her face.

"I'm not saying you can't be, but you better keep my name out your mouth. This my last warning. You told that girl what I did when I was only trying to help yo ass out."

I chuckled maniacally. "Fuck all that. You might wanna be careful with your lil threats shawty."

"Oh trust me boo, they ain't threats. I'm not playing with you no more. Now get the fuck out of my house!" she yelled.

I turned and headed for the door. On my way out, I glanced back at Kiana one last time before finally leaving. She had me fucked up if she thought I would let her threaten me without any repercussions.

Natalya

Two weeks later…

Bet twenty more I hit the first roll

Run up in your house like I'm commando…

As the music blasted loudly from the speakers, I nodded my head to the beat. At the last minute, Marcellus and I decided to have a small gathering in our backyard. Since our home was so big, it easily accommodated the twenty plus people we'd invited and more if anybody else decided to come. With a cup of coconut rum, pineapple mango juice, and a splash of grenadine on top, I walked through the backyard with a smile on my face.

The black one piece zip up Tammy Rivera bathing suit I was rocking along with my see through sarong had my confidence on one thousand. My big, naturally bouncy hair was freshly washed and pushed back by a yellow flower that adorned the left side of my head. The flat Giuseppe Zanotti sandals with the diamond beaded band set my look off. I was looking too damn cute if I must say so myself.

The weather was perfect; it wasn't too hot or cold. Sashaying up to my man as he handled the grill, I wrapped an arm around his waist and put a big kiss on his lips.

These last couple of weeks for us had been amazing. We hadn't argued at all, and once he put Ariel in her place for pulling that stunt, we hadn't heard shit from her. The only disagreement we had was me trying to keep him off me. He'd been wanting to do it even more than before. I think he was trying to get me pregnant, but little did he know I was on birth control. I was serious when I said I wasn't having no babies.

"Wassup shawty? You looking good as hell," Marcellus complimented. I'd been in the house prepping the sides for most of the morning. I'd just got done getting dressed, so this was his first time seeing me.

"Thanks baby! I got this bathing suit just for you to see me in." I did a lil twirl so he could check out my whole outfit.

Marcellus stroked his goatee as his eyes lustfully roamed my body. "You did good. That body is looking righteous," he told me. I snickered while playfully slapping him on the arm.

"You are a mess."

Marcellus was about to kiss me again, but someone called my name just as our lips connected. When I glanced up, I noticed my cousin Nene and one of her friends walking into the backyard. I couldn't remember the friend's name, but what I did remember is that I didn't vibe with her. Not only was she loud, but she was annoying. We'd all gon' out to a club and her thirsty ass tried to get with every nigga in there.

"Hey cousin! You looking cute," Nene told me as she approached us. "Wassup Marcellus."

"Wassup Nene?" He threw her and the friend a head nod.

"Nothing much." Nene smiled.

"I'mma go holler at Jue," Marcellus announced.

"Ok baby," I responded before pecking his lips. Marcellus ambled off, leaving us to talk.

"You look cute too. I like that bathing suit," I told my cousin.

"'Preciate that gurl. Oh, you remember my bestie Danika, right?"

That's her name.

"Yeah, I remember her. How you doing?" I said looking her up and down. I was trying my best to be polite, but it was just something about this bitch I wasn't feeling. Ol' girl was red bone with a round face, wide eyes, full lips, and an okay shape. You could tell she'd once been bad but had recently let herself go a little.

"Hey girl. Y'all place is nice. I didn't know you was messing with Marcellus," she threw in while glancing around. I could see her silently admiring our house.

"You know him?" I questioned curiously.

"Not personally. One of my homegirls used to talk to him," she said.

I arched a brow. "Really?"

"Yeah, but that was a long time ago," Danika claimed.

"Hmm," I smirked before turning to Nene.

"Anyway, what you been up to?" I wasn't gonna entertain Danika and mess up my day. I was in too good of a mood.

"Not shit. Just working and taking care of them bad kids of mine." Nene worked at the Waffle House as a waitress and had five kids. I think they all had different daddies. "Where the niggas at? I see a few but they all got a woman with them," Nene stated.

"Some of Marcellus' other boys supposed to be coming through in a minute."

"I hope they look like him because I don't do ugly niggas," Danika chimed in.

"Nah, don't nobody look like my baby." I rolled my eyes.

"Damn, too bad. I'mma go swim Nene." Danika switched off, not even bothering to wait on Nene. I frowned as I watched her sit on the side of our pool.

"Wassup with your girl?" I asked Nene.

"Gurl, she just be talking. She don't mean no harm," Nene giggled.

"You should teach her not to say certain shit about another woman's man."

"It ain't even that deep. Don't pay her no mind."

I shook my head. *I guess me beating your friend's ass won't be that deep either*. "I'll be back. I'mma finish making my rounds." I quickly strutted away to go find Marcellus. I spotted him over by the pool talking to Jue and a different woman he was with.

"Wassup y'all?" I said, speaking to Jue and the brown skinned woman that was sitting on his lap. She wasn't as pretty as Hope and she looked a little rough around the edges.

"Wassup Talya?" Jue spoke back.

Marcellus pulled me over to him and wrapped his arms around my waist. "What you about to do?"

"Nothing, I was coming to look for you. Stop," I whined as he literally French kissed my neck.

"What's the problem?" he whispered in my ear.

"You always gotta put on a show," I said. He sunk his teeth into my neck and pulled on my skin.

"Boy don't be tryna put no hickie on me! I don't want my students knowing I'm freaky."

"Well let me put one on your lips then," he told me, and my clit thumped.

"Aye, y'all need to take that freaky shit over there somewhere," Jue teased.

"That ain't me. Check your boy," I said.

"Nigga, this my crib. It ain't a place in this house that we ain't fucked. Matter fact, we just fucked on that chair you sitting in the other day."

Jue scrunched his face in disgust. "Y'all nasty. C'mon shawty let's get in the pool," he told the girl.

"We fucked in there too!" Marcellus blurted.

I was so embarrassed. "Quit telling people our business." I slapped his arm.

"Shit, we grown. People know we be getting it in. Them hips ain't spreading for no reason."

I rolled my eyes. "Would you shut up?"

"Nah seriously, I'm about to roll to the store. I gotta get some more charcoal, lighter fluid, and ribs. Make sure these muthafuckas don't be all in the crib rambling through our shit while I'm gone."

"Un-un, I'll got to the store and you stay here and babysit."

"You sure?" he questioned.

"Yup. I need to get some more Malibu from the liquor store anyway."

"Cool. Go look in the room and grab two hunnids out my wallet. That should cover everything."

"Aight, where your wallet at?"

"In my top drawer."

"Okay. I'll be back in a minute," I said pecking his lips. I started to walk off and Marcellus grabbed my arm.

"Aye, you need to change clothes before you leave. I'on want them niggas at the liquor store trying to holler."

"Boy, I'm not thinking about them niggas."

"I know you ain't, but that's not gon' stop them. I ain't in the mood for no bullshit today. Now do what I said," he ordered.

"Yes daddy. I'll put some shorts on," I grinned. I kissed Marcellus once more before finally going into the house. After tossing on a pair of shorts and grabbing the money out of his wallet, I left for the store.

Marcellus

"Aye, where Talya run off to?" Jue asked.

I was sitting in a lounge chair by the grill sipping on a Corona. The gathering was now in full swing and it was way more people than we'd invited. I wasn't tripping because everybody was cool.

"She went to the store," I said as I nodded my head to the beat of a Drake song that was playing.

"Where shawty go that you had with you?" I questioned.

"Mane, I sent that bitch home. Her ass was trying to act stuck up and shit like she didn't wanna let me fuck," Jue ranted.

"Nigga you cold."

"Fuck that hoe. She knew what it was when I brought her hur'." As usual, I just shook my head at his ass. "Damn, who is shawty in the purple bathing suit?" Jue pointed.

"That's Talya's cousin Nene."

"Damn, they kind of favor. She come with somebody?" He inquired.

"Yeah, ol' girl with the fire red hair and the black bathing suit."

"Wait a minute…Ain't that the broad Danika you used to fuck with?" Jue squinted his eyes to get a better look.

"Yeah, that's her ass," I mumbled.

"Nigga you bold. You got a bitch hur' that you used to bust down?" he laughed.

"I didn't invite her. Hell, I ain't even know Talya knew shawty."

"You better be careful. She keeps glancing over hur'."

"That's why my ass is staying far away from her."

"Dawg this shit is crazy. I'm about to go see what's up with Talya's cousin. I'll be back," Jue announced.

"Aight nigga." I nodded.

As soon as he left, Danika made her way over to where I was. I looked around to be sure nobody Talya knew was watching.

"Well, well, well… It's been a lil minute," she said.

"Yup," I muttered without looking her way.

"I see you finally settled down. How's that working out?"

"Wassup Danika? What you really want?" I questioned as I finally glanced her way. She was smiling hard as hell.

"I just wanted to catch up."

"Why you didn't try to catch up in front of my girl? Why wait until she ain't around?" She looked at me and smirked.

"C'mon now. I'm sure you wouldn't have wanted that. I told her that you used to talk to one of my friends."

"Why you do that?"

"Just in case she figured out we knew each other."

"Is that right?" I asked.

"Mhm." She smiled at me seductively.

"How long you been knowing her?" I questioned curiously.

"I don't really know her. We just hung out with Nene."

"That's wassup. I'mma go into the house for a minute. You enjoy the party," I said and stood up.

I was trying my best to get far away from this broad. She was playing games, and a nigga wasn't trying to get caught up.

When I got inside of the house, I went up to my bedroom to take a leak. After handling my business, I washed my hands before leaving the bathroom. As soon as I stepped one foot into the room, I saw the last person I expected to see in here.

"What the fuck is you doing in my room?" I gritted.

Danika switched over to me and quickly dropped to her knees. Without saying anything, she reached for my shorts and started trying to pull my dick out.

"C'mon, this shit ain't cool. This the room I share with my gal," I said.

She gazed up into my eyes. "Let me just taste him for old time's sake?"

"Nah, this ain't right."

Danika and I had fucked several times in the past. The last time was about a year ago. No doubt she was a true freak, but I wasn't trying to go out like this. I did my dirt and all, but even this would be a bold move for me.

"C'mon baby, just for a lil while," she pleaded as she kept grabbing at my dick. At that moment, I was seriously battling with myself to do the right thing. My head up top was telling me to put this bitch out, but the head down below was telling me to go for what I know.

Damn! Why was I always being tested?

Natalya

It had only taken me a little over ten minutes to get the items Marcellus needed. Once I took the things back to the car, I walked over to the liquor store which was a few doors down from Schnucks. I grabbed two bottles of Malibu Coconut Rum and some Peach Schnapps for a drink I wanted to mix. After paying for my items I walked out of the store.

Just like Marcellus said, all types of dudes tried to holler at me. I paid their thirsty asses no mind as I went back to my car. Right when I was a few feet away I heard a car behind me. I glanced over my shoulder to see if I was in its way. It was a black Maxima with dark tinted windows. When I saw that I was in the person's way, I moved over to my left to let them go pass. Instead of them keeping it moving, the car just followed closely behind me. I looked over my shoulder again and signaled my hand for them to go around.

"Go around," I waved, but the person continued to sit there. I was suddenly getting a weird feeling. Hurriedly, I tried to rush back to my car. I was almost there when I heard the Maxima revving its engine. Out of nowhere it sped up like it was going to hit me and didn't stop until they were a few inches away. My heart dropped to the pit of my stomach as I started screaming to the top of my lungs.

"Ahh! Ahh! Somebody help me!" I yelled. The car continued to inch closer and closer. I was now stuck between it and the big truck parked next to me. I had nowhere to go.

"Help!" I screamed again.

"Aye, you okay?" one of the guys who tried to holler at me said.

"The person in this car trying to hit me," I shouted.

The dude started walking towards the car, but it backed up and quickly sped away. I tried to get their license plate number, but they drove away too fast.

"What was that shit about?" the dude asked.

"I'on know but thanks," I mumbled while turning my back to him. With my hands trembling, I hit the locks on my car, hopped inside, and drove the fuck off.

I tried calling Marcellus on my way home, but he didn't pick up. I looked down at my hands and noticed they were still trembling. As soon as I pulled up to my house, I noticed more people had arrived. I spotted Kiana's little car parked behind Marcellus' Benz. I jumped out and ran inside. I bumped into Kiana on the way to the kitchen.

"What's wrong with you?" she asked, noticing the scared look on my face.

"Somebody just tried to run me down again."

"What?" she exclaimed.

I told Kiana what happened, and she was pissed. "Where is Marcellus?"

"I don't know. I just got here a little while ago. Let's go find him so we can let him know what's up." Kiana spat. She was right on my heels as I marched out into the backyard in search of Marcellus. When I spotted Jue and Nene sitting together, I went over to them. "Have y'all seen Marcellus?" I asked. I was so shaken up I didn't even focus on them being together.

"I saw him go in the house not too long ago. Errthang straight?" Jue asked.

"It's cool. I need to holler at him about something." I walked off before he could say something else. When I got back inside of my house, I checked the downstairs area and didn't see him there, so I went up to our bedroom on the second floor. Just as I got to our door, I thought I heard a female's voice.

"Who the fuck in your room?" Kiana asked me.

"I don't know but I'm about to find out," I snarled while busting in the door. My eyes immediately zeroed in on Marcellus and Danika.

"Oh hell nah!" I shouted.

Danika was down on her knees in front of Marcellus. He was completely dressed, but from what I saw it looked as if she was trying to suck his dick. When Marcellus noticed me, he immediately tried to explain.

"I was in the bathroom and when I came out, she was—"

I held my hand up to stop him. "Ain't no need to explain. I know exactly what the fuck is going on. This bitch was trying to be on some grimy shit, and I'm finna whoop her ass!" I yelled.

Marcellus looked surprised that I wasn't going in on him. Why would I? It was obvious he wasn't doing anything by the way he held Danika hands like he was trying to pull her up. Plus, I'd heard him loud and clear tell her that she needed to leave.

Before Danika had the chance to open her mouth, I was over to her in less than a second, ramming my fist into her face. The disrespectful bitch had the nerve to try and swing on me, but I dragged her by that fake ass hair and slammed her head into the wall. Thankfully, Marcellus and

Kiana didn't try to stop me. They knew I needed to release this rage I had pent up inside of me. As Danika kicked and screamed, I beat the brakes off that bitch. When I had enough of that I started to kick her. She was now yelling at the top of her lungs.

"Shut up bitch!" I slammed my fist into her face once again.

"Aight shawty, that's enough," Marcellus said, finally breaking it up.

"Y'all better get this bitch outta here!" I boomed.

Just as Kiana grabbed Danika by her arm to escort her ass out, several people ran into the room. It was Nene, Marcellus' momma with Kacen on her hip, Jue, and a few other people.

"What the hell is going on in here?" Marcellus' momma asked.

"What you doing up here Danika?" Nene questioned.

"Your trick ass friend was just trying to fuck Marcellus," I barked.

"Oh shit," Jue mumbled as he walked out. Everybody quickly followed behind him. I guess they ain't want no parts of what they thought was about to go down. Nene was the only one to stick around.

“Say what now?” she asked with her face full of shock as she glanced at Danika.

“You heard me. This bitch was just in here trying to fuck my man. Didn’t I tell you she wasn’t to be trusted?” Nene balled up her face.

“C’mon Danika, this my cousin. Why would you do som’ shit like that?”

Danika ran her hands over her hair trying to get herself together. “Fuck that bitch. I saw the way she was staring at me with that stank ass look. And don’t think I’on know about you calling me thirsty and shit. Since you wanted to talk shit, my thirsty ass said I would fuck your man. If you wouldn’t have busted in, I would probably have my juices all over your sheets.” She smirked.

I tried to rush that bitch again, but Marcellus yanked me back. “Let me go Marcellus,” I boomed.

“Shawty calm down. Nene, you better get this bitch out of hur’ before I let her loose,” He threatened.

“Danika, you need to chill. That’s my cousin. Talya I’m so sorry,” she apologized.

“Wow! You gon’ take her side? I been your best friend since we were younger. You said she might not even be your real cousin ‘cause her momma was a hoe back in the day. Your uncle might not even be her real daddy.”

"Shut up Danika." Nene glanced at me with an embarrassed look.

"Nah, don't tell me to shut up now. Keep it real with yo 'cousin."

"Talya, let's just beat both these bitches' asses," Kiana gritted.

"Nah, that's okay Kiana. Let her friend just keep blasting her ass."

"Talya." Nene raised her hands.

"Bitch, get the fuck out of my house right now and take that stank ass hoe with you."

Nene walked over and angrily snatched Danika by her arm. "Stop, don't pull on me. I know how to walk."

"Well hurry your ass up!" Nene spat. They argued as they left the room.

"I'mma go check on everybody," Marcellus said as soon as they were gone. I nodded as Kiana walked over to me. She pulled me in her arms and hugged me.

"I know you're hurt because you were trying to build a relationship. But to be honest, I'm glad everything came out. I didn't like that sneaky hoe anyway. She was jealous of you."

I laughed a little. “Well at least I know I can trust you,” I said, and it was true. It seemed Kiana was the only one who hadn’t tried to cross me.

Saadiq

One week later…

"Ma stop crying. It's aight," I told her.

"I'm just so happy to see you baby." she sniffled.

"I know, and I'm happy to see you too. But you gon' have to chill with the tears. You know I hate to see you cry."

"I'm sorry. You been okay? Nobody tried to touch you in here, have they?"

"Ma chill. It ain't none of that going on." I frowned.

"I'm just checking."

I glanced at Adore'. "'Preciate you bringing her hur' for me."

"No problem, it was my pleasure. Besides, it was time for us to finally meet."

Momma stopped wiping her eyes and glanced between me and Adore'. "Why was it time for us to meet?" she asked.

I had Adore' to swing by and pick up ma dukes so she could come to visitation with her. We'd been staying in touch by phone, but we hadn't seen each other. When she asked if she could come visit, I told her she could.

"Go ahead and tell her Saadiq." Adore' grinned.

"Tell me what?" Momma looked confused as hell.

"Aight ma it's like this… Me and Adore' are together," I admitted.

"Oh you are?" She looked at me before slowly glancing at Adore'.

Adore' eagerly nodded her head. "Mhm, we made it official about two months ago," she finished for me.

"Well congratulations," Momma uttered. The look on her face didn't match the words coming from her mouth. She was team Talya so I knew she would feel some type of way. That's why I'd waited until we were face to face to tell her the news.

"Thank you, Ms. Kamen. I will make your son very happy," Adore' squealed. On the low, I saw momma roll her eyes.

"Aye, go get us some snacks and let me holler at her for a minute," I told Adore'.

"Okay baby." She hopped up and switched away. As soon as she was gone, momma started right in on a nigga.

"I don't like her," she said.

"How you don't like her, and you just met her?"

"I can't put my finger on it, but it's something about her that doesn't seem genuine."

I chuckled while running my hand down my face. "You don't like nobody."

"That's not true. I like Talya." I shook my head.

"Well me and Talya ain't together no more."

"I know that, but it doesn't mean you can't get back together. How do you start a relationship with someone and you behind bars anyway?"

"Easy. Adore' been there for me since day one," I grumbled.

"Talya would have been here too, but you didn't let her."

I chortled. "I swear you been around her too much. Y'all starting to sound alike."

"Don't change the subject. Do you really like this girl, or is this just something you're doing 'because you're bored?"

"Nah, I think she cool."

"I didn't ask you that. I said do you really like her."

"I guess," I mumbled.

"You guess? Boy, I swear you haven't changed a bit. You got that same attitude you had when you were with Sunday. Why don't you wanna be with Talya anymore?"

"Ain't she with somebody else?"

Momma looked shocked. "Yes, but that doesn't mean nothing either. Right now y'all both are just being stubborn."

"Being stubborn is not answering the phone for somebody when they call or some small shit like that, not going out there popping out another nigga's seed.

"What are you talking about?" Momma frowned.

"I'm talking about your precious daughter having a baby by somebody else. How come you didn't tell me? We been in contact for a lil minute now, and you ain't said shit. I guess you gonna find some way to justify that too, huh?"

"Look Saadiq, I wasn't supposed to tell you this but—"

"Baby they didn't have those chips you like so I got you some baked Doritos, a Snickers, a Slim Jim, and this Gatorade." Adore' handed me the snacks that she'd gotten from the vending machine. She tried to give momma a bag of chips and drink, but she turned it down.

"No thanks." She waved her hand.

"What I miss? Why do you look like that baby?" Adore' asked glancing between us.

"You didn't miss nothing. We were just catching up." Mama gave her a fake smile.

"Oh okay." Adore smiled.

"Adore', tell me about yourself. Do you have any kids?" Momma asked out of nowhere.

"No ma'am."

"How old are you?"

"I'm thirty," she said.

"Mmm. That's like a six year age difference. Don't you think you a little too old for him?"

"No ma'am. Saadiq is very mature for his age."

"I guess. Are your parents still together?" Momma continued.

"Unfortunately not. My mom moved to Colorado when her and my dad separated. My dad raised me," Adore' explained.

"Aight ma, that's enough questions," I told her.

"No that's okay. I don't mind."

"Well I do. This ain't what the visit is supposed to be about."

"Okay I'm done." Momma threw up her hands. I knew her feelings were hurt but I wasn't about to let her keep grilling Adore'. She would just have to get over the fact that me and Talya wasn't rocking no more. I didn't like it either, but that's just how shit was.

Kiana

A few days later…

"You got some pretty ass feet," Lex told me as I sat on the couch and put my feet in his lap. We were at my house having movie night. This had become sort of a weekly ritual for us. Since Macy's grandmother kept her on the weekends, Lex would just come over here and we'd spent time together. If he had an appointment to tattoo, I would go to the shop with him if Aunt Delano had Raegan.

"Thanks," I smiled. "Mmm." A moan slipped from my lips. His hands were so damn strong.

"Let me ask you something," Lex said.

"What?" I breathed heavily. His touch was making me horny.

"Are you really feeling me?" he questioned.

"You know I am. Why you ask that?"

"Because I been thinking…"

"Thinking about what?" *Was he about to tell me he was ready to have sex*?

"It's been a minute since we been kicking it. We've both gotten to know each other on a deeper level, and I'm really feeling you too. What you think about being my girl?" he asked, and I smiled so hard that my cheeks hurt. No one had ever asked me to be their girlfriend. I wanted to scream hell yes, but I didn't want to come off as desperate.

"Are you sure you ready for that?" I questioned.

Lex looked me dead in the eyes with a straight face and said, "I wouldn't have asked if I wasn't ready." My heart literally skipped a beat.

"I mean, I guess we can do that," I mumbled. I was trying not to sound too eager.

"You guess?" He roughly squeezed my foot.

"Oww. Yes Lex, I'll be your girlfriend. Is that better?" I laughed, and he nodded.

"Aight then, it's official." Lex moved my feet from his lap and leaned over to seal our new relationship with a kiss on the lips. The kiss was so sensual it made my nipples stiffen. When his hands started to roam my body, my panties got wet. Lex gently pulled me down on the couch as his sucked on my tongue.

"Mmm," I let out as I pulled his shirt over his head and ran my hands over his hard chest. While slowly tracing the bold letters of his daughter's name, I gazed into his eyes.

"You ready for this?" he asked.

I quickly nodded my head to let him know I was ready. Once we'd both stripped out of our clothes, he grabbed a condom from his wallet. While holding his solid, long dick in one hand, he rolled the rubber down over it. At that moment I started to salivate. His penis was so fuckin' beautiful. It was the same brown color as him with just the right size mushroom head, and his pubic area was nicely groomed.

I licked my lips as eyed his privates. When he looked up and saw me staring, he flashed that sexy grin I loved so much. Grabbing my legs, Lex pulled me down on the couch and slowly rolled his penis up and down my slit. Once I was soaking wet, he plunged deep into my tunnel.

"Oh yes!" I screamed as my eyes rolled to the top of my head. My mouth fell into an O shape with each thrust he took. Lex took both my legs and placed them on his shoulder, going deeper than anybody had ever gone before. It hurt a little, but it was a feel good type of hurt. As he drew one of my nipples into his mouth, he started a rhythm. He would slow roll for a little while then he would deep stroke me. He did that for about a good ten minutes before he went in, beating this pussy up.

The sound of our skin clapping sent me into a complete frenzy. I'd never felt anything as good as this before. I don't know if it was because of the feelings I had for Lex or what. All I knew was I didn't ever want this moment to end. After an hour of changing positions several times and having multiple orgasms, we both lay spent on my couch with him still deep inside of me.

"Damn girl that shit A1," he mumbled.

"Boy quit playing?"

"Nah, I'm serious You got a nigga hooked already. I'mma have to hurry up and get my energy back so I can get some more," he said, kissing my lips. He slowly pulled out of me and sat up on the couch.

"You wanna take a—" I started to say but my phone interrupted me. I jumped up to see who it was. When I saw that it was my auntie, I let the call roll to voicemail.

I turned to Lex to finish what I was saying but once again my phone rang. My eyebrows raised when I saw that it was my aunt calling for the second time. "Give me a minute baby. This is auntie"

"Go ahead. Take care of that," Lex told me while cutting on the TV.

"Hello?" I answered.

"Kiana get over here right now!" she barked into the phone.

"What's the matter auntie? Is something going on with Raegan."

"No, she's fine. I just need you to get over here right now," was all she said before she hung up in my face. I pulled the phone away and looked at it strangely. Something had to be wrong for her to call me Kiana. It had been years since she'd referred to me by my real name.

"Errthang straight?" Lex asked with a confused look on his face.

"I'on know. My aunt said I need to get over there right now."

"Well gon' and get dressed and I'll take you by there."

"Okay, I'll be ready in just a minute." I took off towards the back to throw on some clothes. I had no idea what was going on, but from the sound of my aunt's voice she was pissed about something.

***

Twenty minutes later I was walking into Aunt Delano's house. I'd left Lex in the car waiting for me. Auntie met me in the living room. From her bloodshot eyes, I could tell she'd been crying. "What's the matter auntie?" I asked.

"Sit down," she ordered.

I took a seat on the couch and looked up at her. "I'm only going to ask you this once and I want you to be honest."

"Okay, what is it?" I tried to search her face, but it was stoic.

"Were you the one that used my social security number and got all those credit cards in my name?" she questioned. For a split second my heart stopped beating. I had no idea this was what I was walking into.

"Who told you that?"

"It doesn't matter. Did you do it?" she gritted.

"Um…I-I…uh—" I stammered.

"You what? Please tell me that you didn't do that Kiana. My head is telling me you did, but my heart is saying my baby wouldn't do this to me. After everything we've been through, it's just not possible. Please tell me my head is wrong. Let me know this is all just a big misunderstanding." More tears welled in her eyes as she stared at me.

Brisham must have told her because he was the only other person who knew. "Look auntie, I can ex—" She held up her hand to stop me.

"Explain what, how you broke my heart? You of all people are aware of everything I went through with that mess. My credit score was ruined, I had to fight off all those creditors, and I almost lost my house. The fact that you would allow me to go through all of that knowing you were the cause seriously makes me question you as a person.

"When no one else wanted you, I took you in. I didn't throw it up in your face either. Now I may have shown you a little tough love or said some things that you didn't like. Hell, they were all true. You were just like your mother, letting a man ruin your life. That boy used you and in turn you used me. You jeopardized our relationship just so you could say you got a man. Was it worth it?"

"I'm sooo sorry auntie. I never meant to hurt you. I was in a real low place in my life, and I made some stupid decisions. Please forgive me," I pleaded.

"Just save your tears honey, because I don't care 'bout 'em. What you did is unforgiveable. So, what I want you to do is pack up your daughter, get whatever you have left here, and leave my house for good. I don't ever want to see you again. If I had the strength, I would beat your ass down. Right now I'm just too hurt to even look at you." My aunt turned and stomped out of the room. I sat there with a face full of tears, feeling lower than I'd ever felt in my whole entire life.

During the time when Brisham and I were on those Mollys heavy and we didn't have any money, I stole my aunt's social security number. I got a credit card in her name with a five-thousand-dollar limit and sold it to someone on the street for fifteen hundred dollars. I was only supposed to do it once to help Brisham get back on his feet. After I did it the first time, he blew the money on some damn rims and some other bullshit. A few weeks later he came to me and asked if I could do it again. Like a damn fool, I ordered another one. That time the credit card had a fifteen-thousand-dollar limit, and we sold it for thirty-five hundred.

Once all that money was gone we did it one last time, but that credit card company only gave her fifteen hundred. I guess by then the other ones were maxed out, so they weren't giving her as big of an amount as they did before. We took that credit card and bought stuff that we sent to an abandoned house. Once it was delivered, we went and got it. Looking back on everything I'd done, I feel so stupid. Not only did I allow the credit cards to go for super cheap, I never really pocketed a dime of the money. Basically, like my aunt said, I'd ruined our relationship so someone else could benefit.

A few minutes after she left, Aunt Delano returned with Raegan and her diaper bag. "I know I said you could get your stuff, but I changed my mind. I want you out of my goddamn house at this instance. You repulse me and I can't stand to look at your face. You better be glad I got a lot of love for your child because she's the one saving your ass from me calling the police."

I grabbed the car seat with Raegan in it, along with her diaper bag and walked to the door. I tried once again to apologize, but my aunt cussed me out so bad I just left. By the time I got back to Lex's truck, I could barely stand. He got out, strapped Raegan in the backseat, and helped me into the front. He asked what was wrong, but I didn't have the energy or the words to explain to him what I'd done. I just laid my head on the seat and cried all the way back to my apartment.

Natalya

One week later…

"Ugh, what the hell does this hoe want?" I questioned aloud. It was Nene calling me for the hundredth time. She had been calling since everything went down at my house, but I'd ignored her ass. She was the last person I wanted to talk to. I really thought we were cool, but I guess to her I was just someone else she could use. Whenever we went out, I always paid her way and bought her drinks. I'd given her so many clothes and shoes she didn't have to go shopping for at least a whole year.

On top of all that shit, I'd helped that bitch with her bills. She was always saying she didn't have no money, since neither one of her baby daddies helped with the kids. I should have known that bum bitch only hung around me because it benefited her. She wasn't loyal to nobody but herself. So many times she'd told me shit about Danika that I could have brought up, but what would have been the point? I figured I would let them hoes continue to backstab each other.

After sticking my phone in my purse, I walked up to the door. I stood for a minute before finally knocking. My nerves were all over the place. I wasn't sure how this meeting would go.

"Wassup Talya? What are you doing here?" My mother questioned once she opened the door.

"Can I come in for a minute? We need to talk." She eyed me suspiciously before finally opening the door wide enough for me to step inside. When I entered the house, I noticed she changed a few things. She had gotten rid of the old furniture she had since I was a kid and got her a new sofa and love seat. Also, she'd put up some more curtains and had even hung up some nice pictures.

"The house looks good," I complimented.

"Thanks," she mumbled while eyeing me up and down. The look on her face screamed 'get to the point of your visit.'

"How you been?" I asked.

"I been okay," she replied blandly.

"Look, I know you wanna know why I'm here."

"Yup." She folded her arms over her chest.

"Is Gary my real father?" I asked.

She laughed. "Really? You waited all this time to ask me that question."

"Can you please just tell me. I heard that he might not be. I need to know if it's true or not?"

"Yes Talya. Even though his ass ain't been a good one, he is your daddy." I nodded.

"Okay. Why do you hate me?" I blurted out.

"I don't hate you girl."

"Well what is it? I don't think you love me either."

"Is this why you came over, to put me down for something else I didn't do as a mother? If that's the case, you can gon' right back out that door. I got too much going on in my life to be arguing with you." She sighed while falling back onto the couch. Just like any other time, she picked up a blunt and put it to her lips. I walked over and sat down in front of her.

"I'm not trying to put you down, I just need answers. Before the situation with Beenie, you were at least loving. What about all that made you hate me?" She blew the smoke from her nostrils while glaring at me.

"You want me to be honest?" she finally asked, and I nodded. "Why? What is it going to prove? Will it make you stop looking down your nose at me?"

"I don't look down my nose at you."

"Yes, you do Talya. Ever since you were younger, you always had this look on your face like you were embarrassed of me."

"If I looked at you like that, it was because you let men run all over you. But that's not what I'm talking about."

"Look, it wasn't that I hated you… I guess I was jealous."

"Jealous of what?" I frowned.

"For the first time in my life I had a man who supposedly loved me, but he turned out to be a damn pervert. He was attracted to my young daughter who his grown ass had no business even looking at."

"But why be jealous? I'm your daughter, and it's not like I wanted his sick ass to do that to me. It doesn't make sense."

"Because you still had something I didn't possess. You had this innocence, and I knew that's what Beenie wanted."

"What are you talking about?" I asked. To me she was talking in circles.

"Listen Talya…I don't know how to tell you this so I'm just gonna say it. I have HIV. That's the reason I tolerate bullshit from these men because no real man will ever want me knowing I have this disease. Hell, the one time I did try to live a normal life was with Andy. I figured if I used protection and not tell him about the disease everything would be okay. He found out from snooping through my things. That's why he beat my ass. I wasn't trying to protect him when you tried to call the police. I knew I was wrong for withholding that information."

"Oh my God! How long have you had it, and where did you get it from?"

"Beenie," she confessed. "I found out about two years into our relationship. He claimed he didn't know, but I know that's a lie. I was so angry when I found out that I just wanted to kill myself, but I decided not to 'cause I knew I would be leaving you behind. At the same time, it made me resent you because I had to stay around for you. When that shit went down with Beenie, it just gave me another reason to blame you for something instead of hating the person who caused all this pain. I tried my best to recapture my life before it was ruined, but none of that worked. I was only masking the pain I felt, and I just became angrier and bitter."

"Damn," I mumbled. I had no idea she was experiencing all that. "Why didn't you talk to me or try to get some help?"

"Honestly, I felt my life was over anyway. I didn't see no point in trying to save myself. All the hurt and shit just made me want to self-destruct so that's what I did."

"Having HIV is not a death sentence. There are plenty people who have lived a long life with it. You've been killing yourself quicker than the disease has."

"Yeah, well maybe it would be better if I were dead," she uttered, and that broke my heart.

"Don't say that. You have so much to live for. What about me? What about your grandson?"

"My grandson?" she asked with a raised brow.

"Yes, I have a one-and-a-half-year-old son who I know you will love. His name is Kacen, and he's so sweet."

Her face balled up like she was gonna cry, but she was trying her best to hold it in. "Wh.e.re is he?" Her voice cracked as she spoke.

"He's at daycare right now. That's the reason I came by here. I wanted to settle our differences, so you could finally meet him. My life hasn't been easy either. I've dealt with a lot of pain and hurt too, but that doesn't mean I can check out on myself or those around me," I said, and she broke down crying. I got up and walked over to her. I wrapped my arms around her neck and pulled her head to my chest.

"You are so strong Talya. Why can't I be like that?" she sobbed.

"You can be. You just gotta quit running from your problems. That's one thing both of us will have to stop doing. Maybe we can get some help together," I said.

"You would do that with me?" she asked.

"Yes, I will if that's what you want."

She hugged me tighter as the tears freely fell from her eyes. I rocked her in my arms until it was time for me to leave. "I have to go, but I can come back and visit."

My momma sat up and wiped her eyes. "Will you bring the baby?"

"Yeah, I'll bring Kacen," I said, and she nodded. I grabbed my things and started to leave.

"Talya?" my momma called out to me.

"Yeah?" I answered.

"Thank you," she smiled.

I gave her a gentle smile and left. Just as I was about to get inside my car, Ms. Jennifer came rushing up to me.

"Talya, I've been calling you all week. We need to talk asap," she stated.

"About what?" I questioned. I really wasn't in the mood to talk about anything else.

"Just please come to the house and I'll explain."

I sighed. "Aight, give me a minute and I'll be over."

I had to take a minute to recover from the news my mom dropped on me. I felt so bad for her.

Marcellus

Two weeks later…

"Oh shit I feel it in my stomach!" Quandra screamed. She was up against the wall while I drilled her thick ass from the back. For the past hour we'd been going hard in the paint. I had so much stamina built up in me that I had to release it somewhere.

"I'm about to come," Quandra screamed.

"Cum for me shawty," I whispered as I spread her ass cheeks apart. With a smile on my face, I watched my dick slide in and out.

"Mmm I'm coming," she purred. I closed my eyes and drilled into her harder. After several deep strokes, I shot off inside the condom.

"Argh! Goddamn!" I grunted.

Just like always, Quandra went and grabbed a towel to clean me off. Once she was finished, I quickly threw my clothes back on. It was my day to get lil man from daycare since Talya had tutoring.

"You want me to drop that package off at seven-thirty, right?" she asked.

"You can actually get there a lil earlier. That way you can peep the scene out." I'd finally given Quandra a job. After showing her the ins and out for like two weeks, I let her go on her own. She made her first run for me a week ago. Tonight she was meeting up with this nigga who was gonna cop six bricks. I wasn't familiar with dude, but I'd heard he was legit from some reputable sources. Based on that I made my decision to work with the homie.

Quandra was aware if she ever got knocked her ass was not to open her mouth. All she had to do was tell them muthafuckas she wanted a lawyer. I would handle everything from there. Since she'd agreed, I had hope she fully understood the terms.

"Okay daddy, I gotcha. If there are any issues I will let you know." I nodded. Everything with Quandra was smooth sailing. She didn't nag a nigga or put up these high expectations. I often wondered why the fuck it couldn't be like this with Talya.

"'Preciate that girl. I paid the room up for the next two days so feel free to stay if you want to."

"You know I will," she told me. I left and went to handle my business.

***

I was sitting on the couch watching football when Talya finally came into the house. "Hey," she said.

"Wassup shawty?" I threw her a head nod. She walked straight to Kacen's playpen and picked him up. From the corner of my eye, I watched as she showered him with kisses.

"Hey momma's baby! Did you miss me?" she asked. I sat there for a minute wondering if she was going to make her way to me. About ten minutes went by and she hadn't even looked my way.

"Where my kiss?" I decided to ask.

"Huh?" She glanced at me with a confused look.

"I said where's my kiss? You haven't kissed me in a few weeks now. What's up with that?"

"It ain't been that long," she denied.

I bit down on the inside of my jaw. "Mane, you do that shit every time you go through something. You always shut me out."

"What are you talking about? I'm not shutting you out."

"Yeah, you right. I'm just tripping," I piped sarcastically.

"What's that supposed to mean?"

"Nothing mane." I tried to tune back into the game, but she kept talking.

"No, you said it so tell me what you meant."

I sat up on the couch and glowered at her. "How come whenever the smallest thing happens in your life, you use that as an excuse to distance yourself from me?"

"That's not true."

"C'mon shawty. I wouldn't be saying the shit if it wasn't true. I ain't no nagging ass nigga, so I'm not just gon' make up some shit to start an argument. Trust and believe I sit back and peep shit long before I even mention it."

"I peep shit too," she said.

"Whatcha mean by that?"

"I find it funny how Ariel is popping up again and calling you for every little thing. Not only that, but you leave sometimes at night and don't show your face again until the next morning. It's a lot of shit I could toss at you. I haven't said anything though because I'm trying to give you the benefit of the doubt." I shook my head. "What?" she asked.

"Why you always do that? You find a way to make this shit about me whenever I'm talking about you." She burned me up with that.

"Why you always get defensive whenever I mention your baby momma or you possibly creeping?" I let out a deep breath. "Exactly! I'm tired Marcellus. I don't have the energy to fight with you. All I wanted to do was come home, unwind, and spend the evening with my baby."

I ran my tongue across my teeth. "That's exactly what I'm talking about. You don't even include me in your plans. I guess all I'm good for is giving you dick and buying you shit, huh?"

Talya didn't say anything, so I got up and snatched my keys off the table. *Fuck this mane*. I wasn't about to keep putting up with her bullshit.

Brisham

Two days later…

A nigga had just come back from the club where I'd spent the whole night in the VIP with my homies and a few bad bitches. We'd tossed back drink after drink, popped a couple of Mollys, and blazed several blunts. My boy Bird had just dropped me off. His little sister who was in high school was keeping Skylar, so that would give me time to sober up. I was going to need that time because I was too fucked up.

When I finally got to the door, I fumbled with my keys for a minute before I found the right one. "Damn, I'm fucked up," I mumbled to myself as I clumsily stumbled inside. I was just about to close my door when suddenly I heard footsteps running behind me. Out of nowhere I felt my body being pushed from the back. I took about three steps and fell face forward. "What the hell," I grumbled.

I slightly lifted my head, trying to shake the dizziness off. That's when I noticed two shadowed figures standing above me. Whoever these muthafuckas were had on all black clothing with ski masks. "What the fuck y'all want?" I slurred. One of them closed the door.

"What the fuck are y'all doing?" I yelled. They didn't say anything as they ran over and started to jump me. These niggas were kicking and punching me all over my body. Due to my drunken state, it felt like ten muthafuckas jumping me instead of two. I tried to get up but one of them kicked me in the face, knocking my ass right back down. The saline taste of blood instantly filled my mouth. At that moment I had no other choice but to curl up into the fetal position.

They were straight whooping my ass. Every time I thought this shit was about to end, the muthafuckas would seem to gain their second wind. I don't know how many kicks I took to my side, back, face and stomach or how many punches I took to my head. All I know is that the pain took over and before long I ended up blacking out.

***

A few hours later I was laid up in the hospital. After waking up and feeling like my body had been split in two, I called for an Ambulance. Ironically, they brought me to the same hospital I came to when I was shot. Just as before the police came asking questions. This time I was truthful when I said I didn't know who was behind this shit. The possibility of somebody retaliating for that nigga Jacobi popped in my head. Then it hit me I would've been dead if it had something to do with that. Nigga's didn't do no jumping shit nowadays. They were quick to pull the trigger, so I knew it couldn't be somebody from his crew. Besides, I was careful with the situation. No one was aware I even knew his ass. My next thought was that it was somebody trying to rob me, but then I realized they didn't take shit. When I came to, I was still wearing my jewelry that I wore to the club. The only other explanation I could think of was… "Kiana," I said aloud. Her auntie must've confronted her about the little information I sent her. I see the bitch still wanted to test me. "I got something for her ass," I said as I snatched up my phone and dialed her number. I let it ring several times before her voicemail picked up. I hung up and called right back. She still didn't answer. I hung up again and hit my boy Bird.

"Yo, what's going on nigga?" He answered.

"Man, I'm laid up in this fuckin' hospital."

"In the hospital? What happened?" He asked. I ran everything down to him.

"You think she had something to do with this?" He questioned.

"Damn right her ass did."

"That's fucked up. I meant to tell you the other day I peeped som' shit."

"What's that?"

"I saw her out with this nigga named Lex I used to go to school with. The nigga owns a tattoo shop over there not too far from Page Ave."

"Oh yeah?" I asked.

"Yeah. They were at the mall all hugged up and shit with y'all daughter."

"Good looking out on that info. I'mma hit you up later."

"You want me to come scoop you when they discharge you?"

"Yeah, I'll let you know when I get out. In the meantime, listen out for any information you can get."

"I gotcha bruh."

"Aight I'll holler," I told him and ended the call. I hit the call button on the bed and had a nurse to come to the room. When she came in, I told her I needed a favor. I knew Kiana wouldn't answer for me, so I figured I could get the nurse to hit her up.

Kiana

The next day…

"Oh my God, this is so beautiful!" I squealed as I admired the tattoo Lex had given me. He hooked me up with a picture of my momma on my left shoulder. The tattoo was a picture of her when she was younger. He added wings to her back and put the date she died.

"So you like it for real?"

"No, I love it. How did you get it to look so real?"

"I just let my hands do what they do," he stated. I continued to stare in the mirror at the beautiful artwork. Lex was talented as fuck, and it amazed me that he wasn't cocky with it.

"Boy, you are a beast." I smiled as I turned around and faced him.

"'Preciate it baby. Tattooing is like an escape for me. Whenever I'm going through some shit, I come in hur' and do as many tattoos as I can to get my mind off my problems. My artists be like 'Lex, why you in hur' so much and you the owner?' I explain to them that my passion is tattooing and owning this business is just what comes along with it. God forbid something bad happens to my shop, I wouldn't sweat it because I'd still have my gift."

"Damn, that's deep baby. I wish I had something I could use for an escape," I mumbled.

"You can have that escape too. You just gotta find out what it is that you like to do," Lex stated.

"Yeah, you're right." I sighed as I pulled my shirt over my head.

"Do you feel better?" Lex questioned.

"Just a little bit." I glanced at him with a small smile.

"Aight. Since you feel a lil better do you want to tell me what happened? And I'on want to hear that shit about y'all having a disagreement. I know it's gotta be deeper than that because I be seeing the look on your face sometimes."

"How are you able to tell that?"

"Because I'm in tune with you shawty. I notice a lot of shit that you may not think I do."

I looked him in the eyes and spilled everything. By the time I finished the story, I didn't know what to think. Lex wasn't saying anything. "Are you going to say something?" I asked nervously.

He ran his hand down his face. "I mean, you gotta know that was fucked up. Any real man wouldn't have let you burn your family just to come up. He would have gone out there to do whatever was necessary to make sure y'all were straight. At the same time, you grown as hell. He didn't put a gun to your head."

"I know he didn't. Do you look at me differently because of what I did?"

"If I told you I didn't I would be lying," he said.

I swallowed hard as I prepared myself for the next question. "Do you still want to be with me?" I fiddled with my hands as I awaited his answer.

"Why wouldn't I?" he asked with a frown.

"Maybe you think I'll do it to you."

"Nah, that would be me judging you based off your past. As of right now I have no reason to not trust you. You were woman enough to tell me what you did, which means you accept responsibility for your actions. Your honesty trumps whatever bullshit you did. I ain't no saint Kiana. I told you what I did to my daughter's mother with all the cheating and shit. I wouldn't want you holding that over my head when I know I've changed."

"You always have the perfect words." I told him.

"I'm just a real nigga that speaks what's on my mind." I stood up and kissed Lex with everything in me. I loved how he accepted me flaws and all. He understood me like nobody else did.

When we pulled away from the kiss, Lex gazed into my eyes. "Is there anything else you wanna get off your chest?" he asked.

Briefly, I thought about telling him about the situation with Saadiq. I changed my mind at the last minute. Unless it came out another way, I figured I would take it to my grave.

"Nah, it ain't nothing else."

Lex pecked my lips again. "You gonna be aight," he told me.

Ring. Ring.

"Baby let me get my phone right quick. It may be Talya calling about Raegan."

"Go ahead. I'mma clean up so we can get out of hur'."

I quickly grabbed my purse before it stopped ringing. "Hello!" I breathed into the phone.

"Is this Kiana Jamison?" the woman asked.

"Yes, this her. Who dis?"

"Hi Kiana, my name is Pam. I'm a nurse at Kindred Hospital."

"What's the matter?" I cut her off.

"I have Brisham Kamen here. He's been beaten pretty badly. He gave us your number as an emergency contact and asked that we inform you he would like to see you."

"What?" I gasped.

Lex stopped what he was doing and walked over to me. "What's wrong?" he mouthed. I held my finger up.

"Who brought him to the hospital?" I questioned.

"I believe he called the ambulance, but that's all I can tell you over the phone. If you come in, the doctor can explain everything."

"I'm on my way," I told her and ended the call.

"What's going on?" Lex asked again.

"That was a nurse from the hospital. She said Brisham is in there. She mentioned something about him getting beat up, and he asked for me," I explained. "What's the matter?" I asked, noticing the blank expression on his face.

"Ain't nothing wrong," he denied.

"Yes, it is. I can see it in your face. You got a problem with me going to check on him?"

"I'm saying, dude ain't got nobody else?" Lex sighed.

"Ion know but even if he did, I would still want to make sure he's good. He's my daughter's father."

"I understand, but do you think it's a good idea to be there for him after what he did to you?"

"Trust me I'm still pissed about that, but right now none of that matters. He needs me."

"Aight, well go handle your business," he muttered.

"Are you mad at me?" I questioned. We'd just made a breakthrough in our relationship, and I didn't want anything to ruin our special moment.

"Nah, I ain't mad at you shawty. To be honest, I would probably question you as a person if you didn't go check on him. But there is gonna come a time when you will have to decide if being there for him is more important that what we got going on. If we gonna be together, he ain't gon' be able to call on you anytime that he gets ready."

"I hear you baby, and I promise it's not gonna always be like this. I gotta go," I told him as I grabbed my things and ran out of the shop.

***

I ran up to the desk where the receptionist was and asked her to point me in the direction of Brisham's room. After checking my ID, she gave me the room number. When I finally made it to his room, I found him sitting up in his bed eating some mashed potatoes. My eyes immediately scanned his body. His whole face was swollen, his eyes were black, his lips were two times the normal size, and it looked as if he had something in his jaw.

"Are you okay?" I asked as I rushed to his side. I tried to hug him, but he pushed me away. My face balled in confusion. "What's the matter with you?" If anybody should be mad, then it should be me. After what he did, I shouldn't even be talking to his ass.

"Bitch, you don't think I know you was behind this shit?" he growled.

"What the hell are you talking about?"

"I know this was you. I ain't got no enemies," he claimed.

"Well obviously you do if you in hur'. If I wanted you hurt, I would have done it myself after what you did to me."

"What the fuck did I do to you? You talking about that shit I told Kylisha?"

"No, I'm talking about what you told my auntie," I snapped.

"I'on know what the fuck you talking about," he lied.

"You're lying," I yelled.

"I ain't lying," he snarled at me.

Just then, a white, average height doctor with a baby face came into the room. He looked between me and Brisham. As if he could sense the tension in the room he said, "Is everything okay in here?"

"Yeah, everything straight. Can you give us a minute?" Brisham asked.

"Sure, I'll come back through in about thirty minutes."

"'Preciate that," Brisham muttered.

As soon as the doctor left, Brisham glared at me. "For the sake of our child, I been letting you slide. Now all my sympathy is gone. It's cutthroat from hur' on out. You 'bout to meet the side of Brisham I show these niggas on the street," he threatened. I looked at him with a disgusted look.

"I don't know what the hell you're talking about, but I told yo stupid ass I didn't have nothing to do with this. I didn't even know you were here until a nurse called."

"Fuck out of my room mane. I ain't buying this shit," he gritted.

"Brisham, I did—"

"Get the fuck out of hur' before I get out this bed and lay hands on yo' ass!" he roared.

"Fuck you!" I turned around and stomped to the door. Before I could walk out, Brisham stopped me.

"Aye, let that nigga you fuckin' with know he might want to watch his back. I'm sure you put him up to it." His voice was eerie, sending chills up my spine. With my mouth wide open, I turned and faced him.

How the hell did he know about Lex?

"If you go anywhere near him, I swear to God you gon' regret it."

He laughed sinisterly. "Bitch, it's already in the works."

I walked out without another word. There was no way I would allow Brisham to hurt Lex.

Natalya

A few days later…

"Did you get a chance to think on what we talked about?"

"I thought about it… Honestly, I don't think that's a good idea."

I was at Ms. Jennifer house getting Kacen. My day at work had been long, my period had started, and on top of that I hadn't been able to get in touch with Marcellus. He was supposed to pick Kacen up from daycare but didn't show up. I called Ms. Jenny and asked her to do it. Needless to say, I was in a bad ass mood and now I just wanted to go home.

"Talya, you gotta tell him. He really thinks that Kacen is for Marcellus'."

"Well if he was out then he would know he was his son," I stated with an attitude.

"What's going on with you? You were never this combative with me." Ms. Jennifer looked disappointed.

"I'm sorry ma. It's just that I feel so lost. My relationship with Marcellus is hanging on by a thread, and sometimes I just feel like I'mma lose my damn mind. Saadiq ruined everything."

“Ah baby. Come here,” she said, pulling me into her arms. I laid my head on her shoulders as I broke down crying. Everything I’d been going through over the past few weeks was starting to take a toll on me.

“Calm down. Everything is going to be okay.” Ms. Jennifer rubbed my back soothingly.

“It just hurts so bad.” I couldn’t stop crying no matter how much I tried.

“I know honey. You gotta calm down ‘cause I want you to listen to me.” I lifted my head as the tears continued to pour out of my eyes.

“What?” I sniffled as I looked into her eyes.

“I’m going to tell you something and it may offend you. However, I feel as if it needs to be said.”

“Go ahead,” I mumbled.

“I know Saadiq is my son, but chile you give him way too much credit. You gotta stop depending on him for your happiness. I understand you love him with all your heart. At the same time, he ain’t God. He can’t rescue you from everything, and there will be times when he will fail you. You can’t let that get you down. Someway you gotta pull yourself together and stand strong for you and that baby.

“Speaking of the baby, I’mma keep it real with you about that too. Not telling Saadiq about his son is messed up. It was one thing when we had no way of contacting him. Now we have the opportunity again, and I feel you should tell him. I don't like keeping such a heavy secret, but I would rather you tell him since y'all made Kacen. Do you get where I'm coming from?" she asked, and I nodded.

"Now what's going on with you and Marcellus? Why didn't he pick Kacen up today?"

"We had an argument, and I guess he's still mad about it."

Ms. Jennifer sighed. "I don't like that. If Marcellus promised you he would do something, then he needs to fulfil that obligation. No matter how angry he is, he can't take it out on that boy."

"I'mma handle it," I mumbled.

"I know you will. When it comes to my grandson, I know you don't play."

Ms. Jennifer hugged me again right before I gathered up Kacen and headed home. While I was in the car, I tried calling Marcellus again but he didn't answer. I finally gave up and decided I would deal with him once he got to the house. My thoughts were on Saadiq. I'd finally made up my mind. No matter how mad I was with him, he did deserve to know about his son.

Adore'

"Baby girl, what are you in here doing?" my father asked when he barged into my room.

"Ahh!" I screamed.

"Oh I'm sorry. I didn't know you were getting dressed." He quickly covered his eyes as I ran into my closet.

"Damn, don't you knock?" I yelled to him.

"I told you that I'm sorry." I heard my father say.

I can't get any fuckin' privacy around here. It's time for me to move out. While in the closet I slipped into a pair of stonewashed skinny jeans, a silk cold shoulder blouse, and a pair of brown Jimmy Choo sling back heels. Stepping out of my huge walk in closet, I ambled over to my bed and plopped down.

"What you want daddy?" I asked.

"Was that a wedding dress I saw you trying on?"

"Yeah, what about it?"

My father scratched his head. "Did I miss something?"

"Well if you must know, Saadiq and I are gonna get married." I cracked a small grin.

For a while my dad didn't say anything as he looked at me strangely. "Really? He proposed to you?" he finally asked.

"Not yet, but I know he's going to do it soon." I cheesed.

"Baby girl, don't you think you're jumping the gun here? What do you even know about him besides he's a fighter?"

"I know a lot. We talk all the time, and he shares things with me."

"Has he told you he loves you?"

"Not in so many words, but I know he does," I gritted. He was pissing me off.

"If a man really loves you, he doesn't have a problem expressing that. You can't make assumptions."

"Let me get this straight… Basically, what you're saying is that I'm delusional?" I tilted my head and glared at my father.

"C'mon sweetie. You know that's not what I'm saying."

"So what are you saying?"

My dad walked around to where I was and sat beside me. Pulling my hands into his, he forced me to look at him.

"We've been here before, and it didn't turn out good. You remember the last situation, right?"

"Why are you bringing that up?" I snarled.

"Because I have a feeling this is the same thing, just a different guy."

"Nah, it's not the same."

"Listen, I genuinely like Saadiq. There is a lot of myself I see in him, but I have to be honest."

"Be honest about what?" I questioned.

"I don't think the situation with him, and that girl is over," my daddy said.

"Why would you say that?" I snatched my hands away from him and stood up.

"Because I saw the same look in his eyes that I used to have for…never mind. All I'm saying is that I just don't want to see you get caught up in the crossfire. You're my daughter and I'm going to always have your back."

I started to laugh hysterically as my father stared at me. "So now what you're saying is that he's using me? Wow! Tell me how you really feel daddy."

"Adore', what are you talking about now?" he said, becoming frustrated.

"Why are you always doing this to me? Is it not enough you ran mommy away? Now you want to push every guy I date out of the picture." Before I knew it, I had started shouting at the top of my lungs.

My dad pinched the bridge of his nose. "You know I did not run your mother away. She—"

My phone rang so I stomped off to get it. When I saw who was calling, I glanced back at my father. "Don't even worry about trying to explain. I know the truth. Can you leave so I can take this call? And please stay out of my life. I got everything under control."

"Baby, I wish—"

"Now daddy!" I demanded while pointing my finger at the door.

He stood up, glanced at me one last time, and turned to leave my room. A long tear slid down my face, but I wiped it off.

He doesn't know what the hell he is talking about.

My phone rang again. "Yeah?" I barked.

"We need to talk right now," the person said.

"I'll meet you at our usual spot in an hour. Don't have me waiting either." I hung up.

Natalya

The next day…

It had been a whole day and I still hadn't talked to Marcellus. He never did come home the night before. I waited up on him for most of the night until I finally just got tired and went to sleep. When I woke up this morning, I was pissed to see he still hadn't brought his ass in.

I called his momma to see if she'd heard from him. When she told me she talked to him right before I called, I started to see red. However, I kept my temper in check with her. I got up and dropped Kacen off to Kiana. She was gonna keep him while I went to check this nigga.

"Where is Marcellus?" I asked the tall, skinny young dude who worked for him when I got into the building.

"Let me go see if he's busy," he told me, and I frowned.

"I don't give a fuck if he is busy or not," I gritted. All of Marcellus' lil workers knew exactly who I was, so I didn't know why he was trying to play me.

"Look shawty, I'm just doing my job. The boss man told me not to let anybody in," he stated.

"First of all, I ain't your shawty. Second, I don't give a damn what he said. Those rules don't apply to me. Now move out of my damn way," I snarled.

The dude threw up his hands as he stepped out of the way. I pushed the door opened and barged inside.

"What the fuck?" Marcellus said, glancing over at me.

I looked around the room and one person's face caught me off guard. "Brisham, what you doing here?" I asked. I didn't even know him and Marcellus knew each other like that.

Brisham glanced at Marcellus. "Just talking business. How you doing Talya?"

"Not too good," I spat with my eyes shifting to the female in the room. It was this thick girl with a pretty face and a head full of weave sitting in a chair not too far from them. I took note of the smirk on her face as she eyed me up and down. *What the fuck is she smirking about*?

"Talya what you doing hur'?" Marcellus questioned.

I glowered at him. "We need to talk right now."

He sighed. "I'm handling business right now."

"I don't give a fuck about that. We need to talk right now."

Brisham chuckled. "It's cool, handle your business. I got everything I need," he told Marcellus.

"Aight, let me know how that goes," Marcellus told him.

Brisham dapped him up and headed in my direction. On his way out, I noticed the bruises on his face. "See you later Talya," he said. I kept my eyes on him until he disappeared out the door. I was wondering where the bruises came from. Knowing Brisham, there was no telling what he'd gotten himself into. I put my focus on the female wondering why she wasn't leaving too. The bitch was staring dead in my face.

"You might want to hurry up before he leaves you," I said, and she giggled.

"Un-un sweetie, I'm not with him," she muttered. I glanced at Marcellus before looking back at her.

"So why are you hur'?" I asked, placing my hands on my hips.

"Quandra, go ahead and burn. I'll holler at you later," he said, and she stood up.

My eyes roamed her curvaceous body as she sashayed past me and out the door.

"Who the fuck was that bitch?" I yelled.

"That's Quandra. She works for me now," he stated nonchalantly. He had me so fucked up. I wasn't for sure, but I swear it was something with him and that girl. The look on her face told it all.

"Why didn't you come home last night? Was you with that bitch?" I barked. He shook his head.

"Shit, it ain't like you would have paid a nigga any attention. The only person you worry about is Kacen."

"Oh, so that's what this is about? You don't feel that I pay you attention?"

"Act like you don't know mane." He smirked.

"If you felt like that, then all you had to do was tell me. Hell, I'm not a mind reader."

"I been telling you this shit time and time again, but you don't listen to me," he yelled, and I jumped. I had never seen him this angry.

"Well staying gone all night is not gonna solve our problems. How you think that makes me feel, especially when I come hur' and see som' random bitch?" Marcellus looked me in the eyes.

"If you really want me to be honest, I didn't give a damn how it made you feel. I go out of my fuckin' way to keep a smile on yo face, but all you do is give me your ass to kiss. It's a damn shame It takes me ignoring your ass to get your attention. Now you wanna come down hur' questioning me about a bitch I'm working with."

"That's very childish. It's one thing to leave me on stuck but to do it to my son is just fucked up."

"Fuck outta hur' with that. You know I will never take anything out on him. He just as much my son as he is yours. I lost track of time. Once I realized it, I called the daycare and they said he'd already been picked up."

"I guess it would have been too much to call and let me know? You know what? Don't even worry about it. I'm not tripping. You just keep doing you, and I'mma damn sure do me." When I tried to walk off, Marcellus roughly yanked me back.

"What the fuck is that supposed to mean?" he gritted. He was so close that his nose was almost touching mine. "You trying to go fuck with another nigga, huh?"

"Let go. You're hurting me."

"Answer my fuckin' question!" he yelled as he pulled me closer to him.

"You think I'mma sit back and let you continue to disrespect me?" I spat.

"Look hur', shawty. I don' let you slide with a lot of shit, but you got me fucked up if you think I'll let you fuck off with somebody else. I will kill you and that nigga," he spat. His words sent chills up my spine.

"Marcellus, you talking crazy right now." My eyes tried to search his face for some sign that he was just joking, but I didn't see none.

"Nah, I'm talking serious. Play with me if you want to and you gon' see a different side. You feel me?" he said, and I nodded.

He finally let me go, and I ran out of the building. *That nigga is batshit crazy for real.*

Kiana

"What's the matter baby? Why are you looking like that?" I asked Lex when I opened the door. He barged past me into the apartment. After locking the door, I faced him with confusion on my face.

"Somebody broke in my shop and destroyed it!" he barked.

"What happened?" I questioned.

"One of my artists called earlier and told me when he pulled up the window was busted out. When I got there, I saw that my shop was ransacked. All of my equipment was damaged, the pictures on the wall were all broken up and shit, and they stole my register."

"Did you have any money in it?"

"A lil over a thousand dollars. Usually we don't leave money overnight, but since my receptionist went home early, I told her I would deposit it today."

Oh shit. My eyes bucked.

"I don't understand this shit. I been in the same building for over twelve years. Everybody in the area knows me, so why the fuck would somebody violate like this?" Lex ranted. He paced back and forth with his hands on his head.

I swallowed hard as I looked up at him. "I'm sooo sorry baby," I mumbled. *Go ahead and tell him, Kiana.* When I tried to force the words out of my mouth, they wouldn't come out. What if I told Lex and he accused me of setting him up? Then again if I didn't tell him and he found out, he could still think it was a setup. At this point I didn't know what to do.

"It's gonna be okay baby." I pulled him into my arms and hugged him.

"I know it is. Really, I ain't tripping about the physical damage. Insurance will handle that part. I just hate my artist gotta suffer behind this. You know what I mean? I can tattoo out of my place, but they won't have nowhere to go. I know my clients, but I don't want just any muthafucka at my place. From what I hear the shop probably won't be open for about two months."

"Whatever I need to do to help, I will," I told him. My heart felt so heavy because I knew it was partly my fault. I should have just told him a week ago when Brisham first made the threat.

"'Preciate that shawty." He placed a kiss on my lips.

"I'll always have your back," I told him.

Another knock at the door interrupted our kiss.

"You expecting somebody?" Lex questioned.

"That's my best friend Talya. Her son is in the room."

"Damn, my bad. I just busted in hur' without even seeing what you had up."

"It's okay. You know I don't mind. Just give me a minute." I gave him a small smile as I went to the door.

"Wassup girl?" Talya said as soon as she stepped in. Judging by the frown on her face, I could see that things didn't go well with her and Marcellus.

"Hey," I said, and turned to Lex. "Talya, this is Lex. Lex, this is my girl Talya."

Talya's face instantly lit up. "Well, well, well. I finally get to meet the man who's been holding my friend hostage. How are you?" she asked him.

"I'm aight. How you doing?" Lex smiled, showing off his pearly white teeth.

"I'm okay." Talya turned to me. "Bitch, he is fine," she whispered.

"I know, right?" I giggled.

"Where is my baby?" she asked.

"He's in the back with Raegan."

"Well y'all don't mind me. I'mma grab him and get out of your hair."

Talya started to walk off, but I stopped her. “How that situation go?” She glanced at Lex before looking back at me.

“We’ll talk later,” she whispered.

“You sure?”

“Mhm,” she mumbled.

“Aight, cool.”

Once Talya got Kacen they were out of the apartment a few minutes later. I told Lex to follow me into my room so we could chill. We spent the remainder of the night talking. I tried so many times to tell him about Brisham but never found the courage. I finally decided to holler at Brisham and see if he was behind it before I brought it up to Lex.

Marcellus

One week later…

A nigga had started to feel kind of bad about the way I'd been treating Talya. In the last week I still hadn't been home. She called a few times but I didn't answer. I guess you can say I was still in my feelings. To occupy my time, I spent most nights at Quandra's crib. Being with her was cool, but I was missing my shawty. To make up for the way I'd been acting, I hit up one of my boys who owned a dealership.

Talya had been saying for the past few months she wanted a Jeep. I went out and copped her a 2019 baby blue Jeep Wrangler Sahara. This bitch was loaded with everything from power steering, heated leather seats, navigational satellite radio, and a remote starter. I was on my way home to wait for her to get off work so she could see it.

Pulling up to the light, I was just getting ready to turn onto Lindell when I thought I spotted Talya going in the opposite direction. I squinted my eyes to be sure it was her. The Audi was the same color as hers, and the rims were the same ones I purchased when I got the car.

“Hell yeah that’s her ass,” I said aloud as I busted a U-turn in the middle of the street. Snatching my phone off the console, I hit Talya’s line. The phone rang several times before it went to voicemail.

Why the fuck her ass ain’t at work, and why she ain’t picking up her phone? Hanging up, I dialed her number again. Since I was about five cars behind her, it was hard for me to keep up. I tried to get in front of this big Dully truck, but the driver was on some fuck shit. Every time I sped up, his ass did the same. We did that for about three blocks until I lost my patience.

“Nigga, move the fuck out the way!” I yelled while hitting my horn. He looked at me and smirked. “Move nigga!” I hit the horn again.

He finally slowed down and allowed me to get over. By now Talya was a good distant ahead of me. I zipped in and out of traffic until only two cars were ahead of me. When I was almost near her, I noticed the area we were headed to was over by the county jail.

Why the fuck she over hur’?

It didn’t take long for a nigga to figure out what was going on. Ten minutes later she pulled up to the St. Louis Corrections Division and parked her car in the visitor’s lot. I stopped my car on the side of the road. When I saw her walk through the lot, I dialed her number again. With anger in my eyes, I watched as she looked at the phone and hit ignore. She then put the phone in her pocket and jogged across the street. For the longest I sat there blowing steam. It was obvious as hell she was going to visit that nigga.

How long this shit been going on?

This was probably the reason she started acting funny. It took everything in me not to hop out of my car, march into that building, and drag her ass back out. I decided to keep it cool for the time being. Like my momma always told me, 'you give a person enough rope and they will hang themselves.' That's exactly what I intended to let Talya do since she thought she was so slick.

Natalya

Fifteen minutes later…

My hands were literally trembling as I watched him walk over to the table. I couldn't believe after all this time he still looked the same. Matter fact, he looked even better than he did before he came in here. You could tell he'd been hitting the weights hard from how his orange shirt clung to his arms and chest

"Hey wassup?" Saadiq said as he sat in the chair across from me. Blankly, I stared at him as if it were my first time seeing him. "You don't have nothing to say?" he questioned.

"I um…" my words became lodged in my throat.

"What?" he asked.

"I guess I'm just happy to see you," I finally admitted.

For a while Saadiq didn't say anything, he just sat glaring at me. "How you been doing?" He finally asked.

"You want me to be honest?" I asked.

He nodded his head. "I could be a lot better."

"What's the problem? From what I hear, you out thur' living yo' best life. Oh yeah, congratulations on your relationship and the new baby." He smirked.

“Saadiq, it’s not what you think,” I said, gazing into his eyes. I already knew he thought Kacen was Marcellus’ son. I don’t know where he got that from, but of course it wasn’t true.

“It’s all good. I told you to move on, so I ain’t trippin’.” He shrugged his shoulders.

“Yeah, you did.” I sighed, and he slightly chuckled while glancing around the room. When his eyes landed back on me, he just looked at me with a blank expression.

“How have you been holding up?” I asked.

“I been straight. Ain’t had no major problems.” He ran his hand down his face. Gazing into his pretty eyes, I found myself getting caught up just like I used to.

The silence between us was starting to kill me, so I decided to speak. “I don’t know how you found out about Kacen, but I think I should explain,” I began. Saadiq shook his head to stop me.

“Nah, you‘on need to explain nothing. You moved on and started a new life. End of story.”

“That’s not it.” I sighed.

“Shit, what else is there? I finally realized what we shared wasn’t as strong as I thought it was. Maybe we both were just trying to force som’ shit that wasn’t meant to be.” I frowned.

“Nothing about our relationship was forced. At least it wasn’t on my part.”

“I doubt that shit. You saying one thing but your actions say something different.”

I tilted my head back. “Excuse you? How the fuck you gonna say some shit like that?”

“Am I lying? The same nigga you fucked with before we got together is the same muthafucka you now got a baby for.”

“First of all, I had no intentions on being with Marcellus. It just happened. But did you forget I damn near begged you to ride this bid out with you? What did you tell me? ‘Go on with your life Talya,” I spat.

Saadiq’s eyes lingered on me before he finally looked off. “I see you still got that attitude,” he mumbled.

“You already know.”

We gazed at one another and then out of nowhere we both started laughing. “This shit is crazy. You know that’s supposed to be my baby mane.” I saw his eyes mist, but he fought not to let the tears fall. My heart became heavy at that moment. I knew I had to reveal the truth.

“What if I told you he is your son?” I said, eyeing him.

“Why would you do that?” he uttered.

“Because it’s the truth.”

Saadiq frowned. “Don’t play with me Talya. I already know he ain’t my seed. You ain’t gotta try to make me feel better. I accept shit for what it is.”

“I’m not playing. Kacen is your son. See, I have a picture,” I told him while removing a small 4x6 picture out of my pocket. It was a photo I had done when Kacen was five months old. He looked identical to Saadiq on the picture. Saadiq glanced down at the photo once I slid it to him. Nervously, I sat back and watched as his face changed about six different times. He had all type of emotions going through him.

“He looks just like my damn baby pictures!” he practically yelled.

“Shhh.” I shushed him while glancing around.

“Fuck that! Why y’all keep this a secret?” he asked, and I pursed my lips together.

“When were we supposed to tell you Saadiq? You shut me out right before I found out I was pregnant.”

“My momma knew he was my son, didn’t she?”

“Yes, but I told her not to say anything because I wanted to tell you.”

Saadiq sat back in his chair and just gazed at the picture. Suddenly, his face flashed a smile. “How old is he?”

"He's seventeen months."

"Damn. Is he walking yet?"

"Yes, he just started walking not too long ago. And his bad ass is getting into some of everything." Saadiq laughed, but he didn't say anything else. He stared at that picture so long I think he forgot I was sitting with him. When he finally glanced up, he had the saddest look on his face.

"I apologize Talya," he whispered.

"For what?" I lifted a brow.

"Not being there for y'all. I feel like I don' already missed a big part of his life."

"Saadiq—" I tried to stop him, but he cut me off.

"Let me finish. I know you think I was selfish, but I seriously did that shit for your own good. I knew I fucked up, and I just wanted you to be happy. I hope you can forgive me." He pleaded with his eyes.

Tears fell from my eyes. After all this time, a huge weight had been lifted from my shoulder. I needed to hear him explain why he shut me out to stop feeling resentment for him.

"I do forgive you," I said, and he nodded.

For the remainder of the visit, Saadiq asked me a dozen questions about our son. I happily answered each one of them. To see the smile on his face made my heart swell.

Once the visitation came to an end, he asked if I could come back with Kacen and I told him I would. By the time I left the jail, I felt much better than I'd been feeling in the past few months. I was actually looking forward to our next visit. Now I just needed to find out why Marcellus had been blowing up my damn phone.

Brisham

"Domino!" I yelled.

"Damn, how you win again?" Valencia asked. Valencia was a cute lil chick with a dark complexion, pretty face, and a slim body. Shawty was a little different from the females I was used to dealing with. She barely had ass and didn't have no titties. On top of that, she was sort of on the shy side. We met at the daycare about a month ago. I was picking up Skylar, and she was picking up her niece. I thought she was cute, so I asked for her number. We talked a few times on the phone, and I asked her to come over. She wanted to hang out and shit, but a nigga really just wanted to fuck.

My doorbell rang so I got up to get it.

"I'mma be right back," I told Valencia.

"Okay," she said.

Before I got to the door, I stopped by the couch and grabbed my pistol from behind the pillow. I wasn't expecting no company. Tipping over to the door, I checked the peephole. When I saw who it was, I cracked a grin. *I knew it wouldn't be long before her ass came over here.*

"You muthafucka!" Kiana barked while charging at me. "Why would you do that?" Her little fist started flying everywhere as she cursed me out.

"Aye chill out," I chuckled.

"You think this shit is funny? Why would you do that to him?"

"I already told you what was gonna happen. You got that nigga around my daughter." I grabbed Kiana's arms and held them over her head.

"Let go of me!" she bellowed.

"Well calm yo ass down."

"Fuck you Brisham! I hate you!" She screamed.

"I told you I wasn't fuckin' with you no more."

She snatched her arms away from me. "I hate I ever fucked with your bitch ass," she went off.

"Shit, the feelings are mutual," I muttered.

"I'm not gonna let you get away with this shit," she spat.

"So you threatening me again?" Fire shot from my eyes as I glared at her. Didn't she learn the first time not to be threatening a nigga?

"Nope, this time it's not a threat it's a promise. You wanted grimy, well nigga I'mma show you the grimy bitch I can be."

I stood there for a minute then I grabbed hold of Kiana's neck. Taking my gun, I put it to her temple. "Bitch, what the fuck you plan on doing?" I growled.

"Brisham, get this damn gun away from me," she gritted.

"Keep playing with me Kiana, and you gon' find out how real shit can get for you. That lil situation with your nigga was just the beginning. You see what happened to that nigga Jacobi. I suggest you get your fuckin' mind right if you don't wanna end up like him."

Tears welled in her eyes as her body trembled. "I hate you!" she cried.

"Brisham?" I suddenly heard Valencia say behind me. I glanced over my shoulder and noticed her standing there with a confused look on her face.

"Go back in the room shawty," I told her.

"What are you doing?" she asked.

"Help me," Kiana whispered. Valencia eyes darted to Kiana and the gun in my hand.

"Brisham, do you hear me? What are you doing to that girl?" her nosey ass pressed.

"Just go back in the fuckin' room!" I boomed.

Valencia took off running back to my room. I looked back down at Kiana. "This is how this shit is gonna go down. I want you to stay away from that nigga. If you don't, be prepared to deal with his blood on yo' hands. You understand what I'm saying?" She quickly nodded her head.

I gave her a sly grin. "Aight. Now go get my daughter and y'all go home."

"I have to go to work." Her lips trembled.

"Well go to work and when you get off, I want you at home with my daughter. I'mma check up on you later."

"Okay," she mumbled.

I finally let her go and she ran out. I chuckled as I closed the door. *I don't know why everybody wanted to test me.* Now I had to go make sure everything was cool with Valencia. Stepping back into the room, I noticed her putting on her shoes. "Where you going?" I asked.

"I'm going home. Your ass is crazy," she spat.

"I thought we were gonna play another game?" I cracked a grin.

Valencia gazed up at me as she grabbed her purse. "Yeah, you're really fuckin' crazy." She shook her head and tried to stomp out of the room. I grabbed her arm, pulling her back to me.

"So you just gonna leave?"

"Brisham, get your damn hands off me. I'm leaving. Lose my number." She pulled her arm back.

"C'mon shawty," I said, but she kept going.

"Fuck that bitch. She didn't want to give me no ass anyway," I mumbled as I fell onto my bed. Snatching a blunt from the ashtray, I sparked it up just as I heard my front door open and close.

Natalya

A few days later…

"So it ain't nothing you can do?" I asked.

"Not without any real proof. You sure there is no one that you've had a problem with?" the young white female officer asked me.

"Nope. There is no one that I can think of," I sighed.

"Well, if you ever think of anyone be sure to come back and see us." She gave me a weak ass attempt at a smile.

"Thanks," I mumbled as I walked away from the desk. I'd come to the police department to file a report. Last week I could've sworn I saw somebody following me in that same black car. Then, when I came out of Kacen's daycare two nights ago, I noticed my tire was flat. Marcellus claimed it didn't look like it was tampered with, but I didn't know what the hell to think. I felt all this was getting out of hand.

"Talya?" I heard someone say behind me.

I turned around and spotted Saadiq's uncle Cordea. It had been a minute since I last saw him. He used to stop by to check on me, but his visits stopped shortly after Saadiq was sentenced.

"Hey," I said.

"What are you doing here?" he questioned.

"I just needed to handle something." I didn't feel like going through all the details. It wasn't as if he could help me.

Cordea looked at me strangely for a minute. "Is there anything I can help you with?" he asked.

"Nope. I got it all figured out."

"I see. Well how you been holding up?" he asked.

"I've been okay." Once again, he looked at me with this strange expression I couldn't read.

"Have you spoken to my nephew?"

"No, I haven't," I lied. I don't know why but for some reason I was starting to feel uncomfortable. Before now I hadn't realized it, but he was weird to me.

"Oh that's right, you have a new boyfriend," he said with a sly grin. See what the hell I'm talking about? *How the fuck does he know that*?

"Well it was nice seeing you. I'm going to get out of here," I announced.

"Alright, I'll see you later." He smiled.

I walked off and headed for the door. "Talya?" Cordea called out to me.

"Yes?" I asked as I faced him.

"Take care of yourself and that little boy." He winked his eye at me.

"Thanks," I mumbled. Call it intuition or whatever, but something was up with that man. I didn't get a good vibe from him at all.

Saadiq

Three days later…

"There go da da," Talya told Kacen.

For a minute lil man looked at me then he reached his hands out like he honestly knew who I was. It took everything in me not to break down.

"C'mere man," I said, taking him from her.

"Is it okay for you to hold him?" she asked, looking around.

"Yeah, it's cool. The guards don't give me no issues."

I put my focus on my son and just stared at him. Everything about him was all me. He had my nose, lips, eyes, curly hair; hell, he even had my fingers. It didn't seem Talya played no part in making him except carrying him. The shit was crazy. All this time I had a son and didn't even know it. A huge part of me felt bad for even thinking Talya would do me that way.

"Hey, are you okay?" Talya asked, breaking my thoughts.

"A nigga just thinking. I'm up for parole in a few months, I can't wait. I feel it's too long to be without him."

"Are you really? I can't believe it's been that long."

"Yeah, too damn long," I mumbled.

"Can I ask you a question?"

"Wassup?"

"Do you ever talk to Brisham? I was wondering because I never hear you mention his name," she said, and I gritted my teeth.

"Nah, I haven't talked to him."

"But why? Y'all were so close," she said.

"I mean, I'm in hur' and he out thur'. We don't see each other."

"I just knew he would've come to visit," she said.

"Nah." I shook my head while looking off.

"That's crazy. So you don't know about him and Kiana breaking up?"

"Nope." I was trying to keep my responses short so she wouldn't keep asking questions.

"They broke up a little after you…" She glanced at me and paused. It was like she'd just realized she was about to bring up the situation. "So anyway, Kacen is big, huh?" She changed the subject. I was thankful for that.

"He gon' be a big boy just like his daddy." I winked, and she blushed.

"But he gon' be cute like his momma," she shot back.

"Gon' on with that cute shit, shawty. You can say handsome."

"What's wrong with being cute?"

"Cute is for females," I spat. Talya giggled.

I leaned back in my seat and looked at her for a minute. She was looking good. Her hair looked freshly done, her makeup was on point, and the red two-piece jogging outfit she sported gave her this laid back but sexy look. "What your man gotta say about you coming to visit me?" I decided to fuck with her.

"Huh?" she asked as if she didn't hear me. I smirked.

"Do he know about you coming to visit or about our phone calls?"

"Um, he knows Kacen is your son," she stammered.

"But do he know about us talking?"

"I haven't had the chance to tell him yet."

"Why not?"

"I'on know." She shrugged. I chuckled while shaking my head. "What Saadiq?"

"It ain't nothing. You look good by the way," I told her, changing the subject.

She looked down at herself. "I just threw this together but thanks." She smiled.

"You wild shawty." My eyes roamed her body before they stopped at her big titties. I remembered the last time I sucked on them things. Just thinking about Talya in that way was making my dick hard. *I bet her pussy still felt the same way it did when I was last in it.* Suddenly Kacen pulled on my chin hair.

"Wassup lil man? You want some attention?" I asked.

My son smiled, and that shit melted my heart. Even with me in this hellhole I never felt more content than I did at the moment. I think it was every man's dream to have a son he could teach to be better than he ever was. For Talya to give me this gift made me love her ass that much more.

"Thank you!" I looked up and told her.

"For what?"

"For giving me the best gift ever…my son," I said, and she smiled. "What made you decide to go through with having him once I was sentenced?"

"Because I felt having him would give me a way to be close to you again," she explained.

"I can dig it," I nodded with a big smile.

For the rest of the visit we spent time talking while I played with my son. Our conversation felt just like it did before all this bullshit happened. It was just like old times.

The only thing I didn't do was tell Talya about Adore'. I didn't really know how to break that news to her.

Kiana

It had been a few days since Brisham's bitch ass pulled that gun on me. I swear if it wasn't for Raegan I would have his ass killed. That was a straight up fuck boy move. Normally I wouldn't wish bad on anybody, but I was praying for the day he got his. He'd ruined Saadiq's life, my life, Talya's, and even our kids. Not only that, but I had to end my relationship with Lex because I didn't want Brisham to do anything else to him.

Lex had been calling me, but I hadn't found the courage to tell him it was over. Instead, I just put his number on block so I wouldn't be able to see when he called. Since I was under so much stress, I'd reverted to popping Mollys again. I know it wasn't the best solution, but it's the only way to keep my sanity.

"Hey Kiana. You have a visitor," one of my coworker's named Heather said to me.

"Is it a patient?" I questioned.

"No, it's a police officer. What did you do?" she joked.

"Not shit," I said. I tried to play it off, but a bitch was nervous. Why would a policeman be here to see me? Heather giggled.

"I'll let him know you're coming," she told me as she left.

After discarding of my trash, I left the breakroom and headed for the front. As soon as I got in the lobby, I spotted the last person I expected to see here.

"What are you doing here?" I asked Brisham's daddy.

His shifty eyes roamed my body before he plastered on this fake ass smile. "Can I talk to you outside?"

"About what?" I questioned nastily.

"I'll explain everything once we get outside."

"Aight c'mon," I sighed as I followed him. "What you want?"

"First, how is my granddaughter?" He asked.

"She's fine," I spat.

"Glad to hear that. The reason I'm here is because I want to know have you said anything." Suddenly his smile dropped and his face got serious.

"You know I haven't said anything." I rolled my eyes.

"You're lying. I saw your friend Talya down at the precinct the other day."

"Okay and?" I snaked my neck.

"Why would was she there if you haven't opened your mouth?"

"The hell if I know. She was probably applying for a job," I lied.

He looked at me suspiciously. "You sure about that?"

"If I said something, you wouldn't be standing here right now." I pursed my lips together while glaring at him.

He laughed. "Yeah, I guess you're right. Besides, I don't think you would do anything that would put you and that baby in harm," he said, and I frowned.

"Muthafucka, are you threatening us?" I cocked my head to the side.

"Why would I threaten my granddaughter and her mother?" He tried to play dumb as if I didn't know how to read between the lines.

"Because obviously you and your son are just alike. I'm so sick of y'all and this bullshit. Why the fuck can't y'all just leave me alone?" Before I knew it, I had lost it.

"Whoa calm down." Mr. Kamen tried to grab my arm, but I snatched it away.

"Don't put your hands on me," I gritted, no longer giving a damn he was an officer. His ass was crooked anyway.

"Alright, I won't touch you. Tell me what my son did to you," he said.

"Every damn thing. All I want is for y'all to do is stay away from me. I did what y'all wanted. Why is that not enough?"

"I'll talk with him," he claimed.

"Yeah, whatever."

"I'm being honest," he uttered with that cheesy grin.

"Look, is that all that you wanted to discuss? I really need to go back inside. My break is up." I was done with this conversation.

"Yes, that's it. Just to give you a warning before you go, if you do say anything, you'll be considered an accomplice." I shook my head before stomping back to the building. "I'mma make sure to have a talk with my son," he called to me as I went through the door.

I didn't even bother replying. I just kept walking as if I didn't hear his ass. After dealing with that bullshit, I needed a molly bad as fuck.

***

A few hours later…

"Lex, what are you doing hur'?" I asked as I glanced behind him to be sure no one was out. *Damn, is it pop up on Kiana day?*

He looked at me strangely. "What you mean what I'm doing hur'? And what's going on with your phone?" He pushed his way past me and walked inside of my apartment. When I turned to face him, he was looking around like he was trying to see if somebody else was here.

"What's up?" I asked.

He squinted his eyes at me. "Why haven't I heard from you in over a week?"

"I just been doing my thing."

"What's that supposed to mean?" He frowned.

"It means exactly what I said."

"Yo Kiana, you need to chill with that attitude. I just asked you a simple question."

"You shouldn't be here."

"Why not?" He asked.

My voice shook. "Because my boyfriend may have seen you."

"What the fuck you mean your boyfriend?" He snarled.

"You told me to keep it real with you, so that's what I'mma do. Me and my baby daddy got back together. That's why you haven't heard from me. I didn't know how to tell you, so I just stayed away," I lied. It was the only way for me to handle this situation.

Lex slowly nodded his head. "So that's the shit you on?" he asked incredulously.

"You always tell me to keep it real." I shrugged.

He shook his head. "I thought we were building something," he said.

"I thought so too, but I realized I still have feelings for Brisham. I'm sorry."

"Mane, that's bullshit. Even if you didn't wanna be with me, why go back to him? I'm not trying to hate on dude, but he ain't right for you. Ever since you been with me you have changed for the best. You ain't that same girl you were when you were with him. I mean c'mon, Kiana. That nigga had you out there selling ass and stealing from your family just so his bitch ass could come up? Is that somebody you wanna be with?"

A few tears threatened to fall but I held them in. He was right about everything he was saying. I had sold pussy while I was with Brisham. He told me it would only be a onetime thing, but I ended up doing it more times than I would have liked to. I did it all because I thought I was holding my man down.

When Lex and I first started dating I kept it real with him because I didn't want it to come back and bite me in the ass. I thought he would leave me, but he stuck right by my side and never brought it up again until now. This was so hard for me because I liked Lex. Hell, I may even have loved him. At the same time, I didn't want to see him get hurt or take anymore losses behind me.

"Because he knows me, and he accepts me for who I really am."

"And who are you?" he questioned. I swallowed hard.

"A very broken person that you're better off without." I choked back.

Without uttering another word, Lex trudged past me and left my apartment. After closing the door, I quickly went to my bedroom. I tried to call auntie to see if I could talk to her, but just like all my other calls it went unanswered. Therefore, I went to my next best solution. I grabbed my purse, pulled out my Mollys, and popped two of them. If nothing or no one else could help me get through this, I knew that they would.

Brisham

"I got everything under control," I said.

"You got everything under control, huh? Well, why does your baby mother look like she's on the verge of a nervous breakdown?"

"That ain't got shit to do with me." I smirked.

"No, this is all on you. Why must you insist on fuckin' everything up? I had it to where she could trust us, but now I'm not so sure she won't go blabbing about what she knows. What are you doing to her?"

"I ain't doing shit to her. She's just mad because I ran her little boyfriend off."

"Why are you bothering her period? If it's not affecting your daughter, then you shouldn't worry about what she's doing."

I wasn't in the mood to hear this nigga's bitching. I was high and I couldn't get Skylar's lil ass to stop fussing. I think he was missing his momma.

"Brisham, are you listening to me?" my Pops boomed.

"Not really. As long as she got my daughter, she ain't about to have nobody else around her."

"Look here nigga…you obviously don't give a fuck about your freedom. Well I do muthafucka, and I'll be damned if me and your mother go down for this bullshit you created. If you don't stop messing with that girl, I will have your ass locked up," he threatened.

"For what?" I barked.

"Drug charges. Don't think I'm not aware of your illegal activities because I am. I haven't shut it down because I don't want you running to me and your mother to save your sorry ass once again. The less you come around, the less your mother will worry."

"Dawg, you ain't gotta do me no favors," I snarled.

"Shut the fuck up before I knock your head off. You claim you have everything under control, but you don't have shit handled. Did you know there is a missing person's case filed for your other baby momma?"

"Why you didn't tell me that first?"

"Because you should know since you got everything under control." I ignored his smart ass remark.

"Who filed the report?"

"Her mother. She came in the other day. My team is gonna investigate."

I ran my hand down my face. That was the reason I couldn't get in contact with her. Now I kind of felt bad that I put her out.

"Keep me posted on that situation," I told my Pops.

"I hope you didn't have nothing to do with this. I'm not helping you with shit else."

I stood up, walked to the door, and opened it. My Pops already knew what time it was because he grabbed his shit and started to walk out. "Leave that girl alone Brisham. I mean it," he warned again on his way out. I slammed the door without replying. Rushing over to my phone, I picked it up and dialed Kylisha's number. I let it ring five times before hanging up. I needed to find out what the fuck was going on.

Marcellus

Two days later…

"Aye, bring Emani out. I'm pulling up now."

I was at Ariel house to pick up my daughter. It was the weekend, and I'd decided to get all my kids. Since me and Talya were on good terms again, I figured we could take them somewhere fun.

"Can you come in for a second?" Ariel asked.

"For what?" I questioned.

"Just come in. I need to talk to you for a minute."

"Here I come mane. I can't stay long 'cause I got the other kids."

"Okay, it won't take long," she promised.

I ended the call. "Y'all wanna come in or sit our here?" I asked my twelve-year-old son, Princeton and my nine-year-old daughter, Iyana. They were both so into their phones that neither one of them looked up.

"We'll stay in the car," Princeton answered. I shook my head.

"Y'all ain't gon' be on them damn phones all weekend. Go ahead and get your time in now 'cause as soon as we get home, I'm taking them."

"Ah man," my son uttered.

"Ah man my ass," I said as I stepped from the car and ambled to Ariel's door. She lived in a decent house that was located downtown. It was an older house, but it was big as hell. She'd got it on her own, but of course the money I kicked out helped her pay the bills. Ariel was a CNA, and she worked at this nursing home. As much as she begged, you would think her ass was unemployed.

After knocking two times, Ariel came to the door and let me in. "Where Emani?" I asked as soon as I stepped inside of her house. Ariel walked over, sat on the couch, and crossed her legs. She was rocking a little pair of shorts, a small tank top, and some sandals. I looked her over. Ariel was what you called slim thick with natural hair like Talya's, except hers was shorter. She had pretty brown skin with a cute face, and some high cheek bones. Although she was fine, her looks made her ugly at times.

"She getting the rest of the stuff put in her backpack."

"Aight, cool. What you wanted to talk about?"

"I'm late," she mumbled.

"Late for what?"

Ariel pursed her lips together. "Nigga don't play stupid. You know what I mean."

"Why you telling me?" I knew exactly what she was saying.

"Because you're the last person I had sex with," she claimed.

"C'mon that shit only happened twice, and I made sure to pull out both times."

"What does that mean? Maybe your pull out game was weak."

"I'on think you understanding me. I can't have no baby with you Ariel."

"Why, because of your little girlfriend? Nigga, you should've thought about that before you decided to creep."

Angrily, I ran my hand along my head. Ariel caught a nigga during one of them times that me and Talya was arguing big time. I should've used a condom, but I wasn't thinking. "How you even know you pregnant?"

"Besides being late, I been throwing up, my nipples are sore, and I can't stand the smell of certain foods. Those are all the signs I had with Emani."

"How long that's been going on?"

"About three weeks."

I hurled my phone at the wall. "Damn mane! This is bullshit. Your ass trying to trap me again."

"You got me fucked up. What I need to trap you for?" She threw her hands on her hips.

"Because that's the type of shit you do. You want a nigga to be with you so bad that you'll do anything to make sure I'm tied down to yo ass."

"Boy please. I ain't gotta trap you to get what I want. If I open my legs right now, you'll slide between 'em. You can't be faithful to nobody, and you don' proved it time and time again. Why would I put myself through that?" she snarled.

Just then Emani came running into the room. She looked at me and Ariel. "What's wrong mommy?" she asked.

"Nothing baby. Go back in your room while me and your daddy finish talking."

"Nah c'mon Emani. We 'bouta bounce."

"But we ain't don' talking." Ariel huffed as she folded her arms across her breasts.

"We done shawty. You said what you had to say."

"So what you gon' do?" she asked as I walked over and picked up my phone. It was now in several pieces.

Fuck! Now I gotta get a new cell.

"I'mma do what I been doing," I sputtered.

"Whatever Marcellus. This is just like the last time. You're getting mad at me about som' shit we both did," Ariel spat.

I ignored her as I grabbed Emani's hand and walked out the door. She followed behind me talking shit, but I kept walking. After helping Emani into the car, I hopped in the driver's seat and peeled off. I needed to go cop a new cell before I got to the crib. I also had to think of a way I could handle this situation without Talya finding out.

***

Two hours later…

After being at Verizon for the longest, I was finally walking into the crib. Almost instantly, the smell of something cooking hit my nostrils. It had my stomach growling.

"Daddy, what Talya cooking?" Iyana asked.

"I'on know. Probably some chicken or something like that."

"It smells good," my daughter said.

"Hell yeah. C'mon so y'all can go speak to her," I told them. Emani took off running.

"Talyaaaa!" Emani squealed when she saw Talya. Emani and Talya had a tight bond. If it wasn't for Ariel reminding everybody, people would think Talya was her momma.

"Hey baby! I missed you," Talya said and picked her up. Emani wrapped her little arms around Talya's neck and put a kiss on her cheek.

"I missed you too," she said. When Talya put her down she looked at Princeton and Iyana.

"Hey y'all!" she said to them. Iyana walked over and hugged Talya while Princeton just waved. "I guess you too big to give me a hug," she teased. He walked over and gave her a hug.

"Hey baby." Talya looked at me.

"Wassup shawty." I leaned in and gave her a kiss on the lips. "Where lil man?"

"He just went to sleep. Are y'all ready to eat?" she questioned.

"Yes!" all the children screamed simultaneously.

"Aight, y'all go wash your hands while I fix the plates," Talya instructed.

Twenty minutes later we were all sitting down eating dinner. The kids were talking amongst themselves while me and Talya sat listening.

"Pops, Iyana got a boyfriend," Princeton blurted out of nowhere.

"No I don't!" She screamed as her face flushed with embarrassment.

"You better not have no damn boyfriend. I will shoot his ass," I threatened.

"I don't have a boyfriend daddy. Princeton is lying," she spat.

"Yes you do. I see y'all walking together in the halls and every time he comes around you start cheesing." Princeton started making these weird faces and shit, mimicking his sister.

Iyana jumped out of her seat and popped him on the arm. "I don't have a boyfriend!" she yelled.

"Owww! What you hit me for?"

"Because you lying. Tell daddy about all those girls who be calling your phone."

Me and Talya glanced at each other and laughed. "Aye, y'all chill out with that," I told them.

"But he lying daddy," Iyana whined.

I turned to my son. "You got a lil girlfriend mane?" I asked.

"I got a few of 'em," Princeton stated cockily. I cracked a grin.

"Shit, that's what I'm talking about." I reached out my hand and gave him a fist bump.

"Marcellus!" Talya called out.

"What?" I grinned.

"I know you didn't tell this girl you would shoot any boy she brings around, but he can tell you he got a few girls and you congratulating him?"

"Mane, it's different with boys."

"How so?" she asked.

"Yeah how, daddy?" Iyana questioned. I glanced at both of them.

"So y'all just gon' gang up on a nigga like that?"

"Yup! Now answer the question."

"Because that's just how it works. I already explained to Iyana that boys her age only thinking about one thing."

"Okay, so what about those lil girls your son talking to? They're somebody's daughters."

"Yeah, but they ain't my responsibility." I shrugged my shoulders.

"That's double standard and you know it," Talya spat.

"Damn, these pork chops you cooked on point. Is it some more?" I asked.

"Why you trying to change the subject?"

"Because I said what I said. She can't talk to no boys and that's final."

"That's final?" Talya repeated with a raise of her brow.

I shot an evil look at my son. His lil ass was straight rolling like the shit was funny. “See what you did lil nigga?”

“What I do?” Princeton grinned while shrugging his shoulders.

“Don’t worry ‘bout it. I’mma put you up on game later.”

“Oh, you will?” Talya asked.

Just then my phone rang. “Saved by the bell,” I mumbled, and she playfully rolled her eyes.

I chuckled while putting the phone to my ear. “Yeah?” I answered.

“Hey, are you busy?” Quandra asked.

“Not really. What you got for me?” That was code to let her know Talya was around, and to make it quick.

“I handled that business, and everything went smooth,” she said, speaking in code.

“Good looking out. I’ll get up with you later.”

“Okay baby,” she said, and we ended the call.

“Is that the new iPhone?” Talya asked as soon as a nigga hung up. It was like she was just waiting to hit me with that question.

“Yeah, why?”

“When you get that? I thought we were gonna get new phones together.”

I looked down at my phone. “I got it today. Is it some more pork chops?” I tried to change the subject, but Talya ass wasn’t going.

“It’s some more. But why did you get a new phone?”

“Because I lost my other one.” I sighed.

“How you lose the other one?” She just kept pressing.

“I think I sat it on top of the car when I got some gas, or I could’ve left it on the counter at the store,” I lied.

“No, you didn’t daddy,” Emani busted out.

I glanced at her, pleading with my eyes for her not to say shit else. “Yes I did Princess.”

“You didn’t leave it. You broke it at our house,” she said.

“Nah baby girl, I didn’t break it then. Don’t you remember what I told you?” Emani gave me a confused look. She knew I hadn’t told her shit.

“Un huh. Momma told you she was having another baby. You said the d word and then threw the phone at the wall.” My eyes damn near bulged out of my head. I didn’t even know she heard all that.

“Wowwww!” Talya muttered as she glared at me evilly.

"Nah that didn't happen baby girl." I tittered. At that moment my ass was like a deer stuck in head lights. Talya hopped up and stomped towards our bedroom.

"Talya hol' up," I said, chasing behind her.

When we got inside the room, I closed the door. I knew for a fact it was about to go down in this bitch, and I didn't need the kids to hear it.

"C'mere mane." I tried to grab her arm, but she snatched it back.

"You still fuckin' your baby momma?" she asked. I scratched the side of my head. "Answer the question."

Should I tell the truth or lie?

The answer was easy, I was gonna lie my ass off. The number one rule was to never admit shit unless your woman caught you herself. Even then you could still deny that shit. "Hell nah I ain't fuckin' her."

"Wow! So you gonna stand in my face and lie?" She clapped her hands for dramatic effect.

"I ain't lying about fuckin' her."

"Are you lying about breaking your phone?"

"Yeah, I lied about that."

"So why lie about that if you ain't fuckin' her?" Talya asked.

"Because I knew what you would think if I told you the truth."

She shook her head. "You so full of shit. I don't have to put up with this. Matter fact, I ain't gon' put up with this shit." She went over to the dresser and started the same routine she did every time she threatened to leave a nigga.

"Where you going?"

"I'm leaving muthafucka. What does it look like?"

"Listen Talya, I didn't fuck that girl. I only got mad because I know if she has another baby that's probably gon' fall on me too."

"C'mon now, don't try to play me with that lame ass excuse. How is the next nigga's responsibility gonna fall on you?"

"'Cause Ariel don't fuck with nothing but deadbeats. Them niggas be getting what they want from her and then leave. This last nigga she fucked with is already in the wind."

Suddenly, Talya leaped on me and started throwing blows at a nigga. "Aye mane, calm the fuck down," I said as I tried to get control of her flying fist. She was going wild on a nigga. I felt blood leak from my lip, and knew it was busted.

"You lying ass muthafucka! You stuck yo' nasty dick in that girl and came back fuckin' me," she seethed. She hit me in the chest with her fist. I ain't gon' lie, that shit hurt like hell. Talya had a mean ass punch on her.

"Calm down," I gritted while grabbing her arms above her head.

She snatched them down. "Fuck you nigga!" she boomed as she went through the room, snatching all her shit.

"Don't leave shawty. I promise I didn't fuck Ariel."

"Fuck you! Now you and your thirsty baby mammy can be together," she hissed as she picked Kacen up.

"I'm telling you I didn't fuck that girl!"

"And you still lying! Didn't I tell you to watch what you said and did around Emani? Well thank you for never listening to me." With that she stormed out of the room taking lil man with her.

Saadiq

A few days later…

"Wassup ma?"

"Hey baby. How are you?" my momma asked me.

"I'm holding up."

"Glad to hear that. I'm looking forward to our next visit," she said.

"Yeah me too. I'm calling because I'm wondering if you heard from Talya? She was supposed to come visit me yesterday, but she never showed up."

"Nah, I haven't talked to her."

"Damn," I mumbled while scratching the side of my head. Not only had Talya flaked on me, but she wasn't answering her phone. I was looking forward to yesterday because she was supposed to bring my son.

"You want me to call and check on her?"

"Yeah, do that for me. Let me know if you talk to her."

"You want me to call this phone back?" she questioned.

I now had a cell that one of the guards gave to me. Throughout the day I kept it on me but at night I made sure to hide it. The nighttime guards were straight up bitches.

They would put you on lockdown over the smallest shit. I couldn't chance getting into trouble with my parole hearing around the corner. "You can call until about ten. If it's later, I'll just hit you tomorrow."

"I meant to ask you if you got whatever Adore' had to give you?" she asked.

"What you talking about? What was she supposed to give me?"

"I don't know. She called me the other day asking if I could give something to you on my visit. I told her I wasn't coming this week. She said she must have had the days mixed up. I tried to offer to bring it next week, but she hung up on me," she explained. I chuckled while shaking my head.

"I know what that shit was about. She was trying to check up on me," I uttered.

"Why would she be doing that?"

"Because I told her she couldn't come to my visit because you were coming."

"Let me guess she doesn't know about Kacen yet, does she?" my mother asked.

"I haven't gotten the chance to tell her."

"Mmm. I'm sure you haven't," she said.

I cracked a grin. "What's that supposed to mean ma?"

"Nothing. I'mma let you handle your mess. I will say this though, if she come around asking questions, I'm not keeping my grandbaby a secret. You might as well let her know what's up. And since we on the subject—" She started but I cut her off. I knew exactly where she was going with this shit.

"Ma, I'mma call you back later," I laughed.

"Yeah, you knew I was about to get in yo ass."

"I love ya ma."

"I love you too. One more thing, Saadiq."

I sighed. "Wassup lady?"

"Has Brisham reached out to you? I forgot to tell you I ran into him a few days ago. I told him he should come visit," she said, and I gritted my teeth.

"Nah I haven't heard from him. To be honest, I ain't fuckin' with that nigga."

"Why not? That's your cousin," she said.

"I got my reasons."

"What's going on? Every time I mention his name you get angry. Y'all used to be thick as thieves. What's the problem?" She just kept pressing.

"Ma let me hit you back. I think I hear a guard coming," I lied to get off the phone with her.

"Okay baby. Make sure you do." I quickly hung up. If only she knew the real reason why I wasn't fucking with that nigga. She would probably be ready to kill him herself.

After hanging up with her I tried dialing Talya again. When she didn't answer, I hung up and shot her a text. I called Adore' next to check her ass about going behind my back.

Natalya

Three days later…

"Ah shit. Cut that up girl." I hollered. 'Juvenile's Back That Azz Up' had just came on. I immediately jumped up and started to dance. Kiana was right behind me. She bent over with her hands on her knees and bounced her butt to the beat of the music. I laughed as I watched her dance like she was a stripper. When we heard a phone ring, we glanced at each other.

"I think that's yo' phone," she said. I walked to the table and snatched it up.

"Ugh," I sighed as I fell back onto the couch.

"Is that him again?" Kiana asked. She cut the music down.

For the past two days I'd been staying at her apartment. The night Marcellus and I got into it, I called and told her everything. When I mentioned going to a hotel, she made me come to her place. We were having a little girl's night to get my mind off things. We had food, liquor, and music. I was feeling a little better until Marcellus called, putting me right back in that funk I'd been in.

"You already know." I released a deep breath.

"You want me to answer?" Kiana asked, and I giggled.

"Why, so you can curse him out?"

"Hell yeah."

"Don't even worry about it. I'on want his ass to think I'm bothered by this shit."

Kiana picked up the bag of chips we were pigging out on and started to eat a few. "Why can't niggas just do right? Then they won't have to apologize for shit."

"Because they ain't built like that. It ain't like it's gonna get any better. Between social media and these thirsty hoes out here, it makes you wonder if it's possible to have a good relationship."

"You right about that shit. What you gon' do?" she questioned.

"Honestly, I don't know. I don' built a life with this man and now I'mma have to start over."

"Okay… What's wrong with starting over? It's not like you can't do it. You have the means to care for you and your son."

"I know I can do it, but I don't want to," I whined.

"Girl please. You don't need him," Kiana fussed.

"You're right. I just hate being alone. You know what I'm saying?"

"No woman really wants to be alone. But like I said, you ain't gotta put up with his shit."

I looked at my best friend in shock. Usually I was the one giving her advice. "I'm proud of you," I said.

"For what?" She raised a brow.

"You been on your grown woman shit lately. What Lex been over here doing to you?"

She waved her hand at me. "Bitch please, this ain't got nothing to do with him. I'm just calling it how I see it. Marcellus was wrong and he been wrong. No matter what y'all were going through, he shouldn't have ever fucked back with that bitch."

"That's what I'm saying. Then to know he might have gotten her pregnant. Like really Kiana. How he gonna do me like that?"

"That's not cool." She shook her head.

"Let's stop talking about this before I get mad all over again." I picked up my glass that was filled with Cîroc and guzzled it down.

"Damn bitch, you trying to get *wasted* wasted, ain't you?" Kiana giggled.

"I wanna forget all this shit."

"Good thing we fed the kids before we started drinking, huh?" she mumbled.

I snickered. “I know right? Anyway, where your man at? You haven’t mentioned him since I been over here.” Kiana’s whole demeanor changed. “What’s wrong, y’all going through it too?” I wondered.

“We broke up,” she admitted.

I sat up on the couch and looked at her. “Why?”

“It’s nothing. You got your own drama.” She tried to blow me off.

“Girl, you better spit that shit out. You been listening to me go on and on for the past two days. What, he cheated?” She shook her head.

“Brisham threatened if I didn’t leave Lex alone, he would do something to him.”

“But why? Y’all ain’t together.”

“Exactly! His stupid ass just thinks he can have control over my life. You remember when I told you somebody fucked up Lex’s shop?” she asked, and I nodded.

“Wait a minute… Don’t tell me it was him?”

“Yup.”

“What the fuck! Does Lex know?”

“Nah, that’s why I broke up with him. I didn’t want him to think I had nothing to do with that shit.”

“Wow, that’s really fucked up. What I don’t get is why he tripping when he got a baby by a whole ‘nother bitch. So what he gonna do, try to run off every dude you talk to? You can't let him have his way."

"To be honest Talya, I'm scared of him," she whispered, and I could have sworn I saw her eyes glisten. I tilted my head to the side. Never had I heard Kiana say she was scared of nothing.

"Why are you scared of him?"

"Because he pulled a gun on me," she revealed.

"Oh hell nah! I'm about to go over there," I jumped up and stumbled backwards. Kiana grabbed me just in time.

"Girl sit yo drunk ass down. What are you going to do?" She asked with a slight giggle.

"I'mma whoop his ass. That's what I'mma do. He got life fucked up if he thinks he gonna be pulling out pistols on you."

"Don't even worry about it. I told his Cordea to tell him to leave me alone."

"And what did his weird ass say?"

"He claimed he would talk to him."

"I guess," I spat.

"I'm serious Talya. Let me handle this. Don't go nowhere near Brisham," she warned.

I looked into her eyes for a minute before I finally agreed. “Okay. I’ll leave it alone. But if he does one more thing, I can’t be responsible for my actions.”

“I hear ya bad ass.” She laughed.

I fell back onto the couch and sighed. “Why does life have to be so hard?” I asked.

“When you find that answer, please let me know,” Kiana mumbled. I glanced at her. No doubt she was still the same crazy Kiana, but there was this undeniable change I’d taken note of. She was a lot calmer than before. I know she claimed her change didn’t come from Lex, but he’d definitely played a part. We’d both been through some things but if anybody deserved happiness it was her.

“Give me your phone,” I instructed.

“For what?”

“Just give me the damn phone and fix me another glass of Cîroc.”

Kiana looked at me strangely before she slowly stood and walked to the table. After handing me her phone, she took my glass and went into the kitchen. While she was in there, I quickly searched her contacts until I came across Lex’s phone number. Without thinking twice, I pressed the send button. The line rang a few times before his deep voice came over the line.

"Yeah?" he answered.

"Is that how you answer your phone?" I giggled.

The line became quiet before he spoke again. "Kiana?" he asked.

"Nah, it's Talya."

"Ah wassup Talya? Errthang good?"

"Well I was calling because I think you and Kiana need to talk." Once again, the line became silent. "You still there?"

"Did she put you up to calling me?"

"Nope, she doesn't even know that I'm doing this."

Just then Kiana came back into the room with my glass filled to the top. "You know we broke up, right?" Lex asked.

"I know, and that's why I'm calling. I don't think she really wanted to. She had some things going on that she was trying to take care of."

"Who are you talking to?" Kiana asked.

I took the glass while ignoring her question. "Where she at?"

"She just walked back into the room. C'mon, you know you want to talk to her."

"Talya, who are you talking to?" Kiana repeated.

"Aight, I'll talk to her for a minute. Put her on the phone."

"Okay hold on." I cheesed and quickly handed Kiana her cell. When she glanced at the screen and saw the name, her eyes widened.

"I'm going to kill you bitch," she gritted, and I laughed.

"Get on the phone and talk to that damn man," I said and stood up.

"You ain't right," she mumbled before putting the phone to her ear.

"And be nice," I threw over my shoulder as I ventured to her room. Climbing into Kiana's bed with my glass, I pulled my cell out of my pocket. I went to my recent calls and pressed send.

"Now you wanna call a nigga," Saadiq went in.

"That's my bad. I had some stuff going on. What are you doing?" I asked.

"Yeah aight. Where my son?"

"He's sleeping right now."

"Give him a hug for me."

"I will. You never answered my question."

"What's that?"

"What are you doing?"

Thinking about you," he said, and I blushed. *Oh God! I love this man so much.*

Kiana

A few days later…

As soon as Lex answered the door a big smile covered my face.

"Hey," I whispered.

"Wassup?" He nodded as he looked at me with a blank expression.

"Can I have a hug?" I asked, and he held his arms open for me. I walked straight into his arms and took in his intoxicating cologne. I tried to kiss him on the lips, but he turned his head. "You still mad at me?"

"I'm not mad shawty, but we ain't there right now."

I went into the living room while he closed the door. Lex lived in a two bedroom condo in Central West End. It was a nice place that he had decorated with modern style furniture. His little girl Macy's room was made up in Disney theme and there was a full playground set up for her in their backyard. He loved that little girl.

"Wassup?" Lex asked when he stepped into the living room.

"You got some tattoos to do?" I questioned while looking around at the equipment on the table.

"I had three this morning. My last client just left," he answered as he sat down beside me.

"When will your shop be ready?"

"They should have everything finished in the next two weeks. So what's going on? You said you wanted to see me."

"I missed you," I told him.

"Wait a minute. You confusing the shit out of me. One minute you claim we together, the next you tell me that you still got feelings for you baby daddy, and now you saying you missed me. You all over the place shawty."

"Lex, I need to tell you something."

"What's that?"

"I lied about me and Brisham being back together."

"Why you lie?" He slightly frowned.

"Because Brisham said if I didn't leave you alone, he would do something to hurt you."

"What? When he tell you that?" he barked.

"It was the day I went to visit him in the hospital. He accused me of having him jumped. I told him I didn't have nothing to do with it, but he didn't believe me. He told me to tell you watch your back."

"What the hell! Why you didn't tell me this? Hell, you had me around hur' thinking you really wanted to be with dude and all along this nigga been threatening you?"

"That's not it…" Lex gave me a confused expression.

"What else?"

"He's the one that destroyed your shop." Nervously, I bit my bottom lip as I glanced at him.

"What?" Lex said and jumped up.

"Lex, please calm down. This was the reason I didn't wanna tell you because I knew you would be angry."

"Damn right, I'm mad. That nigga fucked with my livelihood. I'on even know dude, but he just made this shit very personal. When I see that nigga It's on."

"Lex no! I know you're upset but let me handle it. I don't want you getting into trouble behind my bullshit. His dad is Chief of police. Let me have a talk with him."

"Fuck that shit. Dude violated."

"I know, and I'm sooo sorry. Please just don't beef with him. I can't take no more drama," I said as I started to cry. He ran his hand down his face while releasing a deep breath.

"C'mere man. You know I hate to see you cry."

"I'm so sorry I brought all this drama into your life," I mumbled.

"Shh, it's gonna be aight. You didn't do this shit, and I ain't mad at you. I just wished you would've told me." He rubbed his hands through my hair.

I pulled away from Lex. "It's not gonna be okay. There is so much shit Brisham has me mixed up in."

"Like what?" He lifted a brow.

I was so tired of holding onto this secret, and I felt I just needed to tell somebody. "If I tell you this you gotta promise not to say anything. I mean you can't tell nobody."

"You know I ain't gon' say shit. That's not even me to go running my mouth."

I took deep breath before I started to tell Lex the story about Brisham and Saadiq.

"Damn Kiana, that's heavy. You gon' have to tell your girl before she hears this from somebody else."

"I know, but how do I reveal som' shit like that without losing her? She's gonna be mad at me."

"Yeah, she gonna be pissed, but you gotta tell her. How would you feel if she was holding a secret from you? I ain't gon' lie, she might not talk to you for a while, but y'all will eventually get back on track."

"I'on know Lex. I'mma have to think about this."

"You gotta tell her shawty."

I gazed into his eyes. "What about us?" I asked.

"Honestly, you wrapped up in a whole bunch of shit," he started.

I put my head down because I knew what was coming next. It was only so much of my baggage Lex would be able to accept. "You know I got my daughter that I'm trying to raise. She don't need to be wrapped up in no drama—" he continued, but I cut him off.

"You don't have to explain. I understand," I whispered.

"Nah, let me finish. Are you still taking those pills?" he asked.

"I haven't taken one in a week."

"You sure about that?"

"I'm sure. I only pop them when I get stressed."

Lex was quiet for a minute before he started to speak again. "I know it's easier said than done to kick a drug habit, but you gotta do it. When my baby momma was killed, I got addicted to lean. I mean I was on that shit heavy. It wasn't until I noticed my actions were affecting my daughter that I decided to make a change. I'on want it to go that far for you, so I'mma do all I can to help you out. You gon' have to put in some serious work."

"I'll put in the work," I promised. "Does this mean you gon' give us another chance?"

Lex sighed. “Yeah, we can try again. I ain’t ready to walk away just yet, but I hope this is it ‘cause a nigga can’t handle shit else,” he said.

“I’ve told you everything.”

Lex raised an eyebrow. “You sure? I mean, you‘on like to have threesomes and freaky shit like that do you?” he questioned.

“What?” I frowned.

“I’m saying, if you into that type of shit I’ll try my best to overlook it.” When he grinned, I knew everything was going to be okay. When Lex used his sense of humor it was always to lighten the mood.

“Boy you wish,” I said giggling uncontrollably.

“That’s fucked up. The one thing a nigga is down with and you don’t like it.” He playfully shook his head.

I jumped up and punched Lex in his arm. He grabbed me around my waist and put a kiss on my lips. We started to kiss passionately before he swept me off my feet. “What are you doing?” I asked as he carried me into his bedroom.

“We got like an hour before Macy get out of school. We finna use that time to make up,” he said, tossing me onto the bed.

A few minutes later we were both stripped down to our birthday suits, fucking each other’s brains out. With my ass tooted in the air, Lex pounded me from the back. He was so rough yet gentle at the same time as he hit my spot.

"Shit Lex. This feels good. Fuck me harder baby!" I screamed.

While Lex went deeper, he roughly grabbed a handful of my hair and pulled my head back. "You want me to fuck you harder, huh?" he asked, slapping my ass.

"Mhm," I moaned.

"You sure you can take it?" he asked, slapping my ass again.

By now I was so fucking wet and turned on. He was making this pussy cream. When Lex pulled out, he turned me over and put me in the buck. My pussy started to fart as he slid in and out of my wetness.

"Mmm…Uhn. This yo' pussy. Fuck it like you want," I moaned.

"This my pussy?" he asked, going harder. I nodded my head as he started to hit my spot. "Damn Kiana, I missed this shit…I missed you. Fuck me back," he grunted as he grabbed my breast and began to stroke it. When I pushed myself up and down his length, Lex went crazy. He started slamming into me harder.

"Argh shit! Here it comes!" Lex grunted while releasing his seeds inside of me. "If you ever think about giving that nigga or any other nigga my pussy, we gon' have some problems. And you better not keep shit else from me," he stated. I snickered. "What you laughing for? I'm dead ass serious," he spat.

"Don't worry baby, this is all yours." I kissed his lips.

***

Two hours later…

I had just got back from Lex's house. After making up with my man, I was now ready to handle my business. As soon as I stepped inside, I spotted the kids playing in the playpen, so I walked over to them. "Hey babies," I said, putting a kiss on each of their foreheads. Reagan reached out her hands for me to pick her up.

"Not right now baby. Momma gotta take care of something," I told her, and she whined. I kissed her again before going into the kitchen.

"I see you made yourself at home," I said to Talya. She was standing at the stove cooking.

"Girl yes. I was tired of eating out. You know I like to cook. You want a drink?" she asked as she finished cutting up some tomatoes.

"Might as well," I mumbled as I sat at the table. My nerves were all over the place. I wanted to back out so bad, but I promised Lex I would tell her.

"How it go with you and Lex?" Talya asked as she handed me a glass of wine.

"We made up."

"I'm so happy for y'all. He is good for you Kiana. Don't mess it up," she warned.

"I'm not." I gave her a small smile. "Talya, can you sit down for a minute? I need to tell you something."

"Okay, let me take these taco shells out of the oven. Dinner is almost ready."

I watched as she took the shells out of the oven and sat the pan on the stove. When she walked towards the table, my heart started beating fast. *C'mon Kiana, you can do this.*

"Wassup girl? You ain't pregnant, are you?" She lifted a brow.

"What? Hell nah, I'm not pregnant."

Talya looked at me strangely. "So why you looking like that? If you and Lex made up, you should be happy."

"I am happy but not about this news I'm finna tell ya."

"Aight, go ahead and tell me."

I swallowed hard as I glanced at my best friend of forever. In all my life, I'd never been as nervous as I was to tell somebody something. "I lied to you," I blurted out.

"You lied to me about what?" she questioned with a puzzled look.

"About what happened the night Saadiq went to jail."

"What are you talking about?" She frowned.

"The night all that shit went down, I didn't pick Brisham up from the strip club."

Talya looked at me sideways for a long time before she finally spoke again. "Quit playing bitch. This ain't funny." She started to laugh while taking a sip of her wine.

"I'm not playing," I said and began to tell her everything from the beginning to the end. "I'm sooo sorry, Talya. I know it's gonna take you a long time to forgive me, and I can't blame you for that. You gotta understand why I did it. They threatened me."

Talya sat her wine glass on the table and finally looked at me. "Let me get this straight… All this time you've been covering for Brisham because you didn't want him to tell auntie about you stealing from her? You let me cry my eyes out about my child's father when you knew the truth all along? Is that what you're telling me?"

I slowly nodded my head. Talya got up from her chair and glared down at me. Before I saw it coming, she reached out her hand and slapped spit out my mouth. She did it like three times back to back. With each hit the sting became more painful than the last. As much as I hated for anybody to put their hands on me, I knew I deserved it.

"Bitch, how the fuck could you do that to me? No matter what you went through, I was always by your side. When bitches tried to jump you for fuckin' their man, who was there to help you? Me! Hell, I just helped you get your man back, even though I know you don't deserve him. But what the fuck do I get in return for my loyalty to yo' hoe ass? I lost my man and my son lost his daddy. If you weren't such a horrible person, you wouldn't have to keep shit a secret. I swear your only loyalty is to dick," Talya spat.

I hung my head. I couldn't do nothing but accept everything she was saying. She was right, I was a horrible person. Now that all my secrets were being exposed, I was seeing just how much shit I'd done to those around me.

"I'm sorry Talya. I know you probably don't believe me, but I swear I didn't mean to hurt you. You are my sister and I love you," I whispered.

"Sister?" she laughed manically. "Bitch, you ain't no sister of mine. No sister would let her sister's man go to prison for something he didn't do. And no godmother would allow her godson to go without his father just to save her own ass."

"Talya listen to me. I get you're upset but you can't say nothing. Brisham and his daddy don't want this getting out. They will do whatever to keep that from happening."

"Fuck you bitch. I'm finna get Saadiq out of jail. He doesn't deserve to be in there." She tried to stomp away, but I jumped up and grabbed her arm.

"Listen," I gritted. She was starting to piss me off because she wasn't listening to what I was saying. "It's gotta be more to the story if Saadiq never said anything. Think about it. They probably threatened him too. Use your head right now. Don't let your feelings cloud your judgment." She looked as if she were thinking about what I was saying.

"Get your fuckin' hands off me," she suddenly snapped.

"Promise me you won't say anything. Please?"

"Stay the fuck away from me. I don't want shit else to do with you. If you come near me I'mma beat yo' ass for real," she snarled before trudging out of the kitchen. I sat at the table and broke down crying. Once I heard her leave twenty minutes later, I picked up my phone and called Lex.

"Wassup baby?" He answered on the first ring.

"I need you," I cried into the phone.

"You told her?" He asked.

"Mhm," I mumbled.

"Aight, I'm on my way," he said.

"Please hurry. I feel like I need to pop a Molly."

"Nah shawty. You don't need to do that. Just sit tight, and I'mma be there in a minute."

I ended the call and started to cry like a baby.

Marcellus

A few days later…

"What brings you by here today?" Ma dukes asked when I walked into her house. A few years ago I'd bought her a big five bedroom house out in Chesterfield. She raised me and my brother who was killed when I was a teenager by a gang rivalry in Baden; one of the roughest hoods in St. Louis. Our whole childhood was spent listening to gunshots and ducking bullets. I told myself once I was able to get my momma away from there I would. For five years I asked her to let me take her house shopping, but she would never let me. She finally gave in when her best friend was robbed at gun point outside of her house. Ever since then she ain't looked back.

"I just came through to see my old lady. Is that a problem?" I questioned.

She looked at me with a smirk. "You must have forgotten that I birthed your ass. I know when something is wrong," she asserted. My momma was in her early sixties. She was a little over average height with a big boned figure and rocked a salt and pepper roller set. She was a retired school teacher who had taught in the St. Louis school district for over thirty years.

"I'm serious, ma." I chuckled while falling back onto the plush leather sofa. Taking out my cell, I pulled up my Instagram and started to go through it. I wasn't big on social media and only checked it a few times a week.

"How my grandbabies doing?" Ma asked.

"Spoiled as hell. Every time I turn around, they got their lil hands out."

She laughed. "You created them monsters. Just like you do with me, you give them kids anything they want."

"Nah, they go overboard." I shook my head and sighed.

My momma walked over and sat beside me. She gently grabbed my phone and placed it on my lap. "What's really going on baby? And don't tell me that it's nothing because I see this sadness in your eyes."

I ran my hand down my face. "You think you know me don't it, lady?"

"I do, so you can't get nothing by me."

"Aight ma. Me and Talya been having major issues," I confessed.

"What kind of problems?" she questioned.

I started from the beginning and told her everything. “Boy, I should beat yo’ ass. Why would you even think it was okay to dip back with Ariel? And if you were gonna mess with her, why not use protection?”

“I know I messed up ma. I’on even like her like that.”

“So why play with her emotions if you know you ain’t feeling her? And why couldn’t you have used protection?” she repeated.

“To be honest, it wasn’t supposed to go down like that. One minute I was sitting over there chilling. We had just finished watching a movie with Emani. After we put her to sleep, one thing just kinda led to another.”

Momma shook her head. “That’s always the number one excuse with you men. It’s the same shit your daddy used to say. I’m disappointed in you Marcellus. History is repeating itself all over again. You did this when you were having issues with Charlotte. When you gonna learn that Ariel doesn’t mean you no good? Any woman who will willingly sleep with her friend’s man is not to be trusted. That should let you know she has no morals. But for some reason you just keep thinking with your lil head down there instead of the one on your shoulders,” she fussed.

“My head ain’t little, ma,” I chortled.

She popped me on the arm. "I don't care to hear all that, and you need to take this seriously. There is possibly another life involved because you out there being careless."

"Nah, she ain't pregnant. I made Ariel take a pregnancy test earlier and it came back negative."

"Well thank goodness! God knows you don't need another child by that girl."

Ariel and momma never really saw eye to eye. Momma said she used Emani as a pawn to get what she wanted out of me, and I didn't disagree with that notion.

"Yeah, I know but it's already out that I messed around with her. Talya took lil man and left like a week ago."

"Well now you gon' have to clean up your mess. You broke that girl's trust, and it's gonna be hard as hell to get it back. Now as far as her still having feelings for her baby father, you gonna have to decide if you'll be able to stick around until she gets over those feelings. Honestly, you have to take some blame in that too because you willingly hooked up with that girl knowing her heart was still with someone else."

"There you go taking her side," I grumbled.

"I'm not taking anybody's side. I'm just speaking the truth. She shouldn't have gotten with you knowing she still had feelings for the other boy, and you shouldn't have voluntarily become her rebound. You all are both to blame in this matter. The only thing to do now is sit down and decide where do you go from here. To fully figure this out, you're gonna have to stop sticking your dick this place and that place. That's not gonna help you resolve your issues," Momma stated bluntly.

I laughed while glancing at her. "You wild ma."

"Shit I'm serious. You gon' mess around and get something yo' ass can't get rid of. And I definitely wouldn't trust Ariel's loose ass. I'm glad my grandbaby is here, but I hate you didn't think twice about messing with her. That girl is pure evil."

"Well that situation is done. She probably only had sex with me because she wanted to make Talya jealous."

"You just now seeing that? Boy, I been peeped she was jealous of y'all relationship. She called here one day going off about how you put Talya before Emani, and how you ain't been doing right by her since y'all got together."

"She lying. No matter who I'm dealing with, my kids always come first," I bellowed.

"Boy, you ain't gotta explain nothing to me. I told her ass to get off my phone with that nonsense. Anybody who knows you is well aware of how much you love them kids."

I shook my head in disgust. “I hate her ass,” I mumbled.

“Nah, you’re just angry because you got caught.”

My phone beeped with a message. When I saw it was from Quandra, I opened it up and read it. I was supposed to be meeting up with her so we could discuss a job I wanted her to do.

“I’mma get out of hur’, ma. I need to handle some things before I head home.”

“Aight baby I love you. Be careful and make sure I see my grandbabies in the next few days. It’s been a while since I last saw them.”

“I’ll bring ‘em by,” I told her as I left.

Brisham

"Why you been avoiding me?" I asked Valencia. I'd just stopped by the crib she shared with her sister and niece to holler at her. Since the gun situation with Kiana, she'd been avoiding a nigga like the plague. After calling for over two weeks she hadn't answered, so I did a quick pop up on her ass. At first I told myself I didn't give a damn, but after shawty went missing I realized just how much I missed her.

"I don't know what you and your baby momma got going on, but I don't want no parts of it." She folded her arms over her chest as she glared at me. I licked my lips as I eyed her soft body. She was wearing a pair of spandex workout pants with a half shirt that exposed her flat stomach. Although she didn't have much, shawty was still sexy. It was something about the way she carried herself.

"So you gon' hold that over my head?" I asked with a smirk.

"Nigga you crazy. You want me to stick around so you can do the same thing to me whenever we have a disagreement?"

I looked her up and down with a sly grin. I was starting to feel Valencia a little bit. Shawty was actually cool people. I found myself opening up to her about my real feelings. I never did that with Kiana or any other female. On top of that, she had a lot going for herself. She was in college, didn't have no kids, and was smart as hell. The few times she was around my son, she was good with him. I could use someone positive in my life to help with raising him.

"I wouldn't do no shit like that to you. Matter fact, I already apologized to my baby momma," I lied. She pursed her lips together.

"I don't believe you."

"I'm serious," I told her as I invaded her personal space. "Why you tripping? A nigga been missing you." I tried to put a kiss on her lips, but she put her hand on my chest and pushed me back.

"I'm not tripping. Why would you do that to her in the first place?"

"Because she did some foul shit."

"But that's the mother of your child." Valencia frowned at me.

"Yeah I know," I sighed.

"Do you still love her?" Valencia questioned as she leaned against the door frame.

"Only as the mother of my child."

"Maybe you should see if y'all can work it out." She suggested.

"Nah, too much shit don' happened between us. Our relationship is toxic as fuck and ain't neither one of us good for each other."

"If that's the case, why don't you want her seeing someone else?" She asked.

I cracked a grin. "Mane you heard all that?"

"Yeah, I did." She snaked her neck.

"That ain't nothin'. She don't use her head when she fucks with these niggas."

"Boy, that's bullshit. You can't control who that girl is messing with."

My phone rang just as I was getting ready to respond. "Give me a minute," I told Valencia. I heard her sigh as I turned my back to take the call.

"Yeah?" I answered.

"Hey baby, are you busy?" the familiar voice whispered.

"Yeah, but I got a quick minute. Wassup?" I asked.

"Can you come see me?"

"Where you at?"

"I'm at the Ramada Inn near the airport. I got something special for you," she said.

I licked my lips. "Oh yeah?" I asked.

"Yes. Are you gonna come through?"

"Aight, give me like thirty minutes and I'll be through that way."

"Okay, I'll be waiting." She hung up.

"My bad. That was something important," I explained as I walked back over to Valencia who had a scowl on her face.

"It's all good. I'm sure your groupies need you," she spat.

"You jealous shawty?" I asked with a raised brow.

"No, I'm not jealous," she denied, but I could see the jealousy all over her face. Shawty was feeling me just as much as I was feeling her.

"You gon' let me see you later?" I asked as I took my hand and ran it along her jawline.

"I don't know. Just call me, and I'll see if I'm free." She pushed my hand away.

"You still trippin' mane." I grinned at her.

"No, you're tripping. If you wanted us to spend time together you would put me first." She tried to close the door, but I stuck my foot out to stop her. “What you want?” she asked with an attitude.

“You need to make time ‘cause I wanna take you out. I ain’t asking either. Be ready around eight-thirty.”

“Boy please.” She cracked a small grin, letting me know I was wearing her down.

“You heard what I said. Be ready when I come back, and make sure you wear som’ sexy for a nigga,” I demanded. She rolled her eyes.

“We’ll see,” she uttered before finally closing the door in my face. I half smiled as I turned and headed back to my car. *Her ass is definitely feeling your boy.*

***

“You like that?” Danika asked as she took my dick and flicked her tongue all around the head. With a big ass grin, I glanced down at her sliding my shit in and out of her wet, warm mouth.

“Hell yeah. Handle yo’ business shawty,” I mumbled as I leaned back and closed my eyes.

Danika is this chick I been messing with for a couple of months now. I bumped into her at the store and knew then I had to have her. Shawty let me fuck the same night I got her number. After she turned me out, I knew I had to put her on my list of freaks to hit up. No doubt I was trying to make shit pop with Valencia. At the same time, we hadn't made it official yet. Until then I was free to do me.

I was brought out of my thoughts when Danika pushed me to the back of her throat and started to deep throat a nigga.

"Argh shit shawty. Suck this dick," I coached her.

Danika looked up at me from behind those long ass lashes and damn near swallowed my shit whole. Right when I was getting ready to bust, she slipped my dick out of her mouth. I leaned up with a slight frown.

"What you doing?" I questioned.

"I told you I got a surprise for you. This was just a sample of what's to come tonight," she grinned.

"C'mon shawty, a nigga shit is 'bout to explode. Finish handling yo business."

"Un-un," she said, sliding off the bed. She quickly disappeared into the bathroom. I laid there hard as a brick, wondering what her ass was up to. A few minutes later Danika returned and she wasn't alone. Standing on the side of her was this light brown chick with the prettiest pink lips. She was wearing a red silk negligee that showed off her thick legs and fat ass. You could see her chocolate drop nipples through the sheer of the lace.

"Who is you?" I asked the broad.

"This is the surprise I was telling you about." Danika smiled.

I looked between her and ol' girl for a minute before I finally cracked a grin. "Ah shit, y'all trying to get *freaky* freaky in this bitch, huh?"

"You already know how I get down. Now lay back and let us show you what we got," Danika instructed. Doing what she told me, I folded my arms behind my head and laid back. From that point, no other words were spoken as they climbed onto the bed and started to turn a nigga out. While one sucked on my dick the other one played with my balls. They took turns doing that for a while until a nigga couldn't hold it no more. I ended up busting down the nameless chick's throat.

Before I could gather myself, Danika had already got my dick back hard. While the nameless chick sucked on her titties, Danika rode my shit from the back. I couldn't lie, they were getting the best of your boy. I'd had several threesomes, but these broads were on a different level. Not one to be outdone, I flipped Danika on all fours while ol' girl laid on the bed. I made Danika eat her pussy while I banged her from the back.

By now we were in a full on freak fest. They may have caught a nigga off guard, but I quickly fell into the swing of shit. We changed positions several times and busted plenty of nuts. I put my dick in every hole on them and neither one complained. They just let a nigga do what he wanted.

A few hours later we were laid in the bed spent. I was trying to see if I could muster up enough strength to go one more 'round, but I didn't think I had it in me.

"Are you falling asleep?" Danika asked just as I was getting ready to doze off.

"Nah shawty, I'm just chilling," I lied.

"Don't go to sleep. We got one more surprise," she said.

"Y'all gon' have to give me like an hour to get myself together." I breathed. I was sure it was past the time for me to take Valencia out. My phone had been ringing off the hook, and I figured it was her.

I'mma just have to make it up to shawty tomorrow.

Danika got up and walked to the dresser. With my eyes at half mast, I watched as she went into her purse and retrieved her phone. She came back to my side of the bed and sat down.

"Hey get up. I need to tell you something," she said.

"Wassup shawty?" I grumbled. I'd just told her ass that I wasn't in the mood for shit else. I needed to rest. My heart was still beating fast.

"I just want you to look at something," she said, handing me her phone.

I took the phone from her hand. "What you want me to look at?"

"Press play," she ordered.

I glanced at Danika, wondering what she had going on. "What's this mane, some kind of flick or something?"

"Just look at it," she giggled.

I shook my head before pressing the play button on her phone. The video popped on and for a minute it was just someone moving the phone around. A few seconds later it settled on somebody laying on the floor. I squinted my eyes to get a better view of the person, and that's when I noticed who it was. "Da fuck!" I exclaimed as I sat up. "What the hell is this?" I asked Danika.

"That's yo baby momma, right?" she asked with a grin.

"What the fuck you do to her?" I questioned. Kylisha was tied up and gagged. She was laying on a dirty floor shivering and crying. Somebody wearing all black walked over and started to kick her. You could hear Kylisha trying to scream behind the thing covering her mouth.

"What are you talking about? We didn't do that to her, you did," Danika stated.

I shot my eyes at her. "What the fuck you mean I did this?"

"Well not actually, but the police will believe you did once they get hold of this video," she stated.

I bit the inside of my jaw as I glared at her. Before I could say anything, I heard a clicking sound behind me. I turned my head towards the sound and found myself staring at a pistol.

"What y'all bitches want?" I barked.

"It's simple," the nameless bitch began. "We want a hundred and fifty thousand dollars, cash."

"Fuck you bitches. I ain't giving y'all shit," I snarled, and the bitch slapped me with the gun.

"Fuck!" I grunted in pain.

"If you don't give us this money, I will send this video to the police with a location where they can find your deceased baby momma. Now are you sure you want her blood on your hands?" She barked.

As I held my pounding head, I thought about the situation I was in. This was not a good look for me. Kylisha had been missing for a while, and I was one of the last people to see her. On top of that, I'd had the altercation with her and the junky couple right before she disappeared.

All this shit would point back to me. As much as I didn't want to, I had to give these bitches what they wanted.

"Aight, I'll give it to y'all," I finally agreed.

The other chick walked around the bed to where Danika was. "Good, we'll let her go as long as I have the money by this Friday at noon. If you try any funny shit, we will kill that bitch," she spat.

I eyed them with the look of murder in my eyes. "I'mma have it to y'all."

"We'll be in touch," Danika said. With that, they both redressed and left the room. I couldn't believe this shit. These bitches had set me up.

Adore'

"How you doing? You look good?" Saadiq told me.

"Thank you, baby. How have you been?" I asked. It seemed it had been a long time since I last saw my man; two weeks to be exact. That was too long for me. *How did women who had men in and out of prison do this?*

"Not too good. I'm ready to get out of this muthafucka," he mumbled.

"It's gonna come soon. You just gotta hang on a little while longer."

"I hope so shawty. Anyway, what you been up to?" He changed the subject. I gave him a sympathetic look. Every time I saw him looking this way it always broke my heart. It just wasn't fair that he was stuck in here.

"I've been working with my dad on getting you some matches lined up when you get out."

"Oh yeah?" Saadiq smiled.

"Mhm," I mumbled.

"What you find out?"

"I've found a few contenders. However, the new trainer said the matches won't be big until he's sure you're ready. Is that okay?" I asked.

"Hell yeah! I appreciate you looking out for me."

"You know I gotcha baby. I know how much boxing means to you, so I'll do all I can to help you get back to it," I told him. "But on another note, to cheer you up, I got something for you."

"What's that?" he asked.

"Look under the table," I instructed.

With a sly grin on his face, Saadiq did exactly what I told him. When he came back up, he was grinning from ear to ear. "That thang is looking right," he grinned mischievously.

I was wearing a dress with no panties underneath it. My vagina was smooth except for the landing strip I left when I got my Brazilian wax. When Saadiq licked his soft pink lips, I could already feel them wrapped around my pearl.

"Let me see again," he said looking back under the table. When he looked up that time, he shook his head. "You gon' have a nigga hard as hell. Let me focus on something else."

I snickered. "Oh, I forgot to tell you I found the perfect spot for us," I threw out. Saadiq hadn't mentioned where he would be staying once he got out, but I figured we could get a place together.

"What made you do that?" he asked. Suddenly, his smile faded.

"I wanted you to have somewhere comfortable to lay your head. What's the matter? I thought you would be happy."

"I'on know if I'm ready for all that. To be honest, I know we ain't so let's just hold up."

"But I already paid the deposit and the first month's rent. I'm moving out of my father's house in like a week."

"You can still move in, but I think I'mma crash at my old lady's crib once I get released."

I frowned. "What's the problem Saadiq? I thought you wanted to be with me?" I asked.

"I do, but it don't mean we gotta live with each other. That shit is a big commitment. I'mma need time to adjust to our relationship outside of these walls before I'm ready to take that step."

You lived with that bitch Talya is what I wanted to say but I allowed him to finish. "Plus, I got som' other things going on that I need to holler at you about anyway."

I glowered at him. "What is it?"

"You remember you told me Talya had a baby?" he asked.

"Yeah, what about it?" I asked.

"I'on really know how to tell you this, but I just found out he's my son," he revealed. Suddenly all the wind was knocked out of me, making it hard for me to breathe. "You aight?" Saadiq asked as I held my chest.

I glanced into his eyes. "When did you find out?"

"A few weeks back. She came to visit."

"Why didn't you tell me this?" I slammed my hand on the table.

Saadiq scrunched his face. "Yo, you need to calm down."

"Don't fuckin' tell me to calm down," I snarled.

"Adore', calm the fuck down or you can bounce," he threatened. I took slow breaths to get myself under control. If I wanted him to tell me everything, I had to remain calm.

"I'm sorry. This just caught me by surprise. I have to be honest, it hurts my feelings that you didn't mention it before now. I mean, how do you even know the baby is yours? Isn't she dating someone else?"

"Trust me, that's all me," he uttered.

"What does that mean?" I scowled.

"It means I know for a fact he is mine. My son is over a year and a half old so it ain't no way he belongs to anybody else. On top of that, he looks just like me," was his explanation.

I didn't ask you that! I screamed inside my head.

"Wow! Why is she just telling you this?" I glanced down at my hands and saw they were trembling. I quickly slid them under the table to hide them.

"She couldn't tell me. Remember I took her off the visitor's list?" he said.

Yeah right. That bitch just wants you back.

"And now you've added her to the list again?" I questioned with an attitude.

"Yeah, she is my baby momma. I need to be able to communicate with her for the sake of my child," he said, and I cringed.

"Okay. Where does that leave us?"

"We still gon' be together."

"Does she know that?" I asked.

"Not yet but I'mma tell her soon," he claimed.

"Really Saadiq? I'm your girlfriend. That should have been one of the first things you mentioned. You don't still have feelings for her, do you?"

"Don't start stressing. This shit was just sprung on me, so I haven't had time to discuss all that other stuff with her. I just been trying to get to know my son. I'm telling you this because I'mma be in his life. If it's too much for you to handle I understand."

Wow. He hadn't even answered my question. I didn't know how to feel about that. "Adore' you good?" He asked.

Plastering on the biggest smile I could muster, I told him, "Of course I can handle it. He is a part of you, so I'll love him just like he's mine."

"That's why I fuck with you the long way," he said, and I smiled. Although my heart was crushed, I had to stand by my man's side.

***

A few days later…

"What brings you by here Adore'?" Franklin asked.

Franklin was the district attorney for the state of St. Louis. He and my dad were old college buddies. They also belonged to the same Masonic club.

"You know why I'm here."

"You come to apologize for the other night?" he questioned with a smirk.

"Nope, I'm not. I want to know where you are with Saadiq's case. Are you going to make sure he gets his parole hearing like we discussed?"

Franklin put down the papers he was reading and glanced at me over the brim of his thin glasses. "Why should I?" he asked. Franklin was an older black man with a nice body, a gentle smile, and a fat ass bank account. For years he'd been trying to get with me behind my dad's back, but I'd always turned him down. Although he was handsome, I didn't do older men.

"Because we had an agreement," I spat.

"We did have an agreement, but you broke it."

I folded my arms over my breasts. "No, I didn't. I told you before I would do anything but that."

"And I told you that was part of the agreement," he shot back.

I walked around to Franklin's side of the desk and dropped to my knees. "Please don't make me do it. I'll do anything else," I said as I looked into his eyes.

As you can see, the tables had turned. I now needed Franklin in a huge way. He'd been telling me for months he would pull some strings to get Saadiq paroled. Of course they came with terms, but I was okay with that. I wanted my man to be released. I hadn't told Saadiq I was trying to get him out because all he would do was tell me to leave it alone. He said that before when I tried to hire him a lawyer.

"Adore', I've already told you. The only way the agreement will work is if you fulfill every single obligation."

"But I feel so weird doing that. Let me do something else to make up for it," I pleaded as I took my hand and cupped his balls.

Franklin shifted around in his seat. "No, that's okay. I would appreciate it if you leave now. Since we can't come to an agreement on this matter, we'll just forget everything."

I rolled my eyes. He was really pissing me off. "I'm not leaving," I said, grabbing his balls harder. From the pleasured look on his face, I could see I was turning him on. He didn't want to admit it.

"No thank you, I'll pass." In one swift motion, I unzipped his pants and pulled his penis through the opening of his boxers. I wasn't taking no for an answer.

"Adore'," he grunted in a throaty tone.

"Just sit back and let me do what I do best," I told him as I leaned in and took him into my mouth. Franklin's dick was like a pencil. Not only was it skinny, but it was almost as long as my arm. Unlike other men, I could never deep throat this ruler. Wrapping my lips around the head, I slid inch by inch into my mouth until I had half of it covered.

"Do you still want me to leave?" I spoke around his dick. Lustfully, he gazed into my eyes as I started to slowly suck him.

"Yes, you dirty little slut. Suck this dick," he demanded as he started to relax. Franklin was a real freak. He'd had me to dress up as a nurse, a nun, a teacher, and even a police officer. He even liked to do things like bondage. Initially I was cool with all his demands, but when he told me to fuck him with a dildo that's where I drew the line. That shit was too weird for me. Since I wouldn't do it, he was now trying to renege on our agreement. I couldn't have that.

"You like this daddy?" I asked as I slipped him in and out of my mouth. Franklin didn't answer, all he did was push my head down further. When I felt the head of his penis touch my tonsils, I started to gag. His dick felt like a stick stabbing me in my throat. I gripped his balls tighter, hoping that would make him pull back. It didn't work because I forgot he liked pain with sex. He just kept pushing and pushing. I had to breathe through my nose just to make sure I didn't vomit. Right when I didn't think I could take anymore, he shot off a load of nut into the back of my throat. I jumped up while gagging.

"Why the fuck would you do that? I told you before I don't swallow!" I barked.

Franklin chuckled as he took the wipes out of his desk and started to clean himself up. "Let's just say you may have made up for that one thing." He smirked.

Angrily, I wiped my mouth. His nut tasted horrible. Most men just put anything in their bodies, and it's the reason I didn't swallow. "You need to eat some fruit," I spat, and Franklin laughed again. "I'm glad you find humor in this shit."

"I do," he said, and I snarled at him.

"Look, are you going to do it or not?" I frowned because I could still taste his sour nut on my tongue.

"Let me think about it," he uttered as he gathered his papers on his desk and began to look at them again. I snatched the papers and tossed them to the side. Leaning close enough so he could hear me, I began to speak slowly.

"Franklin if you don't handle this for me, I will be paying your wife a little visit. I'm done playing games with yo' ass. You gave me your word you would do it, and that's what the fuck I expect. I will tell my daddy how you've been trying to get with me since I was a little girl."

"Bitch are you threatening me?" he asked, leaning forward. Our faces were so close our noses were touching.

"Hmm, I guess you can say that." I told him before walking out of his office. I was very confident Franklin would make that happen, or else his wife and colleagues would find out just how sick and demented his ass was.

Kiana

"Kiana, what do you do for a living?" Lex's mother, Beverly, questioned.

"I'm a receptionist at a doctor's office."

"That's nice. How do you like it?" she asked.

"I really like it. Everyone is close there."

"Do you come from a big family?" she asked.

We were at Lex's mom's house. This was our first time meeting. His sister was on the way over so I could meet her too. About a week ago I went to his father and stepmom's house to meet them. This was a little overwhelming for me because I'd never met a guy's family.

"I don't have any family besides my auntie. My mom was killed when I was younger, and I never knew my father," I mumbled.

"Oh honey, I'm so sorry to hear that." She gave me a sympathetic look. Lex's mother was a pretty lady. She was about my height, mocha color skin tone, thin frame, and a very youthful face. Her hair was cut low in one of those boy cuts and was platinum blonde. I wouldn't rock the style, but it was very cute on her.

"That's okay. I've learned to deal with her not being here, and my aunt did a good job stepping up."

"I'm glad to hear that. I'm sure it's hard losing a parent. You seem like a lovely young lady. I don't know what you've done to my son, but I haven't seen him this smitten in a long time. You should see him around here, just skinning and grinning when he mentions your name."

"C'mon ma chill," Lex chuckled.

"C'mon ma, what? Am I lying?" she asked, but Lex didn't say anything. He just grinned. I blushed as I gazed at him.

"Kiana, if there is anything you ever need, don't hesitate to let me know, okay?" Ms. Beverly stated, and I nodded. She got up and gave me a big hug. At that moment, I wanted to cry. It almost felt like I was hugging my momma. Her arms were so strong.

"Thank you," I told her, prolonging the hug.

"You're welcome baby. I'm going to finish up dinner. Y'all get comfortable."

"Do you need some help?" I offered.

"No thanks baby. I'm almost finished." Ms. Beverly gave me another smile before walking towards the kitchen.

I turned to Lex. "Your mom is so nice. I like her," I said.

"Yeah, she cool. Why you ain't tell her what you did to hook me?" he asked, and I giggled.

"'Cause I'on be doing nothing. I'mma saint."

Lex looked at me and smirked. "Yo' ass wasn't no saint last night when I was between them legs," he teased while gripping my thigh.

"Boy quit talking like that. The kids in the room," I snickered.

"Raegan don't know what I'm saying, and Macy ain't paying me no attention. Her ass too caught up in that show."

Just then the doorbell rang. "Lex get that for me. I'm sure it's your sister," Ms. Beverly called to him.

"I'll be right back," Lex told me as he got up and ambled to the front of the house. While he went to get the door, I got on the floor and laid beside Macy and Raegan. Macy was sitting on a big blanket, and Raegan was in her car seat. It was so cute how they both were sitting quietly watching TV.

"You like this show?" I asked Macy. I had gotten so attached to this little girl. It was like I had another daughter. She felt the same way about me too. Whenever I came around, she was always under me.

"Mhm," she nodded without breaking eye contact with the television.

"Here she is right here," I heard Lex say as he walked back into the den. I got up to prepare myself to meet his sister. However, when I saw one of the girls that was with Lex, I could have shitted a brick.

What the fuck?

"Bae this my sister, Ivy, and this her best friend, Landi. Y'all this is Kiana," he told them.

"Hey," I whispered as Landi and I locked eyes. She was mean mugging the shit out of me, and Ivy was just looking. I thought his sister was gonna say something slick, but her response was completely different.

"Okay Lex, she's pretty. She kind of favors Lauren London," Ivy complimented.

"Thanks! You're pretty too." I gave her a half smile. *Landi must didn't tell her.*

"I like that dress too," she said.

Ivy looked identical to their mother, only she was just a few shades lighter and her hair was longer. Out of the corner of my eye, I could see Landi smirk. For the life of me I couldn't understand why my past kept coming back to haunt me. What were the chances Lex would be connected to somebody I hated?

"So this the girl you been talking about?" Landi asked Lex. I cut my eyes at her. Other than gaining about fifteen pounds, her dumb ass still looked the same. The new weight gain didn't make her look better either because it was mostly in her stomach.

"Yeah, this her. Why?" he asked.

"Hmph," she mumbled. "Ivy, I'mma go speak to momma," she announced as she walked out of the room.

"Wassup with her?" Lex questioned.

Ivy gave Lex this weird look that I didn't like. It was as if she was trying to tell him something with her eyes.

"I'mma go say hey to momma too. It was good to meet you, Kiana. Macy come with Tete," Ivy said. Macy stood up and ran to her.

I stood there for a minute with my mind wandering out of control.

"You good?" Lex questioned.

I looked him in the eyes. "I know that girl," I mumbled.

"Who you talking about? Landi?"

"Mhm, that's one of the girls I was telling you about who jumped me." I'd never mentioned Landi's name because it wasn't important, but I had told Lex about the situation.

He shook his head. "That's why she started tripping. Let me go holler at Ivy and let her know what's up."

"That's okay. I'mma just leave." I went to grab my stuff, but he stopped me.

"Nah, don't leave," he said.

"Lex, I can't stay in hur' with that bitch. It's best for me to leave so I don't disrespect yo' momma's house."

"I understand where you coming from but don't let her run you off. You didn't do shit wrong in that situation. If anybody should leave, it should be her."

"But that's your sister's best friend. She gon' feel some type of way about you making her leave for me."

"My sister ain't like that. Landi is known to keep up stuff so trust me on this. I'mma handle it," he promised. I shook my head. Everything inside was telling me to leave.

"Aight I'll stick around for now, but if she doesn't leave then I'm gone."

"She gon' leave. Just sit tight until I come back." After putting another kiss on my lips, Lex disappeared from the room.

Ain't this some shit?

***

A few hours later…

"Did you enjoy yourself?" Lex asked.

"Yeah, it was cool," I told him.

We were now at Lex's place. We'd put the kids down for bed and came to his room to chill for the night. True to his word, he got rid of Landi's ass. I was happy about that, but at the same time I was a little embarrassed. Since Landi acted a fool, we had to explain to Lex's momma why Lex was making her leave. I hated she had to hear that bullshit about me.

"Aye, what's wrong?" Lex climbed on top of me and put gentle kisses on my neck.

"I'm just wondering if all this is too much for you." I looked him in the eyes.

"Whatcha mean?" he asked between kisses. He moved his lips up to mine and started to passionately tongue me down.

"You can have any girl you want. Why not be with someone who don't have all this baggage?"

"You right about that," he mumbled, and I pursed my lips together.

"Really Lex?" I hit his shoulder. He cracked a sly grin.

"Nah seriously. You may have done some things I don't agree with, but that still don't change the fact your heart is in a good place. You just needed the right nigga to come into your life and show you what real love is," he stated.

I nodded, liking his answer. "Thank you. That means a lot to hear you say that."

"Ain't no thang. I told you before I'm in this with you. Just as long as you always keep it real like you been doing, I'mma stay down with ya."

"I know you are baby," I gushed.

"Now are we done with this sentimental shit? I'm trying to get between them thighs." While pulling my shirt up, he pushed my legs apart. I giggled as I tried to close my legs back.

"What you doing?" Lex panted as his hands roamed my body.

"I need to take a shower first." Lex pulled up my bra and slipped one of my breasts out. When he licked my nipple, my panties became wet. "C'mon baby I feel dirty," I whined. He slid his hand underneath my dress and started to play with my wetness.

"I can deal with a lil funk," he teased.

"Hol' up now. My pussy ain't funky nigga," I said as I pushed his hand away and slid out the bed.

"I know that, I'm just fuckin' around. C'mon, let's go take a shower." He got up and walked behind me as I headed to the bathroom.

Forty-five minutes later we were back in bed smoking a blunt. We'd done it two times before finally cleaning ourselves. My body was relaxed, and my mind was carefree. I hadn't felt this content in a long time. And just to think, I wasn't even on Mollys. In fact, it had been weeks since I last popped one. With Lex's help, I was trying my best to kick that habit.

"I need to run off for a minute," Lex suddenly announced.

I glanced at him. "Where you going?" I asked.

"One of my clients want me to do a tattoo. It shouldn't take too long."

"Okay baby. We'll be right here." I smiled. Normally I would be suspicious of a man telling me he was leaving in the middle of the night, but for some reason I trusted Lex.

After we smoked for about another ten minutes, Lex got up to get dress. I finished the rest of the blunt we'd been smoking and put it out. With a big smile on my face, I watched him as he moved around the room. His firm athletic calves looked good in the cargo shorts he was wearing, and his strong biceps in that fitted tee just did something to me. I swear I loved this nigga's dirty drawers. "I'll be back in a few," he said before kissing my lips.

"Okay baby be safe," I mumbled as my eyes suddenly became heavy. My sleepiness had just hit me hard.

Lex started chuckling. "Love yo' ass. I'll be back soon." He said it so smoothly I wouldn't have heard him had there been any ounce of sound.

I snapped my head around. "Wait!" I called out to him just as he hit the doorway.

"Wassup?"

"Did you just say you love me?"

"Yeah. Why?" He looked confused.

"Boy, you can't just be dropping that on me like you been saying it all along."

Lex shook his head. "I have been saying it, you just ain't been listening." He smiled.

Brisham

A week later…

"Here the fuckin' money." I slammed the big envelope down onto the car as I shot daggers at Danika and the other bitch. It didn't take me no time to get the money. I had the shit in a safe back at the crib. I figured the quicker I gave these bitches what they wanted, the quicker they would let Kylisha go. They had me meet them at this wooded area right outside the city limits.

Danika slid the envelope off the car and handed it to ol' girl. The broad took a few stacks out and started to thumb through them. "Where the fuck is my baby momma?" I gritted.

"Calm down. We'll get to that in a few minutes," the bitch said with a grin. I wanted to slap the shit out of her ass.

"Nah, fuck all that. You said once I gave you the money you would let her go."

"I know what I said, but first I need to make sure everything is good." After counting the money, she looked back at me. "Thank you, it's all here."

"Tell me where I can find my baby momma?"

"Give us ten minutes, and we'll call you with a location."

"Hell nah. Tell me where my son's momma is right now bitch!" I barked.

"You are so hostile. Danika told me about your lil habit. Maybe you need to pop a pill."

"Fuck you bitch!"

"Mmm, maybe after we handle this business. Your dick game was kind of official" she laughed.

Danika's hoe ass started giggling too.

I tried to lunge at the bitch, but Danika raised a pistol, making me take a step back. "Don't even think about it nigga. I will blow your head off," she threatened. I bit down on my tongue to the point I drew blood. I had my pistol in my waist, but I knew it wouldn't be a good idea to use it. If I killed these hoes, I would never get Kylisha back. Plus, I didn't know if they were working with somebody else on this setup.

"Just sit tight. We'll be in touch in just a few," the nameless bitch said before they dropped down into the car and sped off.

"Goddamn!" I roared, looking around. Now they had the money and Kylisha. What if they did something to her and had no plans to give her back. I felt like a damn fool for giving up the dough without making sure they held up their end of the deal. Impatiently, I sat for about fifteen minutes waiting for the call to come. I kept glancing over my shoulder every few minutes, thinking they would return. Just when I was about to jump in my whip and get the fuck out of here, my cell rang.

"Yeah?" I quickly answered.

"Go back out where you came in. You'll find her to your far left behind the big row of trees."

"How I know you telling the truth?" I asked. I had already got inside of my car and was headed that way.

"I'm not lying, she's there. It was good doing business with you," the broad uttered before hanging up.

I threw my phone on the passenger's seat and started to speed down the dirt road. When I made it to the location she gave me, I parked my car and hopped out. I then ran over to the trees. Almost immediately, I spotted Kylisha laying on her side. I breathed a sigh of relief.

"Brisham," she mumbled with tears falling down her cheeks. Her clothes were disheveled, dirt was on her face, and grass was in her hair. After untying her hands, I picked Kylisha up and carried her to my car.

"It's aight shawty. You safe now," I assured her. Opening the back door, I slid Kylisha inside and put her seatbelt on. I went around to my side of the car and got in.

"Brisham please get me out of here," she started to sob as she looked around frantically.

"I'm leaving right now, and ain't nobody gonna hurt you again." I threw my car into drive and peeled off. It was a long drive back to the city, so I cut the radio up to drown out Kylisha's sobs. I needed to think and couldn't do that with her crying.

***

We had been back at the crib for a little over two hours. After helping Kylisha get cleaned up, I went and got Skylar from daycare. I then picked up some food for Kylisha to eat. She was just finishing her meal and now it was time for me to ask her some questions.

"I understand you just went through a lot, but I need you to tell me everything."

"Like what?" she asked.

"Tell me how you ended up with them?"

She nodded while sitting up in the bed. "When you put me out, I went to Nivea's house," she began. Nivea was one of Kylisha's homegirls. "I was staying over there for about a week when she introduced me to Danika. Since she would come over to the house every day, I got comfortable with her. Before I knew it, we were hanging out more than me and Nivea.

"One day she asked me to take a ride with her to pick up some money from this dude. When we got there, I didn't think much of it when she asked me to come in with her. It wasn't until after we got inside of the apartment I found out it was a setup. The other girl ambushed me. Brisham, she put a gun to my head. She told me she would kill me if I didn't tell them where you hung out at. I wouldn't tell them the address here. I didn't want them hurting Skylar."

"Did they tell you how they knew me or what problem they had with me?" I asked.

"Nope. They didn't tell me nothing, and whenever they did talk it was always out of earshot."

"So how long did they have you?"

"I don't know. I think it was about three weeks. It could have been longer."

"Was it just them?" I questioned.

"No, they brought this dude in to watch over me whenever they weren't around."

"What he look like?"

"I don't know. They had me to wear a blindfold whenever he was around. I just heard his voice."

"Why did they beat you up?"

"I'on know. I guess it was to show you they weren't fuckin' around."

"Did they keep you at the same spot?" I continued to hit her with question after question.

"Nah, they moved me the first day after we went to that apartment. C'mon Brisham. I'm really tired and just want to spend some time with my son before I go to sleep. How much longer do we gotta do this?" she whined.

"Just answer this last question. Did Danika ever mention the other broad's name?" I was trying to get all the info I could on these bitches. I didn't know where Danika laid her head. Anytime we fucked, it was always at a hotel. I guess neither one of us trusted the other to give up where we lived.

"Nah. She never said her name, but I think she was the one running errthang. She was always yelling at Danika."

I figured that.

"Are we done now? I just want to forget about all this shit."

"We done shawty. Tomorrow you need to call your momma. She been worried 'bout you. She filed a missing person's report."

"I'll call her," Kylisha mumbled as she rolled over and cuddled up to our son. I sat there for a minute looking at them. Even though I didn't like Kylisha in that way, I still didn't want shit to happen to her. She was Skylar's momma.

"Aye, I'mma be back in a minute. I need to go check on some things." I finally got up to go handle my business.

"Wait, you leaving us?" she squawked.

"Just for a minute. I'mma be back soon."

"Please come back soon. I'm really scared," she whined.

"Don't worry about any of that. While you were gone I got an alarm and camera's put up. I can check on y'all while I'm out."

"Okay. Thank you for putting up the money for me. I'm sorry about what happened. I shouldn't have let them come in your house, and I should have been a better mother to my son."

"Don't worry about none of that now. Just get you some rest, and I'll be back."

Natalya

"You look good," Marcellus stated as I sat down. He had me meet him at TGI Fridays downtown so we could discuss the state of our relationship.

"Thanks," I said, but my face remained stoic. Although I'd agreed to this dinner, I was still feeling some type of way. I didn't even plan to be here long. Kacen was with my mother because she had been begging for me to bring him by. I thought tonight would be the perfect opportunity for them to spend time together. I couldn't lie, a big part of me was nervous to leave him, and it wasn't because of her disease. She hadn't dealt with a baby since I was one. I just prayed that everything went okay.

"So how you been?" Marcellus questioned. I had to admit he was looking good. He was rocking a denim shirt with black jeans and a fitted cap.

"Not too good. It's hard living out of a hotel with a baby. I need to find a place quick."

"You can just come home," he said, and I smirked.

"That ain't happening no time soon," I spat.

"So when you think you will be ready to come home?"

"I told you before that ain't my home."

Just then the waitress came over and took our orders. After telling her what we wanted, she left to put in our request.

"Listen Talya, I apologize again about what I did. That shit wasn't cool."

"No it wasn't. You broke my trust. I can forgive you, but I won't ever be able to forget."

"I'm not asking you to. But let me ask you this… Are you ever gonna take responsibility for your part?"

I frowned. "I'll never accept responsibility for you sticking your dick in another woman."

Marcellus shook his head. "That ain't what I mean."

"What do you mean?" I snarled.

"So you didn't use a nigga to get over your heartbreak with dude?"

"I didn't use you."

Marcellus sat back in his seat and stared at me. "How you expect me to keep it real, but you ain't doing the same?" I sighed.

He was right. It wasn't fair for me to put this all on him. Don't get me wrong, he was foul as hell for fuckin' off. At the same time, I did play a part in this.

"If you feel I did then I apologize. That wasn't my intention, I really did care for you," I told him.

"Let's just start over fresh," he said.

"That ain't gon' happen. You have another baby on the way with your baby momma. You expect me to just accept that."

"She ain't pregnant," he said.

"How you know?"

"Because I made her take a pregnancy test in front of me," he uttered. I shook my head.

"Hmm. Well good for you," I spat.

"Shawty we can work this shit out."

"How you expect us to do that? Even though she ain't pregnant, you still slept with her without using a condom. I had to go to the doctor just to make sure I didn't have any diseases. If you don't value your own life to wrap it up while you out in these streets, how do you expect me to trust you with mine?"

"Cause I'm done with all that. You ain't ever gotta worry about me fucking off again."

"Tuh! The lies you tell."

"I'm serious. Just give me another chance and I'll prove it to you." He looked into my eyes. It sounded sincere, but I wasn't sure. This was Marcellus we were talking about here. Could he ever be faithful?

"Ion know Marcellus, I need time." He sighed.

“I can respect it.”

“Can you?” I lifted a brow.

“I’on like it, but I can respect your decision. Just promise you won’t get with nobody else until we figure our situation out.”

“Trust me, I ain’t thinking about another relationship.”

He gave me a small grin. “How your momma doing?” he asked moving the conversation alone. I’d mentioned to him about her condition. He was very sympathetic and told me to let him know if she needed anything. That’s what had me so confused. Even with this other shit, Marcellus was always there for me.

“She’s doing okay. Just taking it one day at a time.”

“That’s wassup. You just need to be there for her when she needs you.”

“Yeah, I agree,” I nodded.

“Emani asked about you.”

“For real? How my baby doing?” I asked with a small smile.

“Being bad as usual,” he joked.

“She is not bad. Don’t say that because she bust you out.”

Marcellus shook his head. “It ain’t got nothing to do with that.”

Suddenly, my phone rang. I looked at the caller ID and noticed it was Nene calling. I rolled my eyes as I put the phone back on the table. When I glanced at Marcellus, I could tell by his facial expression he was wondering who it was. I didn't give him the satisfaction of revealing shit. He'd lost his privilege of knowing what I had going on.

The waitress returned with our food. After making sure we had everything, she left us to enjoy our meals. Marcellus and I made small talk about nothing in particular as we ate our food. When we were finally finished, he paid the check and left the waitress a tip.

"I had a good time," he said as he walked me back to my car.

"Yeah me too." I was honest about that. It was cool talking like we used to before we started having all those issues.

"Where we go from hur'?" he asked.

"Just give me time like I asked," I mumbled while glancing down at the ground. Marcellus lifted my chin with his hand, and gently placed a kiss on my lips.

"I'mma make it up to you," he promised.

I pulled away and got into my car. "Just call me," I said as I started my car and drove off. It was so weird, but I was actually having mixed emotions about him. I got ready to turn onto this side street when I noticed bright lights in my rearview mirror.

"Damn, cut them bright lights down," I said aloud as I tried to focus on the road in front of me. The car sped up, getting closer to me. "What the hell?"

I looked into my rearview mirror again. It was hard to see what kind of car it was because of how bright the lights were. I sped up thinking they were just trying to get around. When I did that, they sped up too but didn't go around. By now I was panicking. Picking up my phone, I quickly dialed Marcellus.

"Wassup shawty," he answered.

"I think somebody is following me," I said.

"Where you at?" he asked.

"I'm almost at Pine Street," I told him as I glanced up again. The car was now coming closer and closer.

"Aight, go to the nearest gas station and let me know where you at." As soon as he said that, the car sped up again. Right as it was about to hit me it shot down a side street. My nerves were all over the place. I literally saw my life flash before my eyes.

"Shawty what's going on," Marcellus brought me out of my thoughts.

"They drove off," I breathed.

"Go to the gas station like I told you. I'mma still meet you." I nodded as if he could see me. "You hear me Talya?"

"Yeah…yeah. Okay, I'm going there now."

"Stay on the phone," he instructed.

"Alright," I mumbled as I did what he told me.

Saadiq

A week later…

"Thank you for joining us Mr. Kamen. I'm Mr. Davison. I wanted to let you know that we've reviewed your case and your time here at the jail. In our opinion we feel you are rehabilitated. You haven't been in any trouble since you've been in here which is commendable. However, we want to hear what you have to say. Are you remorseful for what you've done, and do you feel as if you are ready to step back into the free world?" the older black man asked.

I held my breath as I glanced at the panel of parole board members. There were two other men; one black and the other white. There was also two white women. If everything went good today, I would soon be a free man. I needed this shit to work in my favor because I was ready to get to my son. Talya had went MIA again, and I wanted to find out what the hell was going on.

"Yes sir I'm ready. I've sent numerous letters to Jonathon's mother apologizing for my role in the death of her son. Jon-Jon was like a brother to me. I feel bad about what happened. Going forward, I plan to make better decisions. Also, I recently found out that I have a son myself. I've already missed so many of his milestones, and I don't want to miss another minute of his life. My place is not here anymore. It is with my son so that he doesn't go down the same road I did." I was laying this shit on thick, telling these muthafuckas everything I felt they needed and wanted to hear. I figured this was the only way they would let me out.

"Congratulations on your son. What are your plans to support him once you're released?" Mr. Davison asked.

"I'mma go back to boxing. My girlfriend been working with her dad to get fights lined up once I'm released."

"It seems you have everything figured out. With that, I'm comfortable in knowing you won't make the same mistake, right?"

"No sir." I shook my head.

"Well I don't see any reason to keep you here. Do we all agree?" he turned to the other members of the board.

"We agree," they all stated in unison.

I released the breath I was holding. This news was like music to a nigga's ears.

Mr. Davison looked at me. "Alright, let us get everything started. We'll have the sentencing judge to sign off on your release. You should expect to hear back from me soon with your release date," he explained, and I nodded with a half grin.

Shortly after Mr. Davison dismissed me back to my cell. The first thing I did was hit up ma dukes and let her know what was up. Next, I called Adore' and told her the news. After hollering at her for a minute, I hung up and called Talya. She still didn't answer. I didn't know why she was avoiding me, but I was about to find out real soon.

Kiana

"You still haven't talked to your girl?" Lex asked. I passed him a towel as he stepped out the shower. I wasn't sure what he had planned for us, but he told me to get ready. He said he wanted to take us somewhere. I'd already got the girls together and took my shower. I just needed to put on my clothes.

"Nope," I replied. Whenever I called Talya, she would send all my calls to voicemail.

"Just give her some time baby."

"I guess," I mumbled. Lex walked up behind me and put a kiss on my neck.

"Hur' up and get ready. I'm ready for you to see this surprise."

I giggled. "Why can't you tell me now?"

"It wouldn't be a surprise if I told ya. Now hur' up and get dressed," he ordered while slapping my ass.

"Keep yo hands to yourself." I pushed him, and he pretended to be hurt.

"You are so damn dramatic." I shook my head.

Thirty minutes later we were riding in the car to our destination. I glanced over my shoulder to see what the kids were doing. Raegan had fallen asleep and Macy was watching her iPad. I turned back around and opened my Instagram page. The first thing that popped up was a throwback picture Ivy posted of her and Lex. Even after all that shit went down with Landi, she still sent me a follow request. At first I thought she was just trying to lurk, but every time I made a post she always liked it. Sometimes she even made comments on my pictures.

"Did you see this picture?" I held my phone up so Lex could glance at it.

"Damn, she posted that?" he laughed.

"I know right. Y'all look like Kid and Sharane from House Party."

"Don't hate on us shawty. We were fly as hell."

"You wish nigga," I mumbled as I went to the comments. I don't know why, but something just told me to read them. A lot of people were saying how cute they looked while others made fun of their hair and outfits. A few comments down I noticed Landi's name. She had put two heart emoji's and a flame. On another comment she put, 'My favorite people. Even though I'm mad at your brother, I still love him. Tell him when he drop that bitch we can pick up where we left off.'

"Pick up where they left off? What the fuck she mean by that?" I looked to see if Ivy responded, and she had.

She told Landi she was a mess. Landi came back with another comment saying that if her brother wasn't tripping she was supposed to be her sister. She also told Ivy to tell Lex 'quit trying to save these hoes.' Ivy responded one last time with some crying laughing emojis.

I looked up from my phone with a serious attitude. *Should I check this nigga over this shit*? From what I saw, it looked like Lex and Landi had something going on. What I wanted to know was if it was before me or had his ass cheated. Is that the real reason why Landi got mad at his momma's house? Another thing, why didn't he tell me about any of this? All these thoughts were swirling through my head when I noticed us pull up to a big brick and red house. It had a two car garage and a nice big yard.

"Where are we?" I asked with an attitude.

"We're in Jennings County."

"Why?" I asked. Jennings was a city in St. Louis with a mixture of all ethnicities. It was actually a better part of the city.

"Quit asking all these questions and get yo' ass out," Lex told me.

I rolled my eyes as I slipped from the car. While he got the girls out the backseat I walked towards the house. It looked even better closer. I turned to Lex. "What is this?"

"This our new place." he smiled.

My eyes bucked. "What?"

"This all us shawty. I'm ready to take our relationship to the next level."

At that moment, I couldn't contain my smile. It was as if all the anger I was feeling was quickly forgotten.

"When we move in?" I asked.

"Whenever you ready, I got the keys right here."

I leaped into his arms. "Thank you! I love you."

Lex kissed me on the lips. "I love yo' ass too."

I was still mad about Landi, but this news was enough to make me put that situation on the back burner for now.

Natalya

Three weeks later…

Saadiq's mom called earlier today and asked if I could come over for dinner. She said she wanted to see Kacen. Even though I wasn't in the mood to leave this room, I knew I couldn't keep her grandson away. For the past couple of weeks I had only been going to work and then back to the hotel. I was still trying to deal with all this shit going on around me.

Aside from someone possibly following me around, I couldn't get the situation with Saadiq and Brisham off my mind. I wanted to know was it some truth to any of it? I guess you can say I was afraid of the answer. That's why I'd been avoiding him. Sooner or later I knew I would have to get to the bottom of this. After getting Kacen dressed, I threw on a pair of Palazzo pants, a fitted tee, and some sandals. I put my hair in a ponytail and applied a little makeup. I wasn't in the mood to get jazzy. I grabbed Kacen's diaper bag and my purse then left the hotel room.

"Hello?" I said, answering my ringing phone once I slid in my jeep.

"Wassup shawty, you good?" Marcellus asked. Since the night at TGI Fridays, we'd been talking more. He was always checking up on me to make sure nothing else happened. For the most part, he gave me space, but I could tell it was killing him that I hadn't agreed for us to get back together.

"I'm fine."

"Where lil man?"

"He's right here."

"Aight, I'm on my way to come see y'all."

"I'm not at the room right now," I told him, and the line got quiet.

"Where y'all at?" he finally asked.

"We talked about this. You gotta respect my boundaries," I sighed.

"Aight mane, just call me when y'all get back to the room."

He now had an attitude. "Okay," I said and ended the call. I wasn't worried about him being angry. He would get over it. Shit didn't work how he wanted it to.

On the way to Ms. Jennifer's house, I kept glancing in my rearview mirror. The past events had me cautious as hell. So cautious that when I noticed the same car following me for too long, I quickly dipped onto a side street. I looked into my rearview mirror again and noticed the car zoom by.

Get it together Talya.

Twenty minutes later I arrived to Saadiq's mom's house. There were a few cars parked in the yard, and I wondered who they belonged to. Stepping out, I went around the back and got Kacen. After grabbing our things, I ambled to the door.

"Mommaaa!" I called as soon as I stepped inside. I didn't see her anywhere, but I did notice several faces from the neighborhood. There were also some people from Ms. Jennifer's side of the family. They were standing around talking, eating, and drinking.

"What's going on Talya?" Uncle Joel said. Uncle Joel was Ms. Jennifer's brother.

"Hey Uncle Joel."

"How you doing beautiful? And how is my great nephew doing?" He grabbed Kacen's hand.

"We're fine. What's all this?" I waved my hand around the room.

You don't know?" he asked.

"Know what?"

Before Uncle Joel could respond, I heard a familiar voice.

"Talya," he said, and my heart briefly stopped beating.

That is not him. It couldn't be. I quickly spun around. There he was out of jail, and right here in front of me. *When and how did this happen*?

"Saadiq," I mumbled.

"Wassup shawty?" He flashed that handsome smile.

"When did you get out?"

"I got out today. C'mon we need to talk," he said.

Twenty minutes later…

Saadiq and I were now in his old room. We weren't saying anything, just looking at each other while he held Kacen. Honestly, I was too shocked to speak.

"C'mere mane and give me a hug," he told me.

Hesitantly, I walked into his arms, and I swear all the stress I was feeling melted away. Being near Saadiq was like no other feeling. When he told me he missed me, all I could do was close my eyes because this had to be a dream.

"I missed you too," I whispered.

"Ion believe you," he said.

I pulled away and took a step back. "Why didn't you tell me you were getting out?"

He smirked. "I did try to tell you, but you ain't been answering."

"I had a lot going on."

"That's all you got to say for not answering my calls? A nigga didn't know what happened. It took me telling my momma to call you over for you to answer."

"Can you take the baby to your momma? We need to talk"

"What a nigga do now?" he asked with a slight chuckle.

"I'll tell you everything when you get back."

"Aight, give me a second." Saadiq walked out of the room with Kacen. When he returned a few minutes later, I got straight to it.

"Is it true?" I asked.

"Is what true?" He looked at me strangely.

"Was Brisham the one driving that truck? And don't lie to me Saadiq."

"Who told you that?"

"Kiana told me everything. Is it true?" I repeated.

He looked me in the eye with a straight face and mumbled, "It's true."

"Saadiq, why did you take that charge if you didn't do it?" I became enraged.

"Calm down before somebody hears you."

"You think I give a fuck about somebody hearing me? This is so wrong. Why would you do that? You ruined your life because of him."

"Listen to me! It ain't as simple as you think. My uncle told me if I didn't take the charge he would do something to you and momma. I had to protect y'all by any means necessary, even if it meant taking a charge for som' shit I didn't do."

I shook my head. "I knew the story didn't add up. You would never be so reckless. What do you plan to do? We can't let them get away with this shit," I fumed.

"I'on know just yet. I'm on parole, so I can't do nothing to get into trouble. They'll send me back to jail. My son needs me."

"That's true, but we gotta do something. Let me handle it. Maybe I can set Brisham up or something."

Saadiq laughed. "This ain't no movie shawty."

"This is not funny. We gotta do something. You can't have this hanging over your head for the rest of your life."

"Hell nah. I'm not about to let you jeopardize your life. Our son needs you too," he said.

"But I—"

Suddenly, I was interrupted by someone walking into the room. When I noticed who the person was, I frowned.

What the hell is she doing here? After staring me up and down, Adore' walked towards Saadiq.

"Baby, I'm so glad to see you. I tried to get over here as fast as I could." She wrapped her arms around his waist and pecked his lips.

Wow. Was I really seeing this? I noticed this uncomfortable look on Saadiq's face. He acted like he didn't want to kiss her back. "What's this Saadiq?" I asked with a smirk.

"I'm so sorry. Where are my manners? Natalya, right? How have you been?" Adore' asked. She tried to reach out for a handshake, but I looked at her hand like it had shit on it. This bitch knew exactly who I was.

I ignored her whack ass. "Is this you?" I asked Saadiq again. He glanced back and forth between me and Adore'. "Yes or no answer," I spat.

"Yes, we're together. I know things didn't work out with you two, but it doesn't have to be any hostility. You're still family to us. You and Kacen."

By now my blood was boiling. Did this hoe just say me and my son was their family as if she'd been around forever? "Nah, ain't none of that. Me and my son ain't shit to you."

Adore' grinned. "Does it really have to be all this? I'm trying to make this situation as peaceful as possible."

"Look bitc—"

"Adore', give me a minute and let me holler at Talya." I was just about to curse her ass out when Saadiq finally found his voice.

"What?" she said.

"Give me a minute. I need to talk to her."

Adore' glared at Saadiq. "But baby, I need to talk to you too," she tried to whisper to him.

"Give me a minute," he repeated.

"Are you serious right now?" she asked.

"Leave now!" he yelled.

"Whatever," she spat as she stomped out of the room.

Saadiq looked up at me. "Look Talya, I apologize for not telling you. Whenever you were around, I could never find the right way."

"It's cool Saadiq," I forced myself to say.

"It's cool?" he asked with a puzzled look.

"I mean It's not like I don't have a relationship too. I just wish you would have given me a heads up." I tried to put up this façade like I was unbothered, but really I was hurting like hell. My heart literally felt like it had been ripped from my chest. *Is this part of the reason he told me to go on with my life*?

“Again, that’s my bad,” he uttered.

“Like I said, I’m good. Enjoy the rest of your party, and I’ll talk to you later.” I tried to walk off, but he grabbed my arm.

“Wait, I thought we were talking.”

“I don’t feel like it anymore. We can talk tomorrow.”

“Where you going?”

“Back to the hotel room,” I spat.

“Why the fuck you staying at a hotel room with my son?”

“It’s nothing.” Once again, I tried to walk off.

“Nah, you need to be telling me something. It ain’t just my son I’m worried about, it’s you too.”

“We’re not together, I don’t need you to worry about me. And our son is good.”

“Talya, quit playing with me. Why you staying at a hotel?”

I gritted my teeth. “I told you it’s nothing.”

“Fuck it you ain’t gotta tell me, but you ain’t taking him nowhere.”

"Excuse me? You been a daddy for all of what…two seconds and suddenly I'm not capable of taking care of my son? He is not staying here with you and that bitch."

"Talya, don't make me go back to jail. I swear that's what you gonna make happen if you try to leave with him. I'on give a damn what you talking about. You need to quit being so damn stubborn."

"Fine Saadiq. Kacen can stay for one night, but I swear you better not leave this house with him. If you leave, he needs to stay with momma."

"You ain't gonna stay?" he asked, and I let out a hearty chuckle.

"Um No," I muttered.

Saadiq shook his head. "You still with the shit," he laughed. I rolled my eyes at him.

"No nigga, you with the shit." I stomped out of the room. I swear nobody could keep it real nowadays.

Brisham

A few days later…

"Who the fuck is you?" I was awakened by loud voices in the living room.

"Who are you?" The other voice shouted.

Quickly I got up and made my way to the front. I found Kylisha standing at the door wearing one of my shirts. She had her finger pointed all in Valencia's face.

"Kylisha, what the fuck is you doing?" I gritted. She glanced over her shoulder at me.

"Brisham, who is this?" Kylisha questioned angrily.

"Why is you questioning me about who coming to my crib? You don't pay no bills in hur'."

She looked at me like she was shocked. I don't know why she was acting like we were together. Just because she'd been kidnapped, it didn't mean shit had changed. I still wasn't fuckin' with her like that.

Kylisha trudged off with an attitude. I shook my head as I walked to the door. "My bad about that shawty. That's my son's momma."

"She's rude as hell," Valencia spat.

"Wassup, what you doing here?"

"Brisham, what's going on? I haven't heard from you in almost a week. I've called your phone so many times, but you never answered. I finally decided to stop by after I got out of school. Is she the reason you were avoiding me?"

"Yeah, but it ain't like that. A lot of shit been going on, and I had to handle it," I explained.

"Well you could have told me. I've been worried, thinking you were probably locked up or something."

"You right, and I apologize," I found myself saying. Shawty was bringing out a different side of me that I didn't know existed. Usually I didn't answer to no fuckin' body. "Why you just standing there? Bring yo' ass in here."

She hesitated for a minute before finally stepping into the house. She looked around as if she were expecting to see Kylisha. "C'mon let's go to my room," I said, grabbing her hand.

When we made it to my room, I shut the door and told Valencia to have a seat.

"Is she back living with you?" Was her first question.

"For the time being. I need to get some shit in order first and then I'mma find her a spot."

"How does this affect us?" Valencia asked.

"I mean, from the way you talk I didn't think you was feeling a nigga." Valencia tried to hide her smile, but I spotted that shit. "So what, you are feeling me?" I asked.

"I don't know," she playfully rolled her eyes.

"Yeah, you feeling me. I been peeped that shit."

"Maybe I am. But if you want to date me then you need to get your life in order."

"Trust me, I'm working on that."

"I hope so because the way you been carrying yourself ain't gonna work. I can look at you now and tell you've been either drinking or getting high. Doing all those drugs is not good. You told me you were slowing down, but it doesn't seem that way. If you don't stop for yourself, at least do it for your kids. They need you." I peeped the sincerity in her eyes and voice.

I stood in front of Valencia and just gazed down at her. She was rocking her scrubs and a high ponytail. It wasn't no makeup on baby's face, but she still looked pretty as shit to me. Her whole demeanor just spoke to a nigga's heart. Plenty times I'd heard that I needed to leave the drugs alone, but it had never been said to me out of concern.

"I gotcha, and I'mma do better," I promised as I gently pulled her up by her arms.

"What are you doing?" she asked when I put kisses on her neck.

"What it look like?"

"No Brisham. I am not having sex with you and your baby momma is in the other room."

"Why not? We ain't together."

She shook her head, but I wasn't trying to hear that shit. In one swift motion I'd turned Valencia around, snatched her pants off, and started to bang that pussy from the back. I fucked shawty so good that by the time I finished my shirt, pubic hairs, and thighs were saturated with her juices. I'd never seen a broad come as hard as she had. While she recovered, I went and took another shower. When I came out to redress, I noticed she was knocked out cold. I left her resting in my bed while I went to handle my business. On my way out the door I checked up on Skylar and Kylisha. She still had a little attitude from earlier, but I paid that shit no mind. I let her know I would be back in a minute and to treat my company with respect.

***

Thirty minutes later…

"Wassup boi?" I said to Dro.

"Ain't shit shaking but the strippers at the club. Come in here and let me show you what I found out."

Dro was a nigga I met about two years ago. My boy Bird put me on to him. He said Dro could help me out in my line of work. Despite his name, Dro's ass was smart as hell. He'd gone to school for years and got several degrees. Although he dibbled and dabbled in some of everything, his main expertise were computers. He could probably hack into the White House shit if he really wanted to. I used him to keep me updated on police cases and other shit like that.

"What you got for me?" I asked.

"You know that video you sent me of your baby mom?" he said, referring to the one when they kidnapped Kylisha. When that broad sent it to me as a reminder to come up off that cash, I sent it Dro. I wanted to see if he could get anything that would help me find Kylisha. He was just now getting back to me.

"Yeah, what about it?"

"Well I did some playing around with it. I was able to zoom in and you won't believe what I spotted. Come take a look at this." He pointed to his computer screen where he'd zoomed in on Kylisha laying on the floor.

"What I'm looking at?" I asked, squinting my eyes.

"Right here… You see her hands? It's nothing holding them together."

I zeroed in on Kylisha's hands and he was right. "Aye, this shit don't make sense. Why the fuck would she just lay there if she could get up?"

"That's not it. Look at this…" Dro fast forwarded to the part where the person walked up and kicked Kylisha. "From a distance it looks as if the person is really kicking her but once you zoom in, you'll notice they stop just before the foot touches the body. On a phone you can't see this. Hell, it took me some time to capture it with my special equipment. I speculate she wasn't in any real danger."

"This shit was all a part of a setup, huh?" I said more to myself.

"Seems that way. If you look closely at your baby's momma face, you'll see she's not really crying," he pointed out.

I bit the inside of my jaw as I glared at the screen. *These hoes thought they were real slick.* "Man, this som' shit. I got this hoe at my crib and been catering to her thinking some shit don' happened for real. Now I'm finding out she was with them too. I should have known not to trust her hoe ass."

“Yeah, I didn’t really know how to tell you this. At the same time if it was my baby momma, I would want to know if she was on some grimy shit,” Dro stated.

“Did you get a hit off the number I sent you?” I mumbled angrily. I still couldn’t get over what he’d just shown me.

“Nah, I didn’t get anything. The number is for a TracFone.”

“At least them bitches were smart enough not to use a phone that would trace back to them.”

“Yeah, they were smart about that. If you can get me anything else to go off, shoot it to me,” he advised.

“Aight mane, I’ll hit you up. ‘Preciate this info.”

“You good homie,” Dro said.

I stood and dapped Dro up. After chopping it up for a little while longer, I left his house and headed back to the crib. I needed to figure out what I was going to do about Kylisha’s lying ass. I knew one thing, this bitch had violated for the last time. She was finna pay for this.

Kiana

A few days later…

"Kiana, did you finish packing up the stuff you wanted to keep in the kitchen? I wanna go ahead and put it on the truck before I leave to get some more boxes," Lex called to me.

For the past week we'd been moving stuff over to our new house. We started with my place first and then moved to Lex's spot. Between both our apartments there was so much shit. I was so exhausted from all this moving, and I couldn't wait until it was over. Thankfully, Lex's momma was keeping the kids for us while we handled everything.

"Yes, I got everything packed!" I yelled.

"Aight cool. Come in here for a minute," he said, and I sighed.

Climbing up from the floor, I went into the kitchen where Lex was. "Wassup baby?" I asked as I eyed him. He was wearing basketball shorts, a white tee, and work boots. He had a towel around his neck to catch the sweat dripping from his forehead. This man was so sexy to me.

"What, you tired?" He grinned.

I pursed my lips together. "What you think?"

Lex walked over to me and wrapped his arms around my waist. "It's almost over shawty. We'll be in that thang fuckin' in no time," he joked.

"Boy get yo' freaky ass away from me. Is that all you think about?" I pushed him back as he chuckled.

"Hell yeah, and you do too. You can't wait until I bend you over that kitchen counter and put this good dick in you," he said, and my clit thumped.

"C'mon Lex, quit teasing me. You know we can't afford to take no breaks. What did you want?" I whined.

"Aight, let me quit playing. Sit down for a minute."

I looked at him strangely as I pulled out a chair. "Wassup?" I asked.

"You remember the picture my sister posted of us?"

"Yeah what about it?" I mumbled. I still hadn't mentioned to Lex about the comments Landi made.

"I was on Instagram a lil while ago and saw some comments Landi put. I'on know if you saw them or not, but I wanted to address it."

"I saw 'em," I uttered.

Lex's face looked puzzled. "Why you ain't say nothing?"

"Oh, trust me I was. I just didn't want to focus on it right now because of the move."

"Is this why you been walking around with an attitude?"

"Yup, I wasn't feeling you because you didn't tell me."

"How you expect our shit to work if we don't communicate? If you have a problem with something, you need to let me know. I can't read minds shawty."

"I've tried to do that in the past, but that shit ain't ever work for me. I figured you would have just lied about it, and then I would have to bust yo head."

Lex pulled up a chair and grabbed my hands into his. "Look at me… The reason you had that problem is because of the niggas you dealt with. I ain't ever made it hard for you to talk to me about nothing, and I ain't ever lied to you about nothing."

"I heard that before. If you so different, why you ain't tell me about you fuckin' with Landi?"

"Would it have made a difference?" he questioned, and I cocked my head back.

"Damn right it would have! At least I would have known."

"What would you have done if you knew?"

"I mean, I uh—" I stammered.

"Exactly. You would have created a problem where it wasn't one, all because of y'all past issues. Besides, I didn't want it to be in your head that she had one up on you 'cause she don't. It was never anything serious with me and Landi."

Even though what Lex said made sense, the stubborn part of me wouldn't let it go. "You still could have told me," I muttered.

"Did you tell me about every dude you had sex with?" he asked.

I rolled my eyes. "No I didn't, and I don't expect you to tell me either. I just feel like you could have mentioned Landi so I wouldn't find out by her taking jabs like she did."

"You right, I guess I didn't think about it that way. When we messed around, it was some month's after Macy's momma passed. I guess you being in the picture must have triggered something. But don't even worry about it, I'mma have a talk with her."

"Uh, no you won't," I barked.

"Why you don't want me to talk to her?"

"What difference will it make? She is obviously miserable. You say y'all ain't messed around in all this time so she making herself look like a fool. Let the bitch have it. You all mine." I smiled, and Lex nodded.

"That's real mature of you shawty," he said.

"I know, huh?"

Lex kissed me. "Hell yeah, and that's why I love you."

The old me would have told him to check that bitch asap, but the new me wasn't trying to be on that. Lex and I were together, and that was all that mattered. For once my life was moving in a positive direction.

***

A few hours later…

After having the talk with Lex earlier, I felt a lot better. Shortly after he left to get some boxes. When he returned, me, him, and a few of the artists from his shop packed up his place. I ordered us all pizza to eat while we finished up everything. Once they left, I hopped into the shower. I was now ready to lay it down with my man, but first I needed to make a few phone calls.

I dialed Talya first, but she didn't answer. I called my auntie next, and she didn't answer either. Going to my messages, I shot them both individual texts, letting them know I loved them and to please call me. I knew it wouldn't do no good, but I at least wanted them to know I was thinking of them. The last call I wanted to make was to Lex's mother. I wanted to Facetime with the girls before they went to sleep. Just as I started to dial her number my phone beeped, indicating it was about to die.

I grabbed my purse to see if my charger was in there. While scrambling through my stuff, I stumbled across the bottle I kept my Mollys in. It had been almost two months since I last had one. There were some days I wanted to pop one bad as hell, but then I would tell myself I didn't need it. Now I realized keeping them in my possession would only give me a reason to come back to them.

"I don't need this shit," I mumbled as I got up from the couch. Once I made it into the kitchen, I popped the top on the bottle and dumped them all into the sink. I then cut on the water and garbage disposal. A huge sense of relief washed over me as I heard them being chomped up.

Walking back into the living room, I searched for my charger but still didn't see it. I went into the bedroom where Lex was. He was sitting on the bed watching TV.

"Bae, have you seen my charger? My phone is about to die, and I want to call the girls before it gets too late."

"Did you ever get it out of the car?"

"Damn, I forgot that's where I left it."

"You want me to go get it?" he offered.

"It's cool baby. I'll go get it."

"Aight, I'mma hop in the shower right quick. When I get out, you need to be face down, ass up." I giggled as I headed back to the front. “I ain’t playing Kiana!” he yelled as I walked outside. I shook my head.

It was now nighttime, and the neighborhood was quiet. After unlocking the door to my car, I leaned inside and spotted my charger in the cupholder. I picked it up, got out of the car, and started to make my way back to the apartment.

“There that bitch right there. I told you she was over here,” I heard someone say. I spun around and came face to face with Landi, and that bitch Kris.

I smirked at them. “What you hoes want? I ain’t fuckin’ with neither one of y’all men.”

“Bitch, I know you had something to do with Jacobi’s death,” Kris barked.

“I’on know what you talking about. I hadn’t talked to Jacobi since the day at Landi’s house,” I lied.

“Bitch quit lying,” Landi snarled. Suddenly, her ass had big balls since she was with her cousin. I guess they had put their differences aside to gang up on me.

“Landi, you are pathetic. You pretend to be this good girl but you ain’t no better than me. The only difference between us is that I own my shit. You was all on the Gram talking greasy ‘cause you knew I would see it. Well guess what bitch? It didn't work. I still got my man, and what you got?"

"I'mma whoop yo a—"

"Hol' up Landi. She gon' get hers real soon. I want this bitch to tell me what the fuck happened to my baby daddy."

"She probably had somebody to kill him," Landi spat.

"Look, I'm not about to stand here and go back and forth with y'all. That was your man, you should have known what he was into." I turned and gave both them bitches my back. Just as I was halfway to the door, I felt a pair of hands grab me. I glanced over my shoulder and saw it was Kris. "Bitch get your hands off me."

I pushed her raggedy ass back. She slapped me across the face, and I hit her with a two piece, causing her to stumble backwards. When she caught her footing, we ran full speed into each other.

At this point we were going blow for blow. Tired of playing around with this hoe, I grabbed hold of her braids and brought her face to my knee. Blood instantly started squirting everywhere. Just as I was getting the best of her, Landi's hoe ass jumped into the fight. She hit me in the back of my head, and I became dazed for a minute. That gave Kris the opportunity to get me down on the ground. They both started kicking me all over my body. I tried blocking most of the kicks, but they were getting the best of me.

"Stupid bitches!" I yelled while grabbing Landi's leg. When she fell on the ground, I used all my strength to get Kris off me before climbing on top of her. Lifting my fist, I brought it down into that hoe's face repeatedly.

"Get the fuck off my cousin!" Kris yanked me by my hair. I stopped hitting Landi to get Kris' hands off me. She was pulling my hair so hard I could feel it splitting from the roots.

"Let go of my hair bitch," I seethed. Just then I felt a piercing pain suddenly shoot through my chest. "What the fuck?" I mumbled. When I looked down, I saw that my white shirt was completely covered in blood. Frantically, my eyes darted to the swiss knife in Landi's hand.

"What now bitch?" she spat, stabbing me again in my stomach. I doubled over in pain.

"Ooooh!" I howled from the depths of my soul. It felt like my insides were on fire. She didn't stop there though. She started to stab me again, and again, and again. At that instance everything became a big blur. Kris must have realized what happened because she let go of my hair and just looked at me. Weakly, I stood up and stumbled towards Lex's apartment.

"C'mon bitch, let's go before somebody sees us," I heard Kris say as I grabbed hold of the doorknob.

"Lexxxxx!" I mustered up enough strength to scream his name. It was so hard for me to breathe. I could tell I was losing lots of blood from how weak I was. By the time I got the door open, I could no longer stand up. I fell face forward on the floor.

"Shawty what you in hur' knocking—Oh shit! Kiana baby!" Lex shouted.

My eyes fluttered, and my body shook. "Help me," I managed to get out.

"What the fuck happened to you? C'mon shawty, don't die on me. Hold on, I need to get some help. C'mon baby." As Lex scrambled to get his phone I thought back over my life. It had been a long tough road for me. Losing those I cared for most was the hardest part, but in the midst of my storm I also found love. Lex had shown me love in a way I thought I'd never experience. He truly was Godsent.

Then there was my daughter. I loved that little girl so much. She was the joy of my life. Who would take care of her if I wasn't around? With each thought I had, my eyes became heavier. I could literally feel my life slipping from me. For a brief second, I wondered to myself if I had to do it all over again would I do anything differently. The answer was easy. Yes, I would. It was just too bad there was no rewind button on life.

Cough! Cough!

"Shit, it's so much blood. C'mon Kiana, hold on. I called for help. They gon' be hur' soon. Just don't die on me shawty. I love you. You gon' be my wife." Lex grabbed my hand and squeezed it in his.

It's too late I tried to say aloud, but no words would come out. At that moment, my eyes closed completely, and I released the last breath I would ever take on this earth.

Natalya

Early the next morning…

It was five o'clock in the morning and someone was beating on my hotel room door. "Who the fuck is that?" I said to myself. Thankfully, Kacen wasn't here. I'd been letting him stay with his daddy since they needed to catch up. I did stress to Saadiq I didn't want his new bitch nowhere near my baby. He claimed he would never do that, but you never know. Climbing out of the bed, I tipped to the door to check the peephole. When I saw who it was, I slightly frowned.

"What are you doing here and where is my baby?" I questioned Saadiq.

He walked into the room before answering. "He cool, he at the crib with ma dukes."

"Is something wrong?" I asked as I turned to him.

"Nah, ain't nothing wrong," he said and walked over to me. Before I realized what he was doing, Saadiq had already picked me up like I weighed two pounds and covered my lips with his. Initially, I was caught off guard, but I didn't protest. For some reason I felt we both needed this. It didn't matter to me that he had somebody else. I wanted to be selfish.

I was brought out of my thoughts when Saadiq lifted my gown and popped one of my breasts out. Like a baby, he took it into his mouth and hungrily started to feast on it. My mouth hung open as his thick tongue flicked all over my nipple.

"Oooh," I moaned. The touch of his hands on my body brought back this familiar feeling. All my senses instantly started to come alive. Before long, we were both attacking one another. By the time we were naked, I was so damn wet. I mean my shit was leaking like a faucet. Spinning me around, Saadiq grabbed my arms from the back as he slid into me.

Like a cup he immediately filled me up. I whimpered because of how good it felt. With this subtle roughness, he pumped in and out of me. He then leaned over and put kisses on my neck and back, causing chills to shoot up my spine. I pulled one hand free and reached between my legs. Gently grabbing his dick, I started to stroke him as he released several low grunts.

"I still love you Talya," he whispered. He had his hand wrapped around my neck from the back as he pummeled into me.

"I still love you too," I said, becoming choked up. I didn't even realize it, but tears were falling down my cheeks. I loved this man so much it was scary at times. Saadiq pulled out and flipped me onto my back. Without giving me time to adjust, he plunged back inside. I wrapped my legs around his waist as he slammed into me.

"Uh! Uhhhh!" I let out. This dick was feeling so good it had me losing my damn mind. Sex with Marcellus was good, but it had never been this passionate. At that moment I felt the hole in my heart slowly close. For the next few hours Saadiq was inside of me like he permanently belonged there. We did sixty-nine and changed several positions before we got into the shower where we made love under the water. I can't tell you how many times I came. All I know is by the time we finished I was passed out, sleeping like a baby.

***

"Mmm, what time is it?" I asked, opening my eyes. I noticed Saadiq was just staring at me. "What are you looking at?"

"You beautiful when you sleep," he said, and I blushed. There was this maturity about Saadiq I'd noticed since I visited him in jail. Usually he would have something slick to say, but as of lately he'd been cool. Not that I didn't like his goofy side, but I enjoyed this side better.

"Thank you," I mumbled. He leaned in and kissed my lips before pulling me on top of him.

"What about Kacen? We gotta get him. Don't your momma gotta work?" I asked. Now that I had time to think, I was starting to feel guilty about what we'd done this morning.

"Nah, she off today so he good."

"Oh," I mumbled as I felt his hardness poke me. I looked down into his eyes. "You gon' handle that?" He asked.

"Mhm," I nodded as he lifted me up and put his dick at my entrance. I slowly slid down his pole. Planting my hands on his chest, I started to rock back and forth. He grabbed my butt cheeks and smashed me into him. As I bounced up and down, I could feel him hitting my spot. My breasts were flopping out of my gown so Saadiq gripped one with his hand. It felt so good that all I could do was lay my head on his chest and enjoy the ride. Ten minutes after we started our quickie, Saadiq was dumping his seeds deep inside of me.

We got up and took a quick shower together. Once we were finished, I thought he was going to leave. Instead, he asked me to take a ride with him. Since I didn't have anything planned and it was the weekend, I told him I would. The first stop we made was to the boxing gym. After Saadiq chopped it up with a few people, we left there and headed to the mall.

Saadiq picked out a few new outfits, some shoes, and got his haircut. He offered to buy me something, but I declined. When I asked him where he got the money from to buy all this stuff, he told me he had it put away. I still didn't feel comfortable taking anything from him since he'd just gotten out of jail. I figured he needed to get back on his feet.

Once we left the mall we went and grabbed a bite to eat. We were now sitting at the Cheesecake Factory as my phone rang with another call from Kiana. She'd been calling me since the night before, but of course I didn't answer. I rolled my eyes as I hit the ignore button. She knew I didn't have shit to say to her ass.

"Who is that?" Saadiq questioned.

"Kiana," I muttered.

"What, you ain't talking to her?"

"Nope."

"Why, because of that shit?" he asked, and I sighed.

"Yes Saadiq."

"That's yo' girl. You gotta talk to her."

"Fuck her," I spat.

"So you don't plan to ever talk to her again?"

"I don't know. I haven't thought about all that. Do you plan to talk to Brisham?"

"That's different," he uttered.

"No, it's not different."

"You being stubborn right now."

"Would you stop saying that, I'm not being stubborn. She lied to me about what happened that night. To me she played a bigger part than Brisham did. All this shit could've been dealt with if she'd told what she knew. I'm not sure if I'll stay mad forever, but right now I just don't wanna talk to her."

"I'm saying tho, I don't blame her for this shit so don't feel like you betraying me by talking to her."

"Look, I don't want to talk about her anymore. What I wanna know is what you plan to do. I think you should go to the police."

"Nah, I can't do that. My uncle got major connections. Before I was released he came and talked to me."

"What did he say?" I asked.

"The same shit he been saying all this time… Don't run my mouth and we won't have any problems."

"This ain't right Saadiq. He needs to be stopped before he does somebody else like this."

"Trust me I know. I just need time to think about everything. Right now, you, my momma and my son are my main focus." I sighed because all this was pissing me off. How could he let them just get away with ruining his life…hell our lives?

"Let me ask you a question?" he said.

"What?" I asked.

"Why you staying at a hotel and not with that nigga?"

I smirked at him. "His name is Marcellus."

"I know what his name is. You can refer to him by his government, but I don't have to. Now answer my question."

"If you must know, we're separated."

"Why is that?"

"Damn, you are nosey. You don't hear me asking you about your relationship."

"Just answer my question, ol' smart mouth ass girl."

"It's complicated," I mumbled.

"What's so complicated?" he continued to prod.

"Damn Saadiq, we broke up because he cheated." I huffed.

"I'm sorry to hear that."

"Yeah right! I know you wanna laugh and tell me how you told me so. Have at it."

He shook his head. “What kind of sucker nigga you take me for? I would never laugh at your pain. If anything, you got me wanting to do somethin’ to dude.”

“No Saadiq, this is my situation. I can handle it.”

“I ain’t gon’ get in it unless he gets out of line,” he uttered, and I let out a slight chuckle.

“Some things never change, huh?”

“You know how I get down. Are you ready to go?” he asked.

“Mhm,” I mumbled.

Saadiq pulled out some money to pay the bill, but I told him I had it. I guess he must have felt some type of way because when we made it back to the car he was still going off.

“Talya if I tell you I’m good, then just accept that.”

“Whatever Saadiq. It’s not that big of a deal.” I waved it off.

“It is a big deal. Yo ass still hardheaded, and don’t ever li…”

I tuned him out when I noticed a familiar car. It looked like the same blue car from the school a while back. The one that tried to hit me.

“What’s wrong with you?” Saadiq questioned.

“That’s them,” I whispered.

"That's who?" he asked.

I ignored his question as I watched two people get out the little blue car. "Oh hell nah!" I spat.

"What? What?" Saadiq asked.

I hopped out of the car without replying to him. Marching over, I approached the people just as they were walking in my direction. "Bitch, you tried to run me over!" I shouted.

Ariel looked up at me with a sly grin on her face. She was with this short light skinned big girl.

"I don't know what you're talking about," she lied through her teeth.

The stupid smirk on her face pissed me off, so I leaped on that bitch and started to beat her ass.

"Get this crazy bitch off me," she shouted as I went in.

Saadiq ran up and tried to pull me off her. "C'mon Talya, let her go. Somebody gonna call the police."

"I don't give a fuck! Let them call 'em," I fumed.

I was banging Ariel's head against the ground as she screamed. It took Saadiq and the girl to break us apart. Looking at her in disgust, I hacked back and spit on Ariel. "Raggedy ass bitch!" I bellowed.

"Aight, you handled it. Let's go now," Saadiq urged, but it was too late. A police cruiser swooped into the parking lot and stopped right in front of us.

Two black officers immediately hopped out. "What's going on here?" one of them asked.

"She just attacked me for no reason. You need to lock her up now!" Ariel screamed.

"Alright ma'am, calm down," the officers told her as she went on a rant.

"Is this true ma'am?" one of them asked.

I slowly nodded my head. "Yes, I attacked her because she tried to run me over with her car."

"That's not true," Ariel lied.

"It is true. She was outside of my job, and this is the car she tried to hit me with." I pointed.

The officers got a statement from the girl who was with Ariel. They tried to get Saadiq to tell them what happened, but he told them he didn't see the altercation. I guess one witness must have been enough because they arrested me. After slapping on some handcuffs, they read my rights before hauling my ass off to jail.

Saadiq

Since I was out on parole, I had to have ma dukes bail Talya out. We took Kacen to Talya's momma, and she told us to keep her updated on everything. Talya's bond was posted for twenty-five thousand which meant we had to pay ten percent. I gave momma the money to take care of it. We were now waiting on them to process her release. As I looked through my phone, I noticed that nigga Marcellus come into the jail. We locked eyes before he went to the clerk's desk. A few minutes later he walked over to us.

"How you doing Ms. Jennifer?"

"I'm fine Marcellus. How are you?"

I shot my eyes at my momma. Even though she'd been knowing Marcellus since the days him and Gee kicked it, I didn't like how comfortable he was with her.

"Do you know what happened? I got a call from my daughter's momma mentioning something about her and Talya getting into an altercation. She told me Talya was arrested."

Momma glanced at me before looking back at Marcellus. "I'm not sure what's going on baby. You will have to talk to Natalya when they release her."

"Aight, I'll do that. 'Preciate it," he said and walked off. He sat in a chair a few seats down from us.

It was obvious me and the nigga didn't fuck with each other because neither one of us said anything to the other. As far as I was concerned, we didn't have to ever hold a conversation. To be honest, dude could go back where he came from because I had Talya covered.

Just then my phone rang. When I looked at the caller ID, I saw it was Adore'. She'd been blowing a nigga up for the past two days. She wanted us to spend time together but right now I wasn't feeling it. "Wassup?" I answered.

"Where are you? I've been calling all day," she said.

"I'm out right now," I gritted. I hated when she called questioning me.

She sighed into the phone. "So when am I supposed to get some of your time?" she asked.

"Just let me handle this business, and I'll let you know," I told her. I liked Adore', but she was too clingy. I couldn't stand that shit.

"I don't like this," she muttered.

"You don't like what?" I questioned with a frown.

"How you keep blowing me off. You're acting like I don't exist."

"I told you I got a lot going on. Plus, I need to spend time with my son. If you don't understand that, I don't know what to tell you. Now let me hit you back."

"Alright Saadiq. Just call me if you ever think about it," she remarked sarcastically.

"Aight mane." I ended the call just as I saw Talya walk from the back.

Me and Marcellus jumped up at the same time and approached her.

"Shawty you good?" he asked her. I bit the inside of my jaw as I ice grilled his ass.

"No, I'm not okay. Your baby momma tried to run me over and I told the police."

"You sure about that?" he asked her, and that shit pissed me off.

"Nigga, she ain't gotta lie," I snarled.

"Look mane, I ain't got no issues with you. I was trying to talk to her," the nigga said.

"Muthafucka, I don't give a damn who you were talking to." I looked him dead in the eyes.

"My nigga, I promise you don't want no beef with me. I said we ain't got no issues but if you wanna take it there it ain't no problem. One thing you need to know about me is that I'on do a whole lot of talking."

"Alright that's enough. C'mon Saadiq," Momma said, grabbing my arm.

"Yes, let me handle this Saadiq. Please go to the car and wait," Talya said, further pissing me off. She was dismissing me like I was some boy.

"I ain't going nowhere. Don't nobody pump no fear in my heart, definitely not this nigga," I raged.

Talya put her hand on my chest. "It's not about that. You just got out of jail, and you don't need to go back. Do this for me please," she pleaded.

"Aight mane I'll go, but hur' up so we can dip. We need to go get our son." I glanced at Marcellus before walking out.

"Saadiq wait up," my momma said as I ambled outside.

"What ma?"

"Listen to me, you need to calm down boy. I understand you feel some type of way about Marcellus being around, but it ain't nothing you can do. Talya gonna have to handle this situation. I don't need you going back to jail over some bullshit."

"It's cool ma," I said as I got into the car.

She grabbed my chin and forced me to look at her. "It's not cool. You have no idea how much I was stressed when you were locked up. Saadiq, I cannot go through that again. It was like I lost a piece of me. Do you understand what I'm saying?"

I glanced into my momma's eyes and saw the sincerity in them. Never had it dawned on me how much this affected her until now.

"I ain't gon' do nothing to get myself in trouble so I want you to quit stressing. Aight?" I pulled her into my arms and hugged her.

"I hope you keep your word."

"You got my word ma," I told her, but honestly that shit was gonna be hard.

Marcellus

"Shawty calm down. I'mma handle this situation."

"How are you going to handle it Marcellus? Huh?"

"I'on know, but I'mma do something."

"How about backing me up with the police, can you do that?" she asked.

"Shawty, you know a nigga don't do the police. Besides, that's Emani's momma. I can't send my baby momma to jail."

She shook her head. "Fuck you and your baby momma. That bitch tried to hit me, and she probably the one who been following me." I grabbed her arm, and she snatched it back.

"Get yo fuckin' hand off me," she seethed. I glanced around. We were now outside of the police precinct. A nigga didn't feel comfortable being nowhere near here, but with that bitch ass nigga Saadiq around I knew I wouldn't be able to get her to ride off with me.

"Talya chill. I ain't trying to be doing all this in front of the police station. I'm telling you I'mma handle everything, but you ain't trying to hear me."

"All you do is say you gonna handle some shit, but you keep letting that bitch slide. I'm done Marcellus."

"What you mean, you done?" I questioned, my face twisted in confusion.

"I can't do this with you no more. I thank you for everything you did for me and Kacen, but this is it for us."

"So now you mad at me for what she did?"

"Damn right! I shouldn't have even let things go this long. When I caught her kissing you I should have walked away then. I guess you can say I learned my lesson."

I understood she was upset, but she was straight pissing me off. "So just like that, you done?"

"Mhm," she mumbled.

"Nah, you ain't even finna tell me this all on me. You want to shit on a nigga since yo boy is out." At first I didn't know why she was avoiding me the past few days, but once I saw Saadiq here I knew what time it was.

"Saadiq ain't got nothing to do with this. It's about you and your baby momma."

I don't know what came over me, but I just snapped. All the shit I'd been through with her ass and she thought I would just let her walk away. I grabbed her by the arm and pulled her over to me. "I told you before you ain't leaving me." I looked her dead in the eyes.

"You can't make me be with you," she snarled.

"Aye nigga! Get your fuckin' hands off her." Saadiq suddenly ran up and pushed me back. We immediately squared up. I swung first, hitting him in the jaw.

"No Saadiq, don't do this," Talya whined.

The nigga countered back with a punch to my temple. I ain't gon' lie, that shit dazed me for a minute. I swung, trying to knock this faggot's head off, but ended up hitting Talya in the back of the head because she jumped in between us.

"Muthafucka I'mma kill you," Saadiq barked. I glanced to my left and noticed his momma marching towards us.

"Saadiq, get your ass to the car before the police come out here," she fussed.

"Yeah bitch boy, listen to your mommy," I chuckled.

He tried to come back for me, but Talya and his momma jumped between us. When I noticed an officer walk up, I got myself together.

"Is there a problem?" the big, burly white officer asked. I glared at Saadiq. "Is there a problem?" the officer repeated.

"Nah officer, ain't no problem. I was just having a lil conversation."

"You all need to move it along," he ordered.

"No problem. I'mma see you Saadiq." I threw over my shoulder as I got the fuck from around there. Hurriedly, I jogged back to my car, jumped inside, and peeled off.

***

Thirty minutes later…

A little while later I found myself at Ariel's house, waiting outside in the car. I was so fucking heated I couldn't put this situation off a minute later. Ariel's hoe ass had put a nigga in a fucked up position. I didn't need these issues in my life.

A few minutes later I saw Ariel pull up. I watched her let our daughter out of the car through the rearview mirror. When she started to approach my whip, I opened the door and climbed out.

"Daddy!" Emani squealed as she ran straight to me. I bent down and picked her up.

"Wassup daddy's girl?" I glanced at Ariel's ass standing there looking stupid with her eye fat as hell. I always knew Talya had a mean ass punch.

"Damn mane, she lit your ass up," I mumbled.

"Whatever Marcellus." Ariel stomped up to her door. I put my daughter down and we followed behind her.

"Daddy, do you want to see my new toys?" Emani asked once we made it inside.

"In a minute baby. Go to your room and let me talk to your momma."

"Okay," she said and shot out the room.

"What do you want Marcellus? I ain't in the mood for this shit." Ariel said with an attitude.

"I'mma ask you this one time and one time only. Was that you that tried to hit her?"

"No! Why would you ask me som' shit like that? Her crazy ass is lying," she yelled.

"I told you I was only gonna ask once."

"Okay, and I'm telling you I didn't do it."

I bit down on the inside of my jaw. "You lying."

"No I'm not," she denied.

"Yo, you lying. I know because the little blue car Talya told me about is the same one Liberty drives," I bellowed. Liberty is Ariel's coworker and friend. They'd been hanging with each other for like six years. Ariel thought she was so slick but was too dumb not to use a car that would be linked back to her. I can't say for sure if she was actually gonna try to kill Talya, or if she was doing the shit to scare her. Either way it went, she had fucked up.

When I noticed the nervous, guilty look on her face I went in. “Ol’ stupid ass girl, why would you do some shit like that? Now you gonna have the muthafucka folks knocking at my door.”

“I’m sooo sorry. I wasn’t really going to hit her,” she said as she began to sob.

“Shut the fuck up! You ain’t sorry. I ain’t going down for yo’ bullshit. You need to take yo’ ass down to that precinct and tell them muthafuckas you ain’t pressing charges against that girl.”

“What if she tries to have me locked up?” She had the nerve to ask.

“Then you take yo’ fuckin’ charges like a woman. Until you handle that, I’m taking Emani. If you get her back depends on your next move. And let me make this shit real clear for you…if you say one muthafuckin’ thing to get me locked up, I swear yo momma gon’ be looking for a black dress. Even on the inside I’mma still have connections,” I warned her.

“Please don’t take my baby Marcellus,” she begged.

“Handle that fuckin’ business.”

Ariel slid on the floor crying her eyes out. If there was one good thing about her trifling ass, she loved the fuck out of our daughter. I couldn’t deny that. Not having her anymore would be like losing a part of herself. After having Emani grab a few things, we left and headed to my house. I needed to figure out a way to get my girl back. I couldn't lose her to that nigga again.

Natalya

Sighing, I fell back onto the couch and closed my eyes for a brief second. This had been one hell of a day. I couldn't believe I went to jail. Because of that bitch I now had a pending case against me. Even though I tried to tell the police what she did, they still said the case would stick if she pressed charges. They stated it wasn't self-defense if I attacked her first.

I was beyond frustrated. Is this what my life had come to, fighting every time I turned around? The silver lining is that I'd finally done something I should have done a long time ago. Breaking up with Marcellus for good wasn't easy, but I'm glad it was over. I no longer had to deal with him or the bullshit he came with. I know Marcellus thought it was because of Saadiq, but I was truthful when I said he had nothing to do with my decision. I was just ready to wash my hands of everything.

"Da da," Kacen suddenly called out. I opened my eyes to look at him.

"What did you say baby?" I asked. He was in his playpen looking right back at me with those big bold eyes.

"Da da," he repeated.

"Talya, did he just say what I think he said?" Ms. Jennifer ran into the living room and asked.

"Yup."

"Ain't that some shit? The first time he says that, and Saadiq ain't even here to hear him."

"I know right?" I smirked, and she shook her head.

"What's the problem?" she asked.

"Ain't nothing wrong," I grumbled with a roll of my eyes.

"Honey, y'all ain't gon' worry me. Between you and my son I'mma have a nervous breakdown. Y'all just need to gon' and make up so I can get some peace around here," she fussed.

I snickered. "He doesn't want me no more momma."

"And if I hear that one more time from either one of y'all, I'mma scream. Just fuck and get it over with."

"Really ma?" I laughed.

"Hell yeah," she said. I giggled.

We already did. That was part of the reason a bitch was pissed right now. After he made love to me the way he did, it was killing me I didn't know where Saadiq was. I was pretty sure he was over there with Adore'. Now I was all in my feelings, wishing I wouldn't have gone there with him.

Ms. Jennifer walked back out of the living room at the same time my phone started to ring. "Hello?" I answered, not bothering to look at the caller ID. I needed a distraction from all these thoughts I kept having.

"Talya?" the deep voice said.

"Who is this?" I asked.

"It's Lex. I been trying to call you from Kiana's phone, but you wouldn't answer."

"She put you up to calling me?" I barked.

"Nah, she um…" he mumbled and then his voice cracked. I wasn't sure but I could've sworn it sounded like Lex was either crying or had been crying. That put me on alert.

"Is something wrong?" I asked with this weird feeling in my stomach. I stood up and started to pace the floor.

"Nah, everything ain't alright. She died Talya," he said, and it sounded like the phone dropped.

"Hello…Hello!" I yelled. *Is this some type of joke*? "Lex, please say something."

Suddenly, there was movement on the other end followed by a familiar voice.

"Talya," auntie whispered.

"Auntie what's going on? Please tell me Kiana is okay." In my heart I didn't feel she was.

"I'm sorry baby, but she's gone. Our Kini is gone," she sobbed. The room started to spin, my vision became blurry, and before I knew it I passed out.

Saadiq

"You want something to drink?" Adore' asked.

"Nah, I'm good," I told her. I stopped by Adore's place since she'd been begging me to come and see her. A nigga really wasn't in the mood for this, but I didn't want to hear her mouth.

"I missed you," she said while walking over to me. She was wearing a short gown with a split up the side, her hair was curly, and she had bright red lipstick on. Now I knew why she'd been blowing me up. She wanted a nigga to break her off some dick.

"Did you miss me?" Adore' asked as she dropped onto her knees in front of me.

"What you doing shawty?" I ignored her question.

"What does it look like?" she asked, unzipping my pants.

Although I wasn't feeling this, I couldn't sound like a bitch by telling her to stop. Instead, I just leaned back in my seat uninterested. She started to stroke my dick with her hands but for obvious reasons he wouldn't salute. Even when she wrapped her lips around it, my shit barely got hard. She was going all in; slurping, bobbing, and even deep throating a nigga. My shit still wouldn't rock up.

"Okay, what's really going on right now?" she asked, letting my dick slip from her mouth. Attitude was present in her tone.

"Trust me, it ain't you. I just got a lot on my mind."

"Like what? You need to tell me something because I'm really feeling some type of way. First, you come over here with this distant look on your face, then you barely give me any affection, and now you can't even get hard."

I gently pushed her hands away while stuffing my dick back into my pants. "Sit down Adore', and let's talk," I told her.

"About what?" she asked.

My phone started to ring before I could respond. I pulled it out and saw it was ma dukes. "Don't answer that Saadiq. We are in the middle of something." I figured I would give her that since I was about to break her heart. After hitting ignore, I slid the phone back in my pocket.

"I think you a cool person, and I do got feelings for you—"

"But?" Adore' snapped.

"This ain't gon' work. I just got out, and honestly I ain't ready for all this."

"Let me guess…it's because of Talya, right?"

"To keep it real, yes and no."

"So you used me?"

"Nah, I didn't use you but if you feel I did then I apologize." I wasn't sure what was going to happen between me and Talya, but I wanted to make sure there was nothing holding us back. In the beginning we wasted so much time getting together, and I just didn't want to go through that again. I knew for a fact she was the only one I wanted to be with.

"You damn right you used me. I was there for you when you didn't have anybody else. I even defended you to my daddy when he said you were basically using me. I put money on your books and wrote you letters. You have no idea the shit I went through for you! Now look at the thanks I get in return."

"I told you I apologize," I said, and she started to cry.

I stood up and walked over to her. "Don't cry mane. Maybe one day we can be friends," I said and hugged her.

She laid her head on my chest as she balled her eyes out. "I can't just be your friend. I love you too much."

Da fuck? I didn't feel this shit was that serious. We had only been dating for like four months. Maybe her ass was just the type to fall quick.

"Why Saadiq? I would have done anything you wanted."

That's the problem. Adore' was a nice girl, too damn nice. She didn't have a backbone and often came off as needy. Not only that, but at times she seemed a little unstable too. We hadn't talked a whole lot about her past relationships. From the little bit she shared with me though, it was always the niggas breaking up with her. Something about that shit didn't sit right with me. It had me wondering what was wrong with her. No doubt I liked a submissive woman, but not to the point I was able to walk over them.

"Aye, not to rush this but I need to get back to the house. You gon' be good?" I asked. This situation was starting to be too much for me. The longer I stayed, the longer she would do this crying shit. I needed to burn before she found a way to guilt me into giving us another chance. Adore' nodded as she stepped back. "Aight. I'mma let myself out."

She looked at me but didn't say anything, so I just left. On the way to my car my phone buzzed in my pocket. I took it out and saw it was my momma calling again.

"What's going on ma?" I asked.

"I need you to come home right now, it's Talya."

"I'm on my way," I told her before ending the call.

Natalya

One week later…

For the past few days I'd been crying so much my eyes were all puffy and swollen. I can't tell you the last time I'd gotten a full night's rest since everything went down. Never in a million years did I think I would bury my sister. At the funeral I was surprised to see just how many people had come out to pay their respects.

Kiana's coworkers from her job was there, old classmates we went to school with, teachers, and even her mom's family that abandoned her when her mom died. The funeral was so sad that not a dry eye was in there. Outside of me, Lex and auntie took Kiana's death extremely hard. It was so bad we had to walk auntie out because she'd broken down while viewing Kiana's body.

"You aight?" Saadiq questioned.

I was at Ms. Jennifer's house in Saadiq's room where I'd been staying since the day I went to jail. I couldn't go back to that hotel room and be all alone with my thoughts. My ass would've had a nervous breakdown if I had to do that.

"I'm okay. Where is Kacen?" I sniffled.

"He in there with momma. I fed him and now he laying down."

"Thank you," I told him.

"Don't ever thank me for doing what I'm supposed to be doing for my son. He's my responsibility too." I didn't say anything. "Get up for a minute and let me talk to you," Saadiq demanded, but not in a rude way.

"I don't feel like it," I mumbled.

"Well don't get up. Just lay there and let me say what I gotta say."

"Go ahead," I sighed.

"I know you feeling real fucked up, but this ain't yo fault shawty. You can't let that guilt consume you. Kiana knew you loved her."

"She called me the night she was killed, but I ignored her call. She even sent me a text. If I had known it would be my last time hearing from her, I would have picked up the phone and let her know I forgave her. Why did this happen Saadiq? It's like déja vu. Her daughter is gonna have to go through the same thing she went through. It's just not fair." I began to sob into my pillow, as Saadiq ran his hand over my back.

"Nah, her daughter ain't gonna go through what she did. You know why?" he asked.

"Why?" I wiped my eyes.

"Because she's gonna have all of us in her life. I give you my word I'mma do all I can to make sure of that."

I sat up and wrapped my arms around Saadiq's neck. "Thank you. It feels good to hear you say that you'll look out for her."

"Kiana was like a little sister to me too, so I wouldn't dare turn my back on her daughter. She's family." I hugged him again. "Everything is gonna be good. I'm here now, and I ain't going nowhere."

Even though I didn't feel it at that moment, I knew he was right. There was a knock at the door. "You expecting company?" I asked, hoping it wasn't Adore'. I hadn't seen her around lately, but I figured Saadiq was keeping her away for my benefit.

"Nah, I ain't expecting nobody."

"Talya you have company," Ms. Jennifer called out.

Saadiq glanced at me. "That better not be that nigga," he said.

I snickered. "I doubt he would come here."

"His ass better not." Saadiq got off the bed.

"Excuse you? She said I had company. I'on need you going to look."

Saadiq looked at me and smirked. “Fuck what you talking ‘bout.”

I got up and followed him out of the room. When we made it to the front, I noticed Lex sitting on the couch.

“Hey Lex. Is everything good?” I asked, and he glanced up at me.

“I came to tell you the news,” he said. I gave Lex the address to Ms. Jennifer’s house and told him to stop by anytime he needed to talk. Raegan was now with auntie for the time being until everything got sorted out. None of us wanted Brisham to get her.

“What news?” I asked.

“They got the people who did it,” he said.

“Who was it?” As of two days ago the police still didn’t have any leads. I pointed them to Brisham since he’d been threatening her, but they didn’t keep him long because he had an alibi for that night.

“My sister’s friend Landi and her cousin Kris. I guess the guilt of what they did made Landi have a breakdown. She confessed to her momma, and she told her to turn herself in.”

“I don’t understand. Why would they do that to her?”

“Jealousy and hate,” Lex mumbled. He then went on to tell me everything that led up to the night of Kiana’s death.

I remembered Landi and Kris from the time when they made Kiana lose the baby. What I didn't know was that before any of this happened, Kiana had gotten into it with them on several other occasions. Apparently, her and Brisham had done some things that caused Landi and Kris to retaliate.

"What's going to happen now?" Ms. Jennifer inquired.

"They charging them with capital murder," he explained.

"Damn," Saadiq let out as he hung his head. I knew he was taking her death hard too.

I went over to Lex and gave him a hug. Even though I was hurting myself, I felt I needed to be strong for him. Being here for him and the kids was my way making it up to Kiana.

Brisham

So much shit was going on a nigga didn't know if I was coming or going. The death of Kiana fucked with me big time. I actually shed some real tears for shawty. We may not have been getting along, but she was still my baby's momma. She didn't deserve to go out like she did. Not only that, but now my daughter was motherless. Hell, you might as well say she was fatherless too. I let the beef between me and Kiana keep me away from her.

When I saw Raegan at the funeral, she didn't even want to come to me. It crushed a nigga's soul to see her clinging on to that nigga Kiana was fuckin' with. I could have easily taken my daughter away from him, but I knew it was my fault she barely knew me. I tried to talk to auntie, but she cussed my ass out. She told me it was on me that her niece was dead.

I left the funeral early feeling fucked up, like somehow this shit was all my fault. All that shit with Jacobi had come back to haunt us. Fucked up thing is Kiana didn't have shit to do with his death. Amongst dealing with that, I had to learn Saadiq was out of jail when I bumped into him at the funeral. The nigga mugged me the whole time I was there. That's another reason I left because I wasn't sure if som' shit would pop off. Don't get it twisted, I was far from scared. I just didn't think it was the time nor the place for us to bang it out.

On the flip side of this shit, Valencia had been riding with a nigga throughout everything. That was a lot more than I could say for my other trifling baby momma. When she heard the news, the bitch didn't even try to pretend like she cared. It was taking everything in me not to choke her ass out after the shit I learned. I told myself to play it cool until I was able to get some answers.

About a week ago I gave Kylisha access to one of my whips to drive. What she didn't know was that I put a tracking device on it. I wanted her to lead me to Danika and that other bitch. So far she'd just been joyriding in my shit. She hadn't led me to nothing until today when I finally spotted her picking Danika up. I followed them to the mall where they stayed in there for about two hours. They came back out with tons of shopping bags and shit.

That pissed me off because I figured they had used my money. After they left the mall, they hit up a nail shop where they stayed for like an hour and a half. Once they left there, they jumped on farty four and went in the direction of Charleston. I hoped it was where the other bitch lived. That way I could take care of all these broads at once. I was ready to get this shit over. It was time to get back my kids and my business.

Adore'

"Hey baby girl."

"Hi daddy. How are you?" I asked.

"Doing okay. I haven't heard from you in over a week. I guess since Saadiq is out he's been getting all your time."

"Mhm. We've been really busy," I lied. My father didn't know Saadiq had broken up with me and I didn't intend to tell him, especially since I was going to get him back.

"Well don't keep him hostage for too long. I want to set up a meeting to introduce him to the new trainer. We need to get this ball rolling as soon as possible."

"Okay I won't," I said in a sugary tone.

"Love you princess."

"I love you too," I said, ending the call.

As soon as I did, I heard my doorbell ring. I was praying it was Saadiq, and that he'd gotten his mind right. Since we'd broken up, I was trying my best to give him space. I figured by not being a headache it would make him miss me, but now he was taking this shit a little too far. He was giving that lil bastard of his and that bitch all my attention. Sashaying over to the door I snatched it open, hoping to see his face.

"What the hell are you doing at my house?" I asked.

"I need to talk to you right now," Franklin said, barging his way inside.

"About what?" I asked, feigning ignorance.

"Why did you send those videos of me to my wife?" he barked.

I turned to him. "Insurance baby."

"Insurance for what? I've already helped you get your little boyfriend out of jail. Are you trying to ruin my damn life?" He snarled.

Ooh, he is big mad. His face was beet red.

"You did, and I appreciate that. But I know your type. Whenever I didn't do what you wanted, all you would've done was find a way to hold that over Saadiq's head. I couldn't chance his freedom in your hand. Now we work on my terms," I spat, and he gritted.

"You fuckin' bitch!" he fumed.

"I've been called worse," I mumbled as I looked down at my nails.

"You won't get away with this," he threatened, and I laughed maniacally.

"You don't want to test me. There are a lot more videos where those came from. The next people I will send them to will be your colleagues. Your life will be ruined. What I suggest is that you go home to your wife and beg for her forgiveness. Trust me, she won't leave or say anything because she doesn't want this to get out. And if you don't want this to get out either, you will do exactly what I'm telling you."

Franklin's face contorted like he had to take a big shit. He shot me an evil look before storming out of my house just as quickly as he entered. He knew my threats weren't idle, I wasn't playing with his ass. I walked over to close my door and noticed the last two people I expected to see coming up the walkway. I frowned.

"What the fuck are y'all doing here?" I asked.

"We here to collect on the rest of our money," she said.

I glared at Danika and Kylisha. "Bitch, didn't I tell you I would get you the money. You shouldn't have come here."

"It's been a week and we hadn't heard from you, so I figured we should pay you a little visit." Danika smirked.

When they came in, I slammed the door behind them. Folding my arms over my chest, I turned and faced them.

"Look, I don't have the money on me right now. I'll get it to you as soon as I can."

"Un-un, that ain't gon' work. We want our money now," Danika's ghetto ass spat.

"Well I don't have it right now. What do you want me to do?"

"You better do something 'cause I'm not leaving until we get it," she snarled.

As you can see, I'm the other person Danika was working with. We were business partners so to say. For years she's been helping me find successful men to have affairs with, and then blackmail their dumb asses into giving us money to keep their affairs hidden. It was so many men we'd done it to that I couldn't even remember the number. This last job with Brisham was more personal than business though. Saadiq confided in me about everything that happened the night he went to prison. He asked me to keep it a secret. I did what he asked, but I also took it upon myself to seek revenge for him.

See, I had a thing for Saadiq since the first time my daddy pointed him out to me. Not only was he fine; I knew he could give me the world with his upcoming success. I wasn't worried about that bitch he was with. I figured I could easily knock her out of the picture. When Brisham tried to take away what belonged to me, I felt it was only right to take it back.

I went to Danika and let her know I wanted to set him up. Of course, she was game because it was money in it for her too. The icing on the cake was that she knew his baby momma Kylisha. She introduced me to her, and we all came up with a plan. Since Kylisha and Brisham were on bad terms, it all worked out perfectly. The only thing now is I didn't want to give them the money. I'm a greedy bitch and would rather have it all to myself. My plan was to kill them. Now it looks like I would have to do it sooner than I'd planned.

"Bitch, where the fuck is the money?" Danika asked, bringing me out of my thoughts.

"I told you I don't have it, but I'll give it to you as soon as I do," I lied.

"Nah bitch, you gonna give me my money right now," she demanded.

"And if I don't give it to you, what the fuck are you going to do?" I asked.

"Let me not walk up outta here with my ends, and you gon' find out," she threatened. "C'mon Kylisha, help me find our shit," Danika told her.

Yeah, I'mma have to gon' and kill this bitch. Danika went storming through my house as if she knew for a fact the money was here. I was just about to follow her when there was another knock at the door. Marching over, I snatched it open. My eyes widened in fear as I stared at the person standing there. I tried to close the door in his face, but he pushed it open on me.

Brisham

"Bitch!" I spat, slapping this hoe across the face with my pistol. She stumbled backwards into the house. Slamming the door with my foot, I aimed my piece at her. She held up her hands like that shit would stop me from putting a bullet in her dome.

"Where them other bitches at?" I gritted.

"I don't know," she mumbled.

I grabbed that hoe by her shirt and pulled her over to me. "Where the fuck they at?" I snarled.

"Back there," she pointed.

I immediately took off while dragging her ass along with me. When I made it to one of the bedrooms, the first person I spotted was Danika. I didn't know what she was looking for, but I could see her tearing the room up. Easing over to her, I put my gun to her head. She jumped when she felt my pistol.

"C'mon bitch, we got some shit to discuss." I could hear her sigh when she recognized my voice.

I now had my pistol pointed at both of them while I looked around for Kylisha. I knew her ass was in here. It took me a few minutes, but I found her hiding in one of the closets. She must have heard my voice and thought she could hide. After making her get out, I took all of them back to the living room where I made them sit down.

“Which one of you bitches set this shit up?”

Kylisha and Danika immediately pointed at the broad whose name I still didn’t know. I turned my gun to her.

“Please don’t kill me. It was Saadiq. He told me to do this,” she cried. Blood was still gushing out of her nose from when I hit her.

“Saadiq put you up to this?” I boomed.

“Mhm, he told me what happened. He said he wanted to get revenge without you knowing it was him.”

“How the fuck you know him?” I questioned. I figured it had to be some truth to what she was saying, but I still needed her to explain this for me.

“He’s my boyfriend. Well he was my boyfriend. After I did all this for him, he dumped me for that bitch,” she spat.

“Talya?” I asked, and she nodded.

“Tell me everything from beginning to end.”

The bitch immediately started to sing like a bird, telling me everything she’d done to me. She confessed as the one who sent them niggas at me. All this time I thought it was Kiana.

After ol' girl finished explaining, I lifted my gun again and pointed it at Danika. "No, no, no!" she shouted as I let off a shot, striking her in the tittie. Her body instantly slumped over, and Kylisha started screaming.

"Shut the fuck up!" I barked as I aimed my pistol at the other broad.

"Please don't kill me. I know a way you can get Saadiq back for what he did."

"Why the fuck should I trust you?" I asked.

"Because he turned on me too. He was just using me to handle his dirty work."

For a brief second, I thought about what she was saying. "I'm listening?" I finally grumbled.

"We can kidnap his family," she uttered with this sinister look on her face. It was like this bitch was creaming in her panties just thinking about this shit. I ran my tongue along my bottom teeth as I looked into her eyes.

"Kidnap his family, huh?" It was a thought to consider. Before any of this, I didn't have no problems with my cousin. I actually felt fucked up about that situation.

"Yes, we kidnap his family and take care of all of them."

“I tell you what. Take care of this bitch and I’ll think about it,” I said.

“That ain’t no problem.” She stood up and walked over to me.

“Fuck is you doing?” I asked as I glared at her.

“I need your gun.”

“Nah, that ain’t happening.” I shook my head.

“C’mon, you can trust me. I know you don’t want to do it because it’s your son’s momma. Just let me do it for you.”

Kylisha was now screaming so loud it was causing my ears to hurt. I knew we had to shut this bitch up before somebody came over here. Without giving it a second thought, I handed my pistol to the broad. She didn’t hesitate to fire one off. The bullet went straight through Kylisha’s heart, killing her instantly. Shawty handed me back the pistol.

“You trust me now?” she asked, and I smirked.

I walked off and headed for the door. “Wait, who is going to clean this mess up?” she asked.

“You gotta figure that shit out. I’ll be in touch,” I told her as I left her house. Saadiq didn’t know it, but he started a war.

Natalya

One week later…

I rolled over and picked up my phone. "Hello?" I answered in a groggy tone.

"Is Natalya Hicks available?" the deep voice asked.

"Speaking. May I ask who this is?"

"This is detective Conner. I'm calling to let you know that the charges against you have been dropped," he said.

"Really?" I smiled.

"Yes. Ms. Brown called this morning and advised us of her decision."

Mmm. Wonder what changed her mind?

"Thank you for letting me know detective." I ended the call with a smile on my face. "Saadiq," I called out, but I didn't get an answer. I got up from the bed and went in search of him. After checking all over the house, I didn't see any signs of him anywhere. I went to Ms. Jennifer's room to see if she knew where he was. She was up feeding Kacen. I walked over and put a kiss on my son's forehead. "Hey momma's baby." He looked at me and grinned.

"Good morning Talya. When he woke up you were sleeping peacefully, so I got him to let you sleep in," she explained.

"I appreciate it. Where is Saadiq?" I wondered.

"I don't know. When I got up, he was already gone. I tried to call him, but he didn't answer."

"Oh," I mumbled.

"You can call him to see if he answers for you," she stated.

"No, that's okay. Do you mind keeping an eye on Kacen for me? I have to make a quick run to get some things for us."

"Girl, you know I don't mind."

"Thanks ma. Oh yeah, the detective just called and said they are dropping the charges."

"That's good news. I wonder why she changed her mind."

"I was thinking the same thing. Anyway, I'mma go get changed before I leave." I kissed Kacen again before going back to the bedroom. After handling my hygiene and dressing, I left the house to handle my business.

Fifteen minutes later I pulled up to the house that Marcellus and I once shared. Since everything went down with Kiana, I'd taken a leave of absence from work. Not leaving the house had allowed me to stretch the clothes I had, but now Kacen and I both needed some more. When I texted Marcellus the night before he told me it was cool to stop by. Stepping out of my jeep, I nervously walked up to the door. I didn't know why but I was nervous to face him. I knocked on the door and he answered a few seconds later.

"Wassup shawty?" he asked.

"Hey." I mumbled. It felt weird seeing him.

"Girl quit acting like that and bring yo' ass in here," he told me. I giggled as I entered the house. "What's going on?" He asked. I walked to the foyer as he closed the door.

"Nothing much really," I sighed.

"I heard about your girl, and I'm sorry for your loss. How you holding up?"

"As best as I can. It's still hard to believe she's gone."

"Yeah, I can feel that. You know if you need me I'm hur'."

"I know, and I appreciate it."

"Ain't no thang. You still my lil baby," he said, and I rolled my eyes playfully.

"I just found out this morning that your baby momma dropped the charges. Did you have something to do with that?" I lifted a brow.

"I told you I was gonna handle it." He shrugged.

“Well about time. Thank you, I guess.”

“You ain’t gotta thank me. Matter fact, I owe you an apology for not listening to you before now. I guess a nigga didn’t wanna believe she would do som’ shit like that.”

“That’s what I don’t get Marcellus. She has shown you time and time again who she is, but you still act like she ain’t capable of half the shit she do. Are you that delusional?”

“I’m far from delusional shawty,” he muttered.

“Well what is it then? ‘Cause I don’t get it.”

“To be honest, I just chose to overlook a lot of shit because of our situation. I always told you I felt you weren’t all in, so I didn’t want to put all my faith in our relationship.”

“I guess you did that because you were afraid of getting hurt?” I asked.

“If that’s what you want to say.” He stuck his hands in his pockets as he looked at me.

I was quiet for a minute before I spoke again. “I guess I can’t really blame you. I mean, I wasn’t the best girlfriend.”

“Nah, it wasn’t all on you. A nigga wasn’t completely one hunnid even outside of the situation with her. In a way I still wanted to have my cake and eat it too,” he finally admitted. In my gut I'd always known he had cheated on me with more than Ariel. However, I chose to overlook it because I knew deep down my heart was still with Saadiq. We both were to blame for a lot of things that went wrong in our relationship.

Marcellus walked over to me and started to stroke my face. "If you give a nigga another chance I'll make it up to you. We can put all this bullshit behind us and start over fresh. Ariel or no other bitch will ever be an issue again," he promised.

Without giving me the chance to reply, he freed his dick from his shorts and lifted the sundress I was wearing. Completely turned on by his sudden dominance, I eyed him lustfully as he ripped my panties off.

"Uh," I let out when the thin material tore on the sides. Marcellus leaned in and covered my lips with his. When he tried to put his dick inside, I stopped him. "Un-un, you need to get a condom first," I whispered. Marcellus took off so fast I thought I saw smoke coming from his feet. About a minute later he returned. He removed the condom from the wrapper while eyeing me. As soon as he put it on, he lifted my leg again and slid inside. "Mmm," I moaned out while wrapping my arms around his neck.

With my back against the wall and my left leg in the crook of his arm, Marcellus fucked me like he'd never fucked me before. He was straight serving me up. All I could do was enjoy this feeling as he brought me to not just one, but two gut-wrenching orgasms. Once he made sure I was satisfied, he turned me around and fucked me from the back to get his nut.

"Argh shit! I'm about to nut!" Marcellus grunted. As soon as he pulled out, I went to the bathroom to clean myself up. Since my panties were torn, I had to throw those away.

"Aye, are you gonna at least think about what I asked you?" he said still breathing heavily.

"I already thought about it," I told him as I got myself together. He glanced up at me.

"Aight, so what you say?"

"I can't Marcellus. Too much has happened, and I think it's best for us to just end right here."

He stared at me with a confused look. I guess since we had sex he thought that would change my mind. I'm sorry, but it wasn't no second chances. He'd actually confessed to cheating on me with more than one person. He had the right game, but the wrong bitch if he thought I'd bounce back after that.

"So what the fuck was all this?" he asked angrily.

"Goodbye sex. I figured I at least owed you that." I smirked.

For a minute Marcellus glared at me like he wanted to snap my neck in two, but then his face suddenly relaxed. "Respect the game, huh?" he mumbled while shaking his head.

"You better know it. I'll come back later and get all my stuff at once." I got ready to walk out the door when I heard him say he loved me. I turned around and looked into his eyes.

"I know, and I love you too," I responded as I walked out and closed the door behind me. I did love Marcellus. It had taken me a minute, but I finally realized it. The thing was I could no longer be in a place where my heart wasn't. Life was too damn short to be unhappy and live with regrets.

***

I was laying across the bed looking at some old pictures of me and Kiana when Saadiq walked into the room.

"You good?" he asked as I wiped my tears away.

"Yeah, I'm good. I know she's at peace."

"That's what you gotta keep telling yourself."

"I know," I mumbled.

"Where you go today?" he questioned out of nowhere.

"I went out."

"Out where?"

I finally turned over and looked at him. "Saadiq, you can't have it both ways."

"Whatcha saying?" he frowned.

"You can't be acting like we're in a relationship, but you haven't even mentioned us getting back together. You either want to be with me or you don't. Let me know now, and I'll move on with my life." I was so tired of the games. I knew I wanted to be with Saadiq, but I wasn't sure how he felt about me.

"Who said I didn't want to be with you?"

"Well you haven't said anything."

"Why you think I broke it off with Adore'?"

"I don't know. You tell me."

Saadiq climbed into the bed and laid beside me. "I guess you thought I was playing when I told you we would be together when I got out."

"Honestly, I don't know. You could have just been talking."

"You know me better than that. I didn't want us to break up in the first place, but you already know why I did it."

"So what are you saying? Are we back together?"

"Yeah, if you completely done with that nigga. Y'all situation was more serious than what I had with Adore'. It wasn't nothing to end that lil shit."

"It's done," I said, and he smirked.

"I'm serious Talya. If you wanna be with me, then whatever y'all had should be dead as of today. It can't be no going back and forth trying to figure this shit out. I'm not about to let you play with my feelings," he said, and my heart dropped.

Wait a minute... Does he know about what happened today? Nah, he couldn't know... *Or did he?* When I came in earlier, he did have this weird look on his face. He asked me where I'd went to, but I acted as if I didn't hear him. "It's over for good," I mumbled.

Saadiq leaned in and kissed my lips. He then pulled me into his arms and held me like he used to do when we were younger. Surprisingly, he didn't try to have sex with me which was odd as hell. It's not like I would've done it anyway, but it did make me wonder. Normally all it took was me breathing on Saadiq and his dick would be hard. I guess I would never know what he knew because I wasn't about to ask him.

Saadiq

I'd left Talya and Kacen at the crib to come work out this morning with the new trainer that Daniel set me up with. When I met with him the day before, we just talked about our expectations from one another. Today he had me to go through some boxing drills. A nigga was sore as hell. Working out in jail wasn't shit like working out at the gym. I was now headed to meet up with Daniel to discuss my first match.

I stepped out my car and walked up to the big house Daniel lived in. After knocking on the door, I waited for him to answer. "Saadiq, what's going on?" he asked as he pulled me into a hug.

"Just maintaining. How you doing?"

"I'm doing good. C'mon in," Daniel said as he held the door for me.

Once I was inside, he led me into this big room he had set up like a movie theater. It was about twelve reclining seats with a big projector on the wall. He even had a bar set up. I glanced at the screen and noticed one of my matches was playing. I smiled as I watched myself in action.

"It seems different seeing it from this side, huh?" he asked.

"Yeah, this shit is crazy."

"It gets better. Just wait until you really blow up. There will be footage of you on almost every screen. Have a seat," he said.

"So you said you got a fight lined up for me?" It had been two years, and I was ready to get back to my second love.

"I sure do. It'll be in two months."

"Cool. Where I'm boxing?"

"In Texas. This guy who I matched you with has a record of 15-0 but don't let that intimidate you. I know you can take him out."

"Oh yeah?" I said, rubbing my hands together. Just thinking about this fight had me hype.

"Damn right," Daniel stated.

"I appreciate you looking out for me. Not too many people would still take a chance on a person after they don' been in trouble."

"Everyone makes mistakes Saadiq. It's not about that, it's what you do to correct those mistakes. You choosing to continue your dream lets me know you plan to turn this all around." He smiled.

"I wanted to tell you something, and I hope it doesn't affect our business relationship."

"Okay, go ahead," he told me.

"Me and Adore' broke up."

"I kind of figured that. She was supposed to deliver a message to you for me, but when I didn't hear from you I knew something was wrong. That's why I reached out to you myself."

"It wasn't nothing I did, or she did—"

"You just realized your heart was with someone else," Daniel said finishing my sentence.

I chuckled. "Yeah, you can say that."

"Let me tell you a quick story. Many years ago when I was your age, I had what you young folks would call the baddest bitch. She was beautiful, smart, stacked in all the right places, down to earth, and most importantly she had my back. The thing was I wasn't ready for all she had to offer. When we first started dating, I'd just gotten my business off the ground.

"Money was flowing in left and right, and I felt I was sitting on top of the world. All the fame I had started to go to my head. I had plenty women after me, and I entertained more than just a few. My lady knew this. Sometimes she would act a fool, and at other times she would just cry. I didn't realize each time I cheated I was breaking her down. A few years into our relationship, I got myself in a jam by doing some underhanded shit in my company. I had the IRS on my back and the Feds. My lady was right by my side. However, there was this other chick I'd been creeping with who was also there promising to hold me down.

"She offered me a deal that I knew I couldn't refuse at the time. To make this story short, let's just say I didn't come to my senses like you did. Two years of us being together and the bitch left me. She realized I couldn't offer her anything because all my money was tied up with lawyers and legal fees. To put the icing on the cake, she decided she didn't want to be a mother to my child."

"Damn, that's messed up. I take it that was Adore's momma?"

"Mhm. And it is messed up but that was the decision I made."

"So did you ever try to get your woman back? I questioned curiously.

"I tried to once I got all that legal shit behind me, but by then it was too late. She had moved on with her life. Saadiq, I love my daughter with all my heart. Believe me when I say that, but I want you to take heed to what I'm telling you. Sometimes the devil doesn't expose himself as a man with a red body and long horns like you see on TV. He can come to you in the form of a five-foot-five body, pretty face, and a lovely smile," he said, and I nodded.

That was real shit Daniel had just spoken, and I couldn't do nothing but respect it. Not only was he letting me know the apple didn't fall too far from the tree, but he was forewarning me about how a person could get caught up in the glitz and fame. I had to remain humble and stay down for the person who was down for me. I appreciated him for dropping those jewels of knowledge.

***

"Wassup baby?" Talya answered.

"Wassup, where you at?" I asked.

"I'm here at the daycare to pick up Kacen."

"Oh yeah? What y'all getting ready to do when you leave there?"

"I'm going to pick up some food from Sweetie Pies, so your momma won't have to cook."

I chuckled. "Ain't you tired of that shit? You eat it at least once a week."

"Nope. I would eat it every day if I could."

"You sure you ain't pregnant? I know you like eating there, but damn you been going hard with it lately."

"No, I'm not pregnant. You know that's my favorite restaurant."

"Fuck around and yo ass gon' be big as a house," I told her.

"And you better still love me!" she spat.

"Damn right I will. Anyway, I'll be back to the house in a minute. I'm ready to see y'all."

"Aww, you miss your family?" Talya cooed into the phone.

"Like a mufucka," I stated truthfully. Talking to Daniel had made me realize just how much I loved this girl.

"We miss you too baby."

"We need to get our own place again. It's cool staying at ma dukes house, but lil man needs his own room. You got him too spoiled. A nigga can't even hit like I want to 'cause his lil ass be waiting to cockblock." Talya started laughing.

"I can't deny that. When you wanna start looking?" she asked.

"We can start tomorrow when I get from the gym. Hopefully, we can find something and get moved before you go back to work."

"That sounds good," she said.

"Bet that. Love y'all, and I'll see you in a minute," I told her.

"I love you too," she replied before ending the call.

Ten minutes later I was standing in front of Adore's house. For the past few days she'd been blowing me up. I finally answered when I left her Pops' house. I figured I would go ahead and end this shit once and for all.

"Hi Saadiq," she smiled seductively when she opened the door.

"Wassup? What was so important?" I asked as I walked inside. I took note of the jumpsuit and tall heels she had on. Her breasts were pushed up high in a leopard bra that was spilling over the top. Admittedly she was looking good, but I wasn't here for all this.

"I think we need to talk," she said.

"About what?"

"You can sit down. I don't bite." She grinned.

"Wassup Adore'? Tell me what's this all about." I wasn't for the games.

"I really need to get something off my chest."

"Go ahead."

"Would you please sit down. I just want you to hear me out. If you don't like what I have to say, you can leave."

I sighed as I glared at her. Already I could see that she was about to be with the shit. Walking over to her all white sofa, I copped a seat right on the edge. There was no need to get comfortable because I wasn't going to be here long.

"I'll be right back," she said, disappearing into the kitchen. When she returned a few minutes later she handed me a tall cup of apple juice.

"'Preciate it," I said, taking a few sips. "So wassup?"

"What is it about me that you didn't like?" Adore' questioned.

I shook my head. "Man, we already discussed this. It wasn't nothing with you, I just decided I wanted to be with my family."

"I know we did but I wanna know. What is so special about Talya?" she asked, and I gritted my teeth.

"To be honest, she's secure with herself. If a person ain't doing her right, she ain't finna accept just anything."

"That's nice, but she's not prettier than me." Adore' smirked.

"That's superficial shit. Looks fade. Once all that goes away, what will you have left to offer?" I asked. I could see I'd stomped her with that question because now she had this dumb look on her face. "That's what I mean. You called me all the way over here to obviously prove you the better woman, but you ain't saying shit. No doubt you are a dime, but you tarnished shawty. Try working on your inner beauty and quit focusing on the outside so much."

Adore's eyes burned with fire as she glared at me. "Wow! I wasn't expecting to hear all that, but I get it. Thank you for being honest." She tried to say it calmly, but I could hear the hostility in her voice.

"I'm glad you understand, but after today we need to dead all communication. My girl ain't gon' be cool with you calling me."

"I thought you said we could be friends?" she asked.

"Nah, I just realized that ain't gon' work. I'll get up with you later." I tried to stand but this dizziness suddenly swept over me.

"You okay?" Adore' questioned as I grabbed my head.

"Nah, I feel dizzy." I started to blink my eyes because my vision was becoming blurry.

"Hmph, maybe you got up too fast." I heard her say.

"I'on know, but something don't feel right." I tried to walk towards the door, but the pounding in my left temple halted me dead in my tracks. I swayed back and forth a few times before I found myself face down on her plush carpet. Adore' walked over.

"Saadiq, what's the matter?" she asked, bending next to me. I blinked my eyes again before finally focusing in on her face.

"You know what the fuck is wrong. You put something in that drink bitch." I tried to reach out and grab her, but it was hard because I was seeing double.

"You damn right I did. Did you think I would let you discard of me like I was some trash? I went through pure hell to get you out of prison and this is how you repay me?"

What the fuck is she talking about? How she get me out of jail? I tried like hell to get up but I kept falling.

"You cr-cr-crazy bitch," I mumbled.

"Oh, you haven't seen crazy yet. This is the last time I let a man treat me like I'm nothing. I'm sick of you muthafuckas," she spat right before bashing me in the head with a heavy vase. Just like that I blacked out.

Natalya

I had just arrived back to the house from picking up our food. As I got ready to step out the car my phone rung with an unknown number.

"Hello?" I answered hesitantly.

"Talya don't hang up," Nene's voice came over the line.

"What do you want?" I snapped.

"I've been trying to call you because I need to tell you something," she claimed.

"Nah, I'm not fuckin' with you." I was just about to hang up when I heard her say something else.

"Talya, I think you're in danger!" she yelled. Placing the phone back to my ear I told her to repeat herself. "I said I think you in danger."

"What the hell are you talking about? Danger how?"

"About two months ago I overheard a conversation Danika had with somebody on the phone. She was talking greasy, saying she was going to get you back for what you did at your house. At first, I didn't think too much about it. I figured she was just mad she got her ass beat. But one day while we were just hanging at her place this girl named Adore' came over.

"We had been drinking and getting high, so I guess they thought I was too faded to pay attention to what they were saying. I wasn't though. I heard the bitch Adore' talking about having something done to you and Kacen. She mentioned som' 'bout having dealings with your BD. Once I heard Danika say she was down, I confronted them bitches. Of course, they tried to downplay it like they were just talking shit."

"Wait, you said the girl's name is Adore'?" I asked.

"Yeah, that's her name."

"How does Danika know her?" I asked curiously.

"I don't know how they met. I just know she been coming around for a minute, and I always get this bad vibe like she be having Danika in som' shit. After I heard them talking about you, I started distancing myself from Danika. I'd already realized she was moving shady. To be honest, I know for a fact she fucked Marcellus a few times."

"I don't care about all that," I cut her off.

"Okay that's cool. I just wanted to let you know to watch yo back," she finished.

"'Preciate the info but let me hit you back."

"Wait Talya," she said.

"What?"

"I'm sorry about everything, and I hope—" she tried to explain.

"It's cool Nene. Let me just call you back," I told her.

"Okay boo." I ended the call before she could say something else. Even though she'd given me the info, I still didn't trust her ass. After hanging up with Nene I quickly dialed Saadiq's number. I put the phone on speaker as I got out the car. The phone rung several times before the voicemail came on.

"Shit," I mumbled, hanging up. I needed to let him know about what Nene just told me. As I grabbed Kacen and the food I started for the house. I continued to call Saadiq. *Where the hell is he?* I wondered when the phone went to voicemail again. This wasn't like him not to answer my calls. I prayed everything was okay. I was so tuned into my phone that I didn't even see the masked person standing in front of me. By the time I laid eyes on them it was already too late.

"Ahhh!" I screamed as I dropped the bag of food.

"Shut up!" the person gritted while throwing something over my head.

"No pleaseee," I whimpered as they snatched me and Kacen up.

***

Thirty minutes later…

I heard the car door open before I was forcefully yanked out by my arms. When I tried to pull away, the person picked me up and put me over their shoulder. By the way he carried me I knew it had to be a man. I fought and kicked, but it was as if my licks weren't fazing him.

As he carried me away, all sorts of thoughts went through my head. Where was he taking me? Was my baby okay? Was I going to die? A few minutes later I heard the person walk through a door. They placed me on what felt like a couch and snatched the cloth off my head. Frantically, I looked around to see where I was. I was now in a house that was decorated as if a woman lived here. It had all white furniture, decorative pictures, and a big screen television. When I glanced to my left, my heart dropped to the pit of my stomach.

"Saadiq!" I cried. He was down on the floor with blood leaking from his head. I couldn't tell if he were dead or alive. The person who brought me in walked out of the house. "Where is my baby?" I yelled but he kept going. Tears mixed with snot slid down my face as my heart beat rapidly.

I had no idea if he was going to hurt my son. When he returned a few minutes later with Kacen, I breathed a sigh of relief. He brought him over and laid him next to me. *Thank God my baby is asleep.*

“Who are you?” I asked him, but he ignored my question as he went to shut the door. I had my eyes on him when I felt someone come up behind me. I glanced over my shoulder and saw that bitch Adore’. I had a feeling she was behind this. She walked around the couch and stood in front of me. In disgust, I glared at her.

“What the fuck do you want with us?” I snarled, and she giggled.

“You’ll find out soon enough.”

“What did y’all do to Saadiq?” I questioned.

Just then the guy returned and stood next to Adore’. “You did good. Why don’t you take your mask off and reveal who you are?” she told him with a sinister smile.

As if I watching a suspenseful movie, I watched the man remove his mask in slow motion. When I recognized who it was, I could have passed out.

“Brisham,” I whispered, and he smirked at me.

“Why would you do this to us?” I couldn’t believe he was working with Adore’.

“Because your nigga set me up.”

"Set you up how?" I asked, and he chuckled like this shit was funny. "It's not funny. That's your cousin. Haven't you done enough to ruin his life?" I snapped.

"Nah, I ain't ruined his life yet," he uttered. I shook my head.

"Alright, that's enough talking. Let's speed this shit up," Adore's bitch ass stated. I eyed her evilly as she walked over to Saadiq and started slapping him across the face.

"Bitch, you better quit hitting him like that!" I yelled, and she glanced back at me.

"What you gon' do?" she asked.

"Untie me hoe, and you'll see." I was so angry that I was damn near foaming at the mouth.

Suddenly, Saadiq lifted his head. When his eyes landed on me and Kacen he tried to get up but Adore' pushed him back down.

"Where you think you going?" she asked. From where I sat, I could see he was in pain. He kept squinting his eyes like he was trying to fight through it.

"Bitch, I'mma kill yo ass," Saadiq snarled at Adore'.

"You ain't gon' do shit." She stood up and walked back to Brisham.

"I'm ready to get this over. Just looking at them is making me sick. Where's the gun?" she asked Brisham.

"Brisham, I don't know what she got you involved in, but you don't have to do this. Think about your family. You and Saadiq can hash out whatever differences y'all have," I told him. Brisham avoided eye contact with me.

"I can't wait to put a bullet in yo ass. You talk too fuckin' much," Adore' spat. I shot my eyes at her before glancing back at Brisham.

"You really gon' let this bitch make you turn on your family, huh? Again?" I asked. He finally turned to me.

"Blame yo' nigga for all this. He set me up to get robbed. It ain't shit else that needs to be discussed."

"Saadiq, tell him that you wouldn't do that!" I screamed.

Saadiq was still over there struggling to get up. He glanced at me over his shoulder. "I ain't gotta explain shit. I'on even know what the fuck he talking about," Saadiq gritted.

Suddenly, Brisham removed a gun from his back and pointed it at Saadiq.

"No, please don't!" When I screamed, I woke Kacen up. He started to crawl on me while crying. "Shhh, it's gonna be okay." I looked down at him.

"No wait! I wanna be the one to shoot him and this bitch. You can do the kid," Adore' told Brisham.

He glanced at her and then at me. "Aight, make this shit quick," he mumbled. When I saw him hand the gun to her, I knew we were in trouble. He'd just put our lives in this crazy hoe's hands. Adore' walked over to me and pointed the gun at my head.

"Saadiq, please do something! She's going to kill us and our baby," I cried. He tried to get up but Adore' pointed the gun at him.

"Sit yo' ass down!" she yelled. Saadiq glared at her.

Once again I tried begging Brisham to do something, but my pleas fell on deaf ears. At that point, I just decided to accept my fate. My family and I were dying in this house and it was nothing I could do about it. When I saw Adore' squeeze down on the trigger, I quickly closed my eyes and began to pray. I was in the middle of my prayer when I heard loud clicking sounds. I reopened my eyes and saw Adore' squeezing on the trigger.

"What the hell is going on? This fuckin' gun is empty!" she roared. Brisham didn't say anything. "Do you hear me?"

"I know it's empty," Brisham finally spoke.

Huh? I looked at him in confusion.

"What the fuck did you do?" Adore' yelled.

Brisham bent down and helped Saadiq up as he glanced at Adore'. "I played you bitch. Just like you tried to play me. My cousin would never send no bitch to handle his dirty work."

Okay, what the hell is really going on? My eyes darted back and forth between Adore' and Brisham.

"You're gonna pay for this shit," Adore' spewed.

"I ain't paying for shit, but tonight yo' ass is gonna die." At the same time Brisham reached for another gun he had in his waist, Adore' snatched Kacen off the couch. She also removed a knife she had and held it to my son's throat.

"Noooo!" I screamed.

Saadiq tried to run towards Adore' but she stopped him. "Don't come near me! I will slice his little neck from ear to ear," she threatened.

"Adore', put the baby down. He ain't got shit to do with this. He is innocent," Saadiq gritted.

"Please put my baby down," I pleaded.

Brisham cocked his pistol and pointed it at her.

"Nah chill." Saadiq held out his hand for Brisham not to make a move.

I was now going crazy. This bitch had my baby and I honestly believed she would kill him. It was as if time stood still while we all tried to figure out how to get out of this situation. Unbeknownst to everyone in the room, I'd quietly removed the tie that was around my hands. As soon as I had the opportunity, I was going to make my move.

"C'mon shawty, put my son down. We can still be together." Saadiq tried his best to bargain with her. I knew he was just telling this crazy hoe what he thought she wanted to hear.

"No, it's too late. You're trying to set me up just like he did," Adore' said while walking backwards.

"Nah, I ain't setting you up," Saadiq lied. He held his hands out in front of him. "Just give me the baby. I'll give him to Talya, and we can leave together."

"Quit fuckin' lying!" Adore' barked.

"I'm not lying," he said.

I glanced at Brisham, and we locked eyes.

Alright Talya here is your chance. In my head, I started to countdown. *Three…two…* When I finally made it to one, I leaped out of my seat and grabbed Adore' from the back. Saadiq ran over and swiped Kacen from her hands.

"Bitch I'm going to kill you!" Adore' screamed. She turned around and leaped on top of me. She dropped the knife, and we both fell on the floor. She wrapped her hands around my neck. Just as she started to choke me, two shots were fired.

"Ahh!" I screamed when she fell on top of me gasping.

After placing Kacen on the couch, Saadiq came over and pushed Adore's body onto the floor. He lifted me up and held me in his arms.

"I love you," he whispered in my ear.

"I love you too." I told him, breathing a sigh of relief.

As soon as we pulled away, I got Kacen off the couch. I wrapped his little body tightly in my arms. Surprisingly, he was still calm. He rubbed his hands over my face while grinning. "Da da da," he said. I smiled.

"Look cuz…I know this can't erase what I did to you, but can you try to forgive me now? I apologize about all that shit." I heard Brisham say to Saadiq. I turned to them while rocking Kacen in my arms. Saadiq stared at Brisham for a while before he finally pulled him into a brotherly hug.

"Nigga, you just saved my family. I ain't got no choice but to forgive you," Saadiq mumbled. I started to smile as they hugged it out.

"Aight, y'all gon' and get the fuck out of here. I'mma take care of—. Talya watch out!" Brisham yelled just as I felt something sharp pierce my back.

My eyes fluttered as I gasped. “Uhhhh!” I let out while falling to my knees.

Epilogue

Three years later…

"Will the defendant please stand," the judge said.

The courtroom became quiet as everyone looked towards the defendant's table. Once he stood up the judge began to speak again. "Mr. Kamen, today you are here to be sentenced on the charges of falsifying documents, accepting briberies, tampering with evidence, and police misconduct. Those charges carry a minimum of five to ten years each. Before I hand down your sentence, I would first like to make a statement," the judge said removing his glasses.

I glanced up at Saadiq and he squeezed my hand. I gave him a small smile before looking back at the judge. "As someone who held a moral obligation to protect this city, you failed big time. You've disgraced your fellow officers. With all that's going on in the country, this is the last thing we need is for people to feel as if they can't trust the law. I'm very disappointed Mr. Kamen. I hope your time in prison will allow you to think about your actions, and how they've affected those around you. With that being said I am sentencing you to the maximum time I'm allowed to by law, which is twenty years. Is there anything you would like to say to the court?" The judge asked.

"No sir," Cordea mumbled.

"Alright if that's it, then you are hereby reprimanded to the St. Louis Correctional Facility where you will serve out your sentence. Bailiffs, please remove the defendant. Court is dismissed," the judge announced. As the bailiffs escorted Cordea out, he glanced in our direction. For a while he just looked at us before hanging his head. I smirked as I watched them lead him to the back.

"C'mon let's bounce," Saadiq told me. I grabbed his hand and we exited the courtroom. When we made it outside there were reporters with cameras everywhere. We had to fight our way through the crowd. One of Saadiq's bodyguard, Buddy walked over and escorted us to the car that was parked in the front. Before we could get in, a reporter stopped Saadiq.

"Saadiq, how do you feel about the outcome of your uncle's sentencing?" The young black man asked.

Saadiq looked at him. "He did the crimes, so he gotta do the time," he shrugged.

"How does the rest of your family feel?"

"I don't know. I can't speak for everybody else, but I feel like justice was served today. My uncle obviously thought he was above the law, but the judge proved he wasn't." Saadiq told him as he tried to get into the car. The reporter stopped him again. "Wait Saadiq…"

"Nah, no more questions. I got a flight to catch for my fight tomorrow. Make sure you check it out. I got something special planned," he said before the bodyguard closed the door on the reporter. "Saadiq. Saadiq," the reporter beat on the window as the car took off. I glanced at him.

"I don't think I can ever get used to that," I told him.

"Shit, me either," Saadiq said, and we both laughed.

Thirty minutes later we were on a flight back to Las Vegas where we'd been living for the past two years. I was looking out the window as Saadiq slept peacefully in the seat next to me. My thoughts were on the last few years of our lives. I'll give you a rundown of everything that happened.

I quit my job as a teacher and opened a youth facility that I run back home. It's called Kiana's Youth Center. It's a non-profit organization where kids could come to hang out, get tutored, and learn trades. I even went old school with the big brother/big sister program. It was the best decision I ever made. The center is doing great. Now, I know you're wondering what happened to everyone. I'll start with Adore' first.

After she stabbed me, I ended up spending two months in the hospital. The knife had punctured my spleen, causing me to have internal bleeding. The doctors stated if I had made it just a few minutes later I could've died. I went through two surgeries before I was able to start healing. I guess I could thank my angel Kiana for looking over me.

Speaking of Kiana, I missed her so much. It wasn't a day that went by I didn't think about her; only now I didn't cry as much as I used to. Lex and auntie shared custody of Raegan. Saadiq and I got her during the summer and some of the school breaks. As for Landi and Kris, Landi hung herself because she couldn't deal with the guilt. Kris was still behind bars where she will be for the remainder of her life. At times I wanted to hate them for taking my friend away, but I realized that was giving them power over my life. I didn't want to live in that dark place forever.

Getting back to Adore', that bitch was now rotting in hell where she belonged. Of course Brisham killed her after she stabbed me. Him and Saadiq then got together and came up with a story for the police. Come to find out, the bitch had been diagnosed with borderline personality disorder when she was younger and suffered from fear of being abandoned. Daniel informed us of her condition once he found out what happened.

He said he thought she was taking meds but learned she hadn't from the toxicology report. He felt bad about everything because he hadn't told Saadiq she had mental problems. We didn't blame him for any of that though. It was all on Adore'. We also found out she was the one stalking me the whole time. The police found pictures of me in her phone that she'd taken on different occasions. Not only that, but her ass had a history of stalking men and their women whenever they broke off the affairs. So much shit came out during that time, but I don't even want to get into it.

Moving along to Brisham. Even though he saved us that night, him and Saadiq never did get back to how they were. Saadiq just couldn't trust him after what he did. It's not like they could've built a relationship anyway. A few months after I was released from the hospital, Brisham was caught driving with four bricks of cocaine in his trunk. He was on his way to make a delivery. Get this, the reason the police pulled him over is because he was swerving in and out of lanes. When they arrested him, he was high as a kite. It was a shame that after everything that went down, he still hadn't learned his lesson.

He was now three years into a forty year sentence. Sad part is both of his kids are without their parents because of his poor choices. As for Cordea, I'll explain a little about what happened today.

Apparently, someone dropped a bug that he'd been taking bribery money from defendants to lessen their charges, or get them off completely. He'd been doing that for the past ten years. It was also some more stuff that he'd done, but it's not relevant. The last I heard about his wife is that she'd left him for somebody she was creeping with. It made you wonder if she was the one who set him up, or hell it could have been Adore'. Who knows what really happened. I was just happy he got what he deserved.

Well, as you can see karma is a real bitch. Even though Saadiq was never cleared of that crime, everything still worked out for the best. Both Brisham and Cordea are now in the same place they put my man. When I asked Saadiq why he never said anything after his uncle's crooked ways were revealed, he told me he didn't want Jon-Jon's mother to relive that night. She'd already forgiven him and moved on with her life. Although I didn't necessarily agree, I respected his decision. To this day I'd never mentioned a thing about it to anybody else.

Lastly there is Marcellus. Since there are no hard feelings, I'll sometimes call to see how everyone is doing. Can you believe he is living the legit life now, and is married? The crazy part is the woman he's married to is Quandra. You remember the one he claimed was working for him? Yeah her. Well that's neither here nor there. I wish them nothing but the best. Also, he has full custody of Emani now. Ariel disappeared about two and a half years ago. I mean homegirl just vanished into thin air. Whenever I tried to ask Marcellus about it, he just changed the subject. I finally stopped asking about a year ago. I have my speculations about that too, but I'll keep my thoughts to myself.

***

The next night…

"Ohhhh!" the crowd roared when Saadiq knocked the guy out.

"Daddy did it, Kacen!" I yelled, and my son started clapping his hands. My baby was now four going on five and was such a big boy.

"Yayyyyy daddy!" he said.

I turned to the rest of our family. On one side of me was Ms. Jennifer, Gee, and his wife. On the other side was my momma. Saadiq had moved our mothers out here to

Vegas with us. Of course, they had their own places. My mom was doing so much better. She'd been attending counseling for the past few years and was learning to cope with her disease. She also worked at the youth center with me. Our relationship had progressed a lot over the years.

Ms. Jennifer jumped up. "Talya, you see my baby up there?" she shouted.

"Mhm, I see my man." I smiled as Saadiq and I made eye contact. He winked at me before taking the microphone from the announcer.

"Thank you to everybody who came out to support me today. I love every one of you," he said, and the crowd went crazy. There was a bunch of '*I love you too*' sent back. Saadiq grinned, relishing in this moment. I was so happy because this was what he always wanted.

"Knockout, will you marry me?" One chick sitting down from us screamed. I threw my hands on my hips and glared at her.

"Sorry shawty, but it's only one woman I want to carry my last name," Saadiq chuckled before turning to me. "Matter fact, come up here Talya," he said.

"You serious?" I asked, looking around.

"Yeah c'mon," he told me. I shook my head as I grinned from ear to ear.

When I made it into the ring, Saadiq grabbed me by the hand. “Talya, we don’ been through a lot together. I didn’t know if we would be able to make it, but you hung in there with me. So in front of our family, everybody here, and all the people watching at home, I want to ask you something,” he said and paused. He turned to his boxing manager. “Where the ring at man?” he asked, and I started to jump up and down. “Hol’ up shawty, I ain’t asked yet,” he said, and everybody laughed. I giggled as I gazed into his eyes. Nobody understood just how long I’d been waiting for this. Now I knew why he’d been saying for the past few days that this night was important to him.

“Natalya Victoria Hicks, will you do me the honor of becoming my wife?” he finally asked once he got down on one knee.

I barely let him finish before I screamed, “Yes, I’ll be your wife!”

“Alright she said yes!” the announcer said. The crowd was still going wild as the cameras went off all around us.

The blogs are going to have a field day with this story. I tried my best to tune all the background noise out, and pretend it was just me and my man by ourselves.

When he slid the five karat princess cut diamond ring on my finger, I stared at it in amazement. Not only was it beautiful, but this thang was blinging. For the longest I just stood there smiling. Although my life hadn't been perfect, I couldn't be happier. I had almost everything that I could ever hope for. I had my family, my new career, and most importantly my guardian angel Kiana.

The End

Thank you for reading. If you will, please leave a review. I like to hear ALL feedback!

*****Author's catalog*****

-Love in The Deep South: A Hood Tale (Books 1-3)

-All I Ever Wanted Was a Love Like Yours (Standalone)

-I Was Everything He Wanted Series (Book 2- I Was Everything He Had)

-All I Ever Wanted Was to Stay Down for You (Spinoff)

-JaQuin & Savannah's Story (Standalone)

-Dear, Promise (Novella)

-Love in The Ring: Round One

*****Coming Soon from Soul Publications*****

-Dear, Serenity

- Beasts (Author Natavia)

*****Already Available*****

- **Dear, Heart**
- **Dear, Honor**
- **Dear, Vanity**
- **Dear, Promise**
- **Dear, Destiny**

Ways to stay connected to the author-

Facebook- N.L. Hudson- Like page

Instagram- n.l.hudson

Twitter- @NLHudson3

Buy signed paperbacks here at my online store-

https://authoressnlhudson.ecwid.com

SOUL Publications

CPSIA information can be obtained
at www.ICGtesting.com
Printed in the USA
LVHW012327120619
621078LV00002B/206/P